# FRED & EDIE

## Jill Dawson

**PARAGON**

CHIVERS PRESS
BATH

First published 2000
by
Hodder and Stoughton
This Large Print edition published by
Chivers Press
by arrangement with
Hodder and Stoughton Ltd
2002

ISBN 0 7540 9136 8

British Library Cataloguing in Publication Data available

£12·99

# FRED & EDIE

Set in ——————————————————————— of
passic ——————————————————————— ial
takes ——————————————————————— or
wome ——————————————————————— th
Thom ——————————————————————— ad
marri ——————————————————————— nd
her ——————————————————————— ng,
drean ——————————————————————— nd
glamc ——————————————————————— in
the r ——————————————————————— er.
Wher ——————————————————————— xy
and i ——————————————————————— le.
Neve ——————————————————————— ve
foresc ——————————————————————— w.
Draw ——————————————————————— od
as w ——————————————————————— Jill
Daws ——————————————————————— ice
for E ——————————————————————— of
her t ——————————————————————— e?
Teasi ——————————————————————— ng
myste ——————————————————————— ng
imagi

For Meredith

'You gave me hyacinths first a year ago;
'They called me the hyacinth girl.'
—Yet when we came back, late, from the
    hyacinth garden,
Your arms full, and your hair wet, I could not
Speak, and my eyes failed, I was neither
Living nor dead, and I knew nothing,
Looking into the heart of light, the silence.
*Oed' und leer das Meer.*

T.S. Eliot, *The Waste Land,*
First published in *The Criterion,* October 1922


Your love to me is new, it is something
different, it is my life and if things shall go
badly with us, I shall always have this past year
to look back upon and feel that 'Then I lived'.
I never did before and I never shall again.

Edith Thompson, 1922

# CHAPTER ONE

## WIDOW'S STORY IN ILFORD MYSTERY

### QUITE HAPPY TOGETHER AND NO QUARREL ... I DID NOT SEE ANYBODY ABOUT AT THE TIME

'I heard him call out "Oh!" and he fell against me . . . We had no quarrel on the way; we were quite happy together . . . I did not see anybody about at the time.'

In these words Edith Thompson (27), widow of the stabbed Ilford shipping clerk, told the police the story of her husband's death. Her statement was read at Stratford court yesterday, when she and Frederick Bywaters, the 20-year-old ship's steward, were remanded on the charge of murder.

Mrs Thompson, said the police, made other statements, and Bywaters also made a statement, but none of these were put in yesterday's hearing.

A large crowd had gathered around the police court in the hope of seeing the couple, but they were brought from Ilford in a cab, and manoeuvred into court before the waiting people knew of their arrival.

WOMAN'S COVERED FACE
Bywaters, who entered the court first, is a tall young man of striking appearance. A plain clothes officer stood between him and the woman, who was helped into court by a woman attendant.

Mrs Thompson was wearing the clothes in which she went to the theatre on the night of the tragedy.

When she entered the dock she covered her face with the deep fur collar of her coat until the magistrate asked if there was anything the matter with her face. She was requested to put the fur collar down, was provided with a chair, and demanded a glass of water. During the hearing she sat with her limbs trembling and hands clutching at her garments.

Divisional Detective-Inspector Hall stated that when he saw Mrs Thompson on Wednesday morning he said to her, 'I understand you were with your husband early this morning in Belgrave Road and I am satisfied that he was assaulted and stabbed several times.'

Mrs Thompson then made this statement:

'We came along Belgrave Road and just past the corner of Kensington-

2

gardens I heard him call out "Oh!" and he fell up against me. I put out my arms to save him, and found blood which I thought was coming from his mouth. I tried to hold him up. He staggered several yards towards Kensington-gardens, and then fell against the wall and slid down.

'He did not speak to me, and I cannot say if I spoke to him. I found his clothing wet with blood. He never moved after he fell . . .

'I ran across the road for the doctor and appealed to a lady and gentleman passing. The doctor told me my husband was dead. Just before he fell down I was walking on the right-hand side of the pavement nearest the wall.

'We were side by side . . . My husband and I were talking about going to a dance.'

The Inspector added that Mrs Thompson appeared to be very agitated at the time.

He took possession of Bywaters' overcoat.

Mrs Thompson had practically to be carried out of court.

Before Bywaters left the dock he asked if he might have legal assistance, and was told the police would give him every help and facility.

DODGING THE CROWD
By a ruse the police succeeded in getting the man and woman away from the building without attracting the attention of the crowd.

The inquest on the dead man was opened at Ilford Town Hall. Only evidence of identity was taken.

*Daily Sketch,* Saturday 7th October, 1922

*Sunday 8th October, 1922*

Darlint Fred,
Here I am. The room is small, as you might expect, but on another matter, the matter of the light, there is more than you might imagine. In fact, it was light that woke me this morning; weak slivers of October light from the oddly shaped window. Today is the official end of British summer time. Now that I have said that to myself the phrase has a strange ring about it. *The end of summer.* The end of our summer. I wonder why I have remembered such a detail? Of course, it's ludicrous, I can't imagine why it matters, but a picture popped into my head as I opened my eyes—a picture of you, somewhere across London in Pentonville, in a grey room with a concrete floor just like this one, lying in bed and

altering your watch, spinning the hands quickly, so that they slip around as they do in a picture show, without regard for convention. The hands on a watch, flashing through hour after hour, or the pages on a calendar, torn and fluttering, time eaten, time flying and time lost. Of course, this is sheer imagining. Your watch has—no doubt—been confiscated, as have all of my belongings.

Freddy, I hope you are bearing up, as I am, and not feeling too afraid. I'm staring at the window, so that I can describe its shape exactly to you. A cathedral-shaped window? No, that doesn't make sense, it's more like the shape of a loaf of bread, if you can imagine that, yet there is something here that reminds me of being in church. A smell rather like school, a smell of the boiled cabbage cooking in the kitchens, also of boiled clothes and sheets, perhaps even boiled skin, and of carbolic soap. I am adequately warm and at the moment there is thankfully, some quiet. It's not a tiny window and it's not high up particularly. The bars would be wide enough to slip a child's hand through. That is, if the glass was not there to prevent such a thing.

Do you remember, Freddy, reading about Lady Constance, about the Suffragettes in Holloway? But no, you would be what, ten or something like that, while I, thinking of myself already as a *young woman* at seventeen, I suppose I took some notice of such things. I couldn't help wondering this morning, if one of those women hadn't been kept in this exact room. After all that starving she did, maybe her hands and wrists did become tiny, maybe they were slim as two sheets of paper and maybe she thought of breaking the glass and slipping a hand right through. But to what avail? She could only have held the bars and stared out. She would have had no strength to do more. Just a thought that crossed my mind, Freddy. A random thought. No doubt you have wondered, too, at who might have slept in your cell before you. It helps, doesn't it, to keep the mind on other matters and not to expend ourselves worrying about our own predicament.

It was the young wardress who brought me my breakfast. She has pale skin like a freckled brown egg and she finds it impossible to meet my eyes. I can tell she is curious about me. (Judging from the crowd yesterday at Stratford, it must have been in the newspapers by now.) I think she would love to stare outright, but she pushes her lank hair behind her ears (they all wear such strange caps, I cannot see that they are use or ornament) and she scuttles out again, with almost—I'm not joking darlint—almost a curtsey. I'm cheery and in fine spirits and I hope this letter finds you the same. I'm still groggy with sleep and last night's crumpled dreams and the dress I slept in.

6

I wear my prisoner's number on a yellow cloth badge on my own dress, which I've been allowed to keep until tomorrow, as they were not quite prepared for me and have had some delay in finding my prison garments. As long as I don't think about the last week, if I concentrate instead on the small details: the shelf, the stool and pail in the corner of the room, the scratchy grey blanket, the white egg-cup painted with a black arrow and the words *Prison Commissioner* on it, the beaker of milk and the dry roll on a tin plate, the pillow which is surely stuffed with something akin to straw (when I mentioned this to the wardress she *snorted* at me), I feel fine. I have found I am in possession of an astonishing capacity to not think, if I so desire. For instance, I believe I have not thought of Percy, not for one moment in twenty-four hours. Is that not remarkable?

I have asked the Governor if I could send this to you and he has kindly replied that I might not. It was an odd experience, stepping out of my shoes and my wonderful crepe de chine in that small office that they call the 'Reception'. I'm now wearing some unspeakable items of underclothing which seem to have been constructed from the sacks used to carry coal.

The officer taking down my details asked: Where were you born, do you know? That might tell you something about the kind of ladies they are used to in here!

I can apparently visit the library—accompanied by a wardress—as often as I like and whilst on remand I won't be put to work and may remain in my room. The Governor has supplied me with paper and plenty of it and a pencil, but no pen, so I am writing anyway in the hope that you can read these words at sometime in the future, when this dreadful mess is cleared up. I am so in the habit of writing letters to you that I find it impossible to stop. Always in my mind, a conversation with you, with my Great Pal, continues. Knowing that your situation is so similar to mine only increases this tendency.

I am not allowed a fork or knife and, of course, you must be in the same position. It will be hard, won't it, to have to eat everything with a spoon? But then again, since twice a day we are given porridge without salt and with a great hunk of bread, I can see that a spoon is the most useful of items.

Darlint, I've promised myself not to remonstrate with you and, as I say, not to think about the last few days which have brought us here, but occasionally it becomes difficult to keep my resolve. A sentence rises up in me, like a bird opening its wings in my chest and then beating them, harder and harder. Then I see you again in your coat and hat, running away down Belgrave Road and I see Percy slipping, slipping and—they have offered me drugs here to keep me from wailing—yes, I admit, I may have been wailing last night, although I can scarce remember—and the sentence is: *Why oh why did he do it?* I believe I know the answer, Freddy, and I believe that when you have the occasion to do so you will explain all to me, reassure me, as you have so often done in the past, so please, forgive me, won't you, for mentioning it just then.

Let us move on to cheerier things. Although I am allowed a pencil, naturally I'm not allowed a knife to sharpen it, which strikes me as funny. After all, I could poke someone's eye out with a pencil, couldn't I, or my own, if self-injury is what they are hoping to prevent. This thought reminded me of the Punch and Judy show we watched, that first summer on the Isle of Wight, do you remember it? *What, Judy, do you mean to cry? Why, yes you hit me in the eye. I'll just lie down and kick, and die!* It must be curious to be a prison governor and to think of people in this way. To think, is this woman likely to do harm to herself or to one of my wardresses, is she a wicked murderess or a careless Baby Farmer or just a poor girl who couldn't pay the rent? So my point is this, that when this pencil is blunt, I must wait until such occasion as I can request permission to have it sharpened. What I am saying, of course, is please forgive me also if this letter has to end abruptly. I don't as yet, understand the routine in here enough to know when I will next speak to someone.

I must end now as I can hear someone coming. Perhaps I will get to sharpen my pencil! Bear Up.
Thinking of you,
Peidi.

\* \* \*

It's strange but if I thought in the past of being in prison, which I have to say, I never did, never believing I would experience such a thing, but if I did in some recess of my mind ever imagine it, which I suppose I must have, given that I have dug up the image I'm about to describe; I realise now that I pictured a hospital ward or a dormitory, a long thin room stuffed with many people, sardines in a tin. I did not picture myself alone like this.

\* \* \*

I need to calculate, to know the precise moment.
Was it the first instant I clapped eyes on Freddy? Was it when I decided to marry Percy? Was it the conversation I had with Freddy the night of the theatre?
If only I could pin-point it. That's what keeps me awake, struggling to land on the exact square—like a child playing hopscotch. Was it when I knocked on Freddy's door, that evening in the late summer of 1921? Or was it

10

earlier than that—the evening the Irish hawker called at the door and made his sly remarks to me?

For there must be one, one tiny moment, and if I could find it, search for it and land on it, it might be possible—just possible—to pick up the chalk and throw it again, so that it falls somewhere else. So that with a hop and a skip and a jump I'm landing with both feet on another square, doing something else.

Not here in my cell, thinking this.

*Monday 9th October, 1922*

Dear Freddy,

A short letter, darlint, which perhaps I will be permitted to send to you. Tomorrow is the day of Percy's funeral. Mother came last night to tell me and to ask what I would like her to write for me as an inscription on the wreath. Can you imagine! What could I say? Mother suggested: *From your Loving Wife, Edith,* but after a lengthy discussion we decided on: *From Edie.* Judging from what mother says of the hubbub at home, the note will be torn up by some irate well-wisher before long.

I am in good spirits again and hope this letter finds you in the same. I did suggest to Mother that she might plant some hyacinth bulbs, for me, on the soil above Percy's grave, which she seemed to think a very odd request.

11

Mother says I cannot seem to get it into my thick head what has happened. Those were her exact words, Freddy! In fact she began shouting. I suppose when I get out of here I will have to plant the bulbs myself.

I know you will find it painful for me to write to you of Percy but today is the first time I have been able to think of him without fainting. Even as I write my hands are perspiring and the pencil slips in my fingers. But I must press on because I have decided it is not a good thing at all to try to survive by not thinking. I am expecting Percy at any minute to walk in here with his navy jacket on and say, Come on, my girl, and then to take over, bustle a little, fill out the forms, do everything necessary to take me home.

I long for cigarettes but I am allowed books and have ordered three novels.

I did so rely on Percy. I can see that now. Perhaps him being those few years older made a difference. He was dreary, and a terrible dance partner, and there's no need to mention to you his temper, after a drink or two! Still, that dreary side of him is something I crave a little just now, after the excitement of the last week or so. If I ever get the chance to again, I will time his morning egg *so perfectly,* and I will not complain at all if he stands over me, squeezing my waist with his big hands, while the egg rattles at the edges of the pan, like something mildly angry, like something about

12

to gently explode.

*Tuesday 10th October, 1922*

Freddy, just a little note. Last night I had such terrible nightmares and I've woken with such a strong sense of fear, feeling all the events of the last week rise up and tumble over me. I did so long to be held and comforted by you and writing to you like this is the closest I can come to that feeling.

The nightmares were brought about by thinking of the funeral today. I suddenly pictured our lovely house at Ilford with the funeral cortege outside of it, and Percy's dreadful friend Harry lighting his pipe and trying to look solemn and my mother with that shocked expression she wears permanently now and Avis, wearing my borrowed black coat and my beautiful embroidered kid gloves. Then I tried to remember who else might turn up for Percy's funeral besides his mother and brother and realised I could think of no one! How few friends he had. Maybe Ernest—the old boy from the Shipping office—and that's the total. I'm not sure Ernest really cared for Percy much, either. There was an awkward occasion one Christmas when Percy had a tipple too many. That was when Percy was the new boy and great things were expected of him. He'll go far, Mother said when I brought

13

him home, tall and broad in his smart black suit. She could hardly stop herself from rubbing her hands together in expectation! I don't suppose you can imagine that now, can you, knowing him only in the last two years? He was judged a promising catch once, you know.

I mention this not to make you feel guilty, darlint, but only because I have no one else to talk to about such things. Percy had no son or daughter to mourn him, he only had me. I kept going over it and over it. Mother said the coffin had white lilies on the top and brass handles and I imagine Percy in there—yes, I have got that far, Freddy, I can picture him now lying in his coffin with his arms crossed and feel only the merest pang of pain when I do so, like a knife faintly drawn across my heart.

I'm sorry I mentioned the knife there. I didn't mean anything by it.

In my imagining of Percy, his arms are folded rather smugly, rather stonily and he has a look which says: I told you so. He has just finished one of those short coughs which announced his every comment. This morning when this thought first came to me, I wept and wept, realising the strange futile pleasure Percy took in being right about miserable things. Then I wanted to laugh out loud and get hold of Percy and say, so you see it was all true, your wife is a Judy indeed and that young

Bywaters came to no good, all as you predicted. I thought I should hate him but instead I had such sorriness for him that his life was worn down to a tiny penny, dull and soiled, and that it should be his pleasure in reducing the lives of others, too. He knew I wasn't happy, didn't he? We often spoke of it and his stubborn response seemed to be: well I am not happy and never have been so what makes you think your life should be different?

If only I could plant some hyacinths here in a bowl to make the room cheery. I am watched night and day—no I don't mean that a wardress is there constantly. I mean that whenever I glance at the spy-hole, someone seems to be passing, just checking up on me. I've discovered that the young one, the freckled, curtseying one is called Eve. I heard her name called by the stout one, Clara, who bustles in with great speed, in fact does everything speedily; ushers a girl in to take out the pail, replaces the tray, reports on events 'outside', announces visitors: Governor's on his way to see you. Or: Your sister's waiting in the visitors' room. Despite her brusqueness (and I've heard her shouting at other prisoners, so I would certainly not like to be on the wrong side of her!) it's Clara I like best. I believe she is sympathetic to us. But I wonder if I'm a poor judge of such things? It seems to me that Eve glances at me slyly. Sometimes I catch her eyes on my waist, on my shapeless self inside this prison dress and I know what she is thinking.

Hyacinths, violets, how much difference it would make to be allowed to have flowers in our rooms! Violets always remind me of that night when we stood under the statue of Eros, and I was saying to you that the sky was snagged on his arrow because when I threw my head back to look at the stars, that's exactly how it appeared. And you said, not listening to me at all, but searching amongst the women at the steps of the statue, Damn these flower-sellers, milling around the place, why do they never have violets? until the prettiest of the lot came to you and said: Sir, I have the most beautiful violets, what'll you give me for 'em? and you said, A good spanking if you talk to me that way again. But, of course, you were laughing and you bought some anyway and she took it in good spirit when I appeared beside you to take your arm, seeing that you were taken.

Those violets lasted very well. They were kept in a beaker of water beside my bed for nearly a week, prompting no comment at all from Percy. Sometimes I think he knew exactly who they were from. In my fondest moments I think that at some level Percy regretted his ban on happiness and thought: Let her have that tiny scrap and no more. That much doesn't threaten me.

But he was wrong, wasn't he? I think that

happiness—once planted—grows roots. Before I was ever happy, I had no idea of what it might feel like. So many people seem to have no idea at all that they might choose to be happy: one only has to look around to see that. Perhaps it only takes the tiniest shoot of true happiness for that to germinate, to exist somewhere and contain the seed of itself, something that might be passed on. For surely it is impossible to feel something if you don't know—if you have never been told—that such a thing exists?

We had our happiness didn't we, the light might shine through it sometimes but it was green and fresh and unbending as a blade of grass, wasn't it, Freddy, while it lasted?

*  *  *

The first time I clapped eyes on Freddy. It must have been then.

Percy carries the cases, of course. We take a number 25 from Cranbrook Road to Victoria station, and sit at the front on the top deck, this being a *treat* to get us into the holiday mood (since we could have just as easily taken a tram) and Percy remarks, more than once, on the heaviness of my case.

What have you in there? he teases, amiably enough. Half of Carlton & Prior?

I return his teasing moments later when I read an advertisement on the side of the bus passing us. FORCE, *a wholewheat breakfast cereal,* and under the picture it reads: *For breakfast try FORCE.*

I nudge Percy. For breakfast, try force! You've been taking that too literally, darling . . .

His head swivels towards me as if on a stick, and at first he looks like someone who has just sat on a bee. Then right after that, he bursts out laughing. (This, I know, might be considered provocative. But when Percy is in a good mood, I like to take liberties.)

So we arrive in good time at Victoria station, where we are to meet Avis and Freddy. We buy our tickets and have a cup of tea and a Sally Lunn in the tea-shop at the station. That's where we are sitting when they turn up. Fred and Avis, I have my back to them; I'm smoking a cigarette.

Percy sees them first. I watch his face register their arrival and then he noisily scrapes back his chair and stands up and it is all a flurry of greetings and introductions. I stub out the cigarette hastily and stand up too.

My first impressions of Freddy are . . . not particularly tall, perhaps, and wearing a long midnight-blue sort of coat, a spotless grey hat? His shoes gleaming and freshly polished.

He is smiling, a charming smile, a smile that tells me he is conscious of his handsomeness and his good teeth. He holds out his hand. If I close my eyes now I can feel his palm— smooth, warm, flat, the texture of a pebble washed smooth by the sea. When I try, *try* as I'm doing now, to bring that moment to mind, I can hear him jingling coins in his pocket, or hear that odd whistling he did. The snap and click of footsteps on a pavement, the hiss and sulphur of a match being lit . . . but that's not right; that's not my first impression of Freddy surely, that's from somewhere else?

Well, we have scarce a moment to acknowledge each other's existence in the run to the platform and with Avis twittering that we had all misjudged the time and that Percy's watch must be wrong. We bundle ourselves onto the train laughing, and Percy takes our coats for us and hangs them up and the train begins moving almost as soon as we sit down.

I'm trying to remember Freddy from school; Avis has told me he was there and how much younger than me he was. Naturally enough, girls of fourteen are not much interested in boys of seven! I'm not having much success.

Avis has brought sandwiches of cured ham and boiled eggs and a flask with more tea, organised as she is, and we are all ravenously hungry and excited, I think, yes, even Percy is talkative and ventures a few jokes, as London fog gives way to green fields and hedges and a blank sheet of cloudless sky.

Freddy doesn't say much to me beyond could I pass him please the salt for his egg, and I'm unsure what impression I've created, or whether I've impressed him at all. I notice the

19

way he eats—the way he always eats—quickly, a little like a wild scavenging animal might eat something, a fox say, with one eye on the look-out for hounds.

It's watching him eating which reminds me. I don't know why but the dip of Freddy's head, the intensity of his concentration, his jaw moving determinedly: all of that brings a picture of Freddy to mind, a memory of the *very* first time I saw him, as a small boy, in school.

Valentine's Lake.

We are swimming, all the children are swimming in Valentine's Lake and Freddy is a small child, one of the youngest. Of course we loathe swimming in the lake—icy and slippery with reeds, sometimes even a water-rat or a duck swimming right into your path to scare the wits out of you, but we all put up with it because it is Mrs Wall who teaches us swimming and terrorises us into compliance. But not Freddy! Now I can see him on the bank of the lake, with a stubborn thrust to his lower lip (a 'pet lip' my mother called such a thing and it was strictly forbidden) there he is, with his skinny legs and his long shorts, refusing, refusing point blank, to go into the water.

We all look on in awe and terror as Mrs Wall seems to rise from the neck of her coat like a swan and then begins to push at him with her stick, screaming: Come on boy, don't waste my time! And still he refuses to go near the water. Some boys call out names, treading water and calling softly, Scaredy Fred, Baby Boy, and other nastier ones, but there he is, undeterred.

Now the funny part is, I can't remember the outcome. I can't picture whether Freddy is forced by the teacher to swim with the rest of us, or whether he runs away, or is caned or whether he escapes punishment. I remember that his hair is curly and dark and not much different at seven than it is at twenty and his eyes like two bright pearly buttons, much too pretty for a boy. Infuriating—the way that memories offer themselves only as fragments or incomplete stories. The end of this incident refuses to relinquish its secrets and so here he is, childish and uncompromising, not minding how much ire he produces in the teacher. Stuck.

Little Freddy Bywaters, seven years old, refusing to dip a toe in the water.

*Wednesday 11th October, 1922*

I am writing this back in my room in Holloway in the afternoon at around 2 p.m. I've noticed that if I begin my letter 'Just a little note' it invariably transforms into a great epistle, so I will restrain myself from such inaccurate beginnings in future! I am going to try again to approach the Governor about writing to you and see if he won't allow this letter—and all my others—to be passed on.

This morning was the most bewildering experience, so strange to be out in the world but yet chaperoned and still not free to go the toilet or wave my arms about or run and skip or do anything without being held tightly by the two wardress bustling me through the mob at Stratford . . . and then to see you standing in court so stiffly, only in fact two feet away from me. I tried not to stare, Freddy, afraid that it might damage our case. (My solicitor has been talking to me a great deal about this, he even approved of the black dress with the beaded apron and neckline this morning because it is 'sober', but that shows how much *he* knows, as it is in fact the most fashionable Parisien dress I own and any woman would realise that straight away. Fortunately there were few women in the court-room. Still, I think he is wrong and there was no harm in my looking my best. That dress is based on a design by Paul Poiret. It floats across the bust and is very flattering.)

You looked pale, as I suppose, did I. I know so well your composed face, your composed posture, the one which tries to disguise the fact that internally you are like the flame from a gas-jet, pure energy and fire shooting upwards, but all the while casting an illusion of something still enough, calm enough to touch.

I only had to glance down at your hands to guess the truth and, as I expected, all your agitation could be seen there, in the way your fingers wrapped themselves around your thumbs in tight fists. I wanted to gently unfold your fingers, the way Mother once unpeeled mine from the school gate when I was small girl and protesting violently at being taken inside. I wanted to kiss each finger and say to you, it's all right, Freddy, bear up.

I really did believe I would be freed by the end of the session. I tried to follow what was said in court this time. Last week was an utter fog and this morning I thought it important to understand. I was feeling fine, quite bolstered up until the prosecutor read my statement from the police station and explained how you and I 'accidentally' met up at Ilford in the police station as I was escorted to another room. There was no accident about it! He and the other policeman *deliberately* engineered it, opening the door at that exact same moment so that you and I were facing each other, only a yard between us. We were like puppets on the hands of the Punch and Judy Professor. I'm sure you know that as well as I, and in the state I was in about all that had happened my mind would not operate fully. I could only drop my mouth open in the most dramatic way like a drawer falling off its runners and stare at you and then moments later utter those words to them, those words that they seized on and wrote down and then read out in court and made us both sound so guilty: Oh God, oh God, what can I do? Why did he do it, I did not want him to do it. I must tell the truth.

But hearing it read out like that, it sounded different entirely, I was incensed! If you saw me whispering to Stern it was because I was asking him if it was possible to interrupt, to tell the court that in fact I had been *told* in the police station by the officer in charge, by that ugly one, with his horrible protruding eyes and a tongue that doesn't seem to fit right in the bottom of his mouth, I was told by him, that you had already confessed to the crime and that I would now be helping you if I told the truth. You must believe that, Freddy. I wasn't trying to save myself from any involvement. I didn't know I *would* be involved, I didn't know I would end up here, I—Freddy, I ask myself over and over—*why* did you do it, why oh why . . .

*(Later)*

I have taken some deep breaths and am trying to compose myself. I know this is no place for recriminations. What you need now from your Peidi is for her to remain cheery, for her to give you her undivided support, her help, her love. And I do, darlint, I offer you all of that. Naturally I am disappointed to be back in here again—I really thought today would be the last day of my custody and have set a lot of store on it all being over by now. It is what has

24

helped me to get through the last week, knowing that when we got to court it would all be cleared up. I have tried not to dwell on Percy, on the events of last fortnight, instead willing myself to concentrate on the future, on how we will both survive this experience. Your behaviour . . . well, I'm not sure what to say here, as I worry now at who might read these letters . . . still, your behaviour is at the least *explicable* when they understand our *circumstances* and how much you tried to protect me.

Now I want to end this letter on a different note so will write to you of other things. Did it strike you as astonishing, the crowds, what, how many people would you say, I can never estimate such things . . . were milling outside the Stratford court? Eve, the younger wardress, has a sister in Manor Park, you might remember the sister, Olive Draper, I think she is the same age as Florrie. Olive was there, Eve, told me. They are all trying to get a glimpse of you Mrs Thompson, she said, in her slightly nasty, sly way, as she was escorting me to the bathing rooms.

Eve is hard to fathom, she does not say what she thinks, unlike Clara, but sometimes her look says it all. She has four children, I discovered, so she is not as young as I imagined. She lost her husband in France, and the children are looked after by her sister. (It occurred to me then, Freddy, that I am now a 'widow'. You might think this discovery a belated one, but the word has never presented itself to me before, and even now that it has, even whilst I might concede intellectually that it is true, the word won't seem to stick, but floats away unattached, like a piece of paper on a stream. Others might think of me as a widow. I wonder if you do? If the word has occurred to you, or the idea?)

The bathing rooms, I wonder if you have to suffer the same indignity? But then, men of course, mind these things far less, and—what am I thinking of—you have spent years on your ship, you can scarcely be embarrassed about performing your ablutions in public! Some of the other prisoners, I can tell, have also now received 'news' of who I am. I have scarcely had a conversation with any of the other women and I am, naturally enough, afraid of them. On walking into their company I have that feeling I often had, whilst working at the shop or at the theatre, or even, now I think of it, from school. It is when parts of myself seem to flake and break apart and reshift, and I wonder with a feeling of pure terror, who I am and where I fit in. I am sure that the women here think I have a 'posh' accent, a 'posh' haircut, that I lived in Ilford with my garden and my job in the city and my big house and thought I was better than them. Of course they don't say that, but I *know* it anyway.

And then in other situations, walking into the Governor's office for instance, or when Lady Rothermere used to come into the shop for her hats, or even Diana Sheperton, you remember her, don't you? Well then, I used to feel so lowly, so ignorant, so ill-bred and petty with silly desires for a 'maid' at Kensington Gardens, when there was only Percy and me to look after and I would see myself for what I was, a girl from Stamford Hill, a child as Percy always said, 'too big for her boots', with ideas above her station. I would think of Mother, and her mania for buying gloves, all kinds of gloves, and never letting anyone but us girls see her hands so that no one else could realise how calloused and rough they were, from *her* childhood, her years of hard work.

You know, Freddy, before all of this, I really expected Mother to be proud of me. I mean, I had a good job and yet when I used to go on a Friday for tea at Shakespeare Crescent, what I felt most strongly even then, was her *disapproval,* the constant questions from Father about the patter of tiny feet, the constant comments from her on the hat I was wearing, or the stockings, or the cigarettes I was smoking. I kept thinking that I had done all she wanted, that is, found myself a solid husband with prospects and a lovely big house and then, to cap it all, started to earn more money than Percy, in fact, earned more in a week than Father used to earn in a month and

27

instead of being pleased for me she seemed, well . . . what was it? Always trying to crush me. I don't want to make Mother sound cruel, which she wasn't. I keep going over that occasion I told you about, the planting of the hyacinths, the way she looked at me. I tremble when I think of it, although I don't understand why.

I feel sometimes as if I am constantly shrinking and then inflating—I am serious here, I know I can talk to you of such things and that you won't laugh at me—I can't seem to remain the same size in any given situation and I still have that sensation, I have it in fact more powerfully lately. In court, I'm sorry to go back to this, but I must—in court, I thought, if only I was educated, like Stern, my solicitor, if only I could make sense of their strange words and see myself the way they see me, maybe then I could understand how I should be, how I should behave, what is *required* of me to make them *understand.*

Well, I must finish this now (my wrist is aching and the pencil is worn down to the stub). I will see you in court in Stratford, darlint, on Tuesday the 17th and now I will begin again my petition to the Governor, begging him to allow me to send you these letters.

All love,
Your Peidi.

*Friday 13th October, 1922*

Darlint,
Avis came to visit this morning, with Mother. She squeezes her hands together and stares at me and the atmosphere between us is entirely unnatural, false. All the time I can see she is thinking: she and Freddy, she and Freddy, *together* . . .

It was, thankfully, brief. I suspect it is Mother who persuaded her to come. I imagine they are worried now, as ever, about *appearances* and wish to present, to God knows who, an image of us as a united family. Father was working and says he will see me Saturday. Actually, on consideration, if I know Avis, she is struggling *not* to imagine you and me together, because such topics give her a queasy feeling at the best of times. It was a tense occasion and the worst of it was a rumour which Avis passed on, in coded way, that your ship has been searched. She said it in such a heavily meaningful way, almost comical, I thought, with her self-importance, she having juicy information from the outside that she knew I was dying to hear. I dread to think what they might find there, if the information is true. I pray that you destroyed my letters as I asked you to, darlint.

This must of necessity be short. The Governor has refused my request to pass these

29

letters to you and it is wearying to continue to write to you like this, uncertain as to when, if ever, you will read my words. The sense of communicating, talking to you, is not strong today. I am afraid I am not in the best of spirits so will write another time, when I am.

I thought of your superstitiousness just then, thinking of the date today if I have got it right (I feel I am losing track), and then thought of your monkey, the one you gave me as a good luck charm. Its stout little body, with the long arms folding over its head. *Hear No Evil.* It struck me (and this is not friendly, Freddy, as I am out of sorts), it struck me that you are like that monkey sometimes. You wish to cover your ears with your hands, if something doesn't suit you. When that is not possible, as it was not with me, since I insisted on talking truthfully to you, you find it very disturbing indeed. Perhaps it is this disturbance which has caused your present predicament.

Yours,
Peidi.


*Saturday 14th October, 1922*

Oh, darling Freddy, please, please forgive my last letter. I know that you suffered a great deal of sadness, over the last year, listening to me and you were the first and last person who did so and understood and took me seriously and thought that my unhappiness mattered at all and I feel terribly guilty. Your Peidi feels dreadful, *dreadful* for writing in such a way to you, when we need all the strength we have inside us right now to face tomorrow *together* and redeem ourselves in court.

Forgive?

*Sunday 15th October, 1922*

Freddy,
My solicitor, Stern, has been to see me today and so, darlint, I know now that you did surrender the key to your ditty box in which were all my letters. Please know that I forgive you, as you are younger than me and must be very frightened.

Stern says that you kept all my letters, there are nearly sixty-five in total. This has given me some pause for thought.

I didn't keep your letters, darlint, not because I didn't want to, but—oh, just because I worried I suppose, that Percy might find them. Now, in some ways, I wish I had them, as your neat cabin-boy's writing would comfort me. But it is probably better for both of us, I mean, where the courts are concerned, that I destroyed them. Most of them—the ones which matter. I may have kept a friendly note from you, addressed to me and Percy, that could not do any damage.

I want to write calmly and not get upset about this. Part of me is flattered at you keeping my letters. I know you did it because you love me. Now that I have written that sentence I find it leaps about on the page, it has picked up some legs from somewhere and is walking around. I can't continue my train of thought until I have followed this sentence. *You love me.* I feel confident writing it, so I must be assured of it. I remember vividly, the first time you told me that you did and I know you will remember, too.

But the reality is, Freddy, I didn't believe it then. It was a sentence from novels I read, a sentence I had always wanted to hear. Of course, Percy said it too sometimes, and I had the same exact response. A kind of disgust. I found the words *disgusting*. Disgust fought with vanity, with triumph, because I knew I had succeeded in igniting your desire for me, I had won you from Avis, but desire, wanting me, that was all I thought you meant. So I took the words and gobbled them up and I grew a little fatter on them and in time, when I *was* fatter, when I was not *starving*, it occurred to me that maybe you had meant something else.

I fear I've put this badly and must write again on the matter when my head is less foggy. Foggy, of course, through anxiety about my letters and who will now read them and whether they will be put in court, which Stern says will be a disaster. He is quite a worrying person, speaks sharply to me when he thinks I don't understand the seriousness of the situation I find myself in, or when I ask too often about you. He says he is going to request that the letters be considered inadmissible evidence because you have taken responsibility for what happened and because there is no prima facie case against me. This should suffice. So I will finish now and see you on Tuesday.

(If I don't write fully about certain events, certain recent events, it is because if ever I get to forward these letters to you I know they will be read by others.)

Your darling Peidi.

\*       \*       \*

The letters I wrote to Freddy while he was away at sea, they're looming up, all written in blue ink on purple tissue paper. They are lying in Freddy's ditty box, crumpled and folded and beginning to look like flowers, like roses, with layers and layers, tighter and more dangerous the closer you get to the centre. And then they are being opened out again by other hands, pale hands, terribly bloodless hands, shredding the petals of the flowers. My words are leaping out and others are reading them, and petal by petal they are not the same, not beautiful at all, ripped apart like that.

A great flush of shame and embarrassment

floods right over me, making my scalp prickle and my legs tremble—*oh, God, I hope that Stern is right and they are never read out in court!*

*Monday 16th October, 1922*
*Holloway*

Freddy. I don't know why I wrote 'Holloway' there—almost a joke, don't you think? As if I might actually be writing to you from somewhere else. From Shanklin, for instance. Wouldn't that be lovely? If I were standing in Rylstone Gardens, near the little cliff walk we took that first morning, with the sound of the grey flat sea below us rolling incessantly and you by my side, smoking a cigarette, luxuriously . . . I am allowed cigarettes here, are you? But only two a day and right now it is six hours until Clara will come in with my next.

Clara is kind, I've decided, and I much prefer her to Eve. When she speaks she makes this sniffing noise first, a little dismissive, to indicate disapproval ostensibly, but I think, in truth, to cover up her strong emotions on the matter. She has never been married and says sharply that she doesn't much miss it, judging from what other women tell of it. This morning she brought my breakfast, the usual roll, glass of milk—I can't stand the tea, it is always so stewed by the time it gets to me and with a dreadful thin scum on top of it—and as she set it down she said, Well, they're all popping off at the rate of flies. Now it's Miss Marie Lloyd, and we discussed this for a while She died apparently the weekend of our arrest, but Clara has only just found out about it, via her brother who works in a music hall as an usher. He met Marie Lloyd many times. I wonder if you have heard about her death, Freddy? I did find it upsetting, particularly the nature of it. Did you know she began crumbling on stage, forgetting her lines, trembling and staggering and the audience only laughed more and more believing it part of the act? That is what disturbed me, imagine laughing at someone else's dying, seeing it happen in front your eyes and being—well, *entertained* by it! I can't imagine being so confused that you couldn't tell which was real and which play-acting, or not able to empathise and feel for the person up there on the wooden boards, not able to remember that she is flesh and blood just like yourself. I'm convinced I should have understood immediately that it wasn't an act, that she was falling for real and needed assistance. This is just what Clara said, too. She said *most people* and then she said sniffily, most *men,* have no great skill in imagining anyone's feelings other than their own—especially a woman's—and the world would be a much better place if they *did.*

Clara is quite a gossip and it is mostly deaths and dead babies which interest her. There is a Baby Farmer in here at the moment, quite a famous one, although I haven't met her yet and tremble at the thought of doing so. I'm sure you find the company you're keeping equally disreputable. Clara says most of the women in here are poor souls really, no danger to anyone else but themselves.

I've thought about what she said of men and empathy. Of course you are the exception to this, darlint, you always understood me when I confided in you, more than anyone, certainly more than Percy, but more than Avis, too. I wonder what gave you this gift, if others, according to Clara, so lack it? I know that you are so close to your mother and I was thinking of Avis teasing you that time when Lily sent you a present, addressed to *The Birthday Boy* and I wonder if this has something to do with it?

Mentioning Lily then gave me pause. She must have been to visit you. I saw her in court with her big hat on, the black straw one with the curved ostrich feather—well, of course we called it 'ostrich', although it wasn't—the one that I sent her from Carlton & Prior only a month ago. Only a month ago! What on earth can have happened to *time,* why does it now stubbornly refuse to obey any rules, why does a day sometimes take an entire week to pass, and this last month feel longer than all the years of my childhood put together? It's as if I'm holding a concertina, alternatively stretching and compressing the minutes in my hands until my head spins with the unexpectedness of every moment, time being something I'm now afraid of, unable to trust. I honestly don't know from one moment to the next if time will pass quickly or slowly. All pattern is shot to pieces.

Surely it is only a matter of hours now, until the 17th and the moment when I'm freed. I know that I shouldn't say such things, when *your* position is so much more uncertain than mine—but believe me, I will do all in my powers to explain the distress you were suffering, the circumstances. Everything will be all right then, darlint, so please don't be envious of my greater chance of freedom.

I haven't dared to think what you and I might do, if we are ever able to have our *one little hour*.

Today I told Clara that I had been having difficulty sleeping and she mentioned that I might visit the Doctor, but I was thinking to myself, there will be no need for that, I will be *outside* soon and I am determined only to think of that and of how to get through the next few hours. Of course, I have to be careful what I write here, but I can freely say that I can't wait until the moment that I see you again in the court-room, darlint. Despite the ugliness of the circumstances, nothing will mar that shiver of delight when I see you tall and erect, with your high forehead and your proud self, always on the edge of jauntiness, *always*, no matter what.

All my love to you, Be Brave, my sweet.

\*　　　\*　　　\*

I thought I was fine about Percy. I had pictured him in his coffin, arms crossed and so forth, I was calm about him, *typically* calm, Avis would accuse me; reconciled. And then one night I'm turning in bed to face the wall, trying to get warm under the stupid scratchy grey blanket and suddenly—here is Percy!

His face, his most angry face ballooning at me, blood trickling from his mouth like a long tongue of black treacle. I spring up with my heart leaping up and down in my body on a string and, of course, Percy disappears. It's dark in here, past lights out, with an occasional scuffle and twitch of movement in the corner of the room. Who's there? I want to say out loud. I tell myself it must be a mouse. I call to Clara—not loudly, tentatively—but nobody comes.

All night he won't leave me. He is sobbing and lonely and all alone somewhere and he taps at the wall in the corner of the room and he wants me to let him in. There are shadows flickering on my tightly closed eyelids and silhouettes in the weak yellow light of the lamp and then Freddy running and me falling and Percy falling and Percy never getting up again and the lamp going out. Lonely, he says. I'm lonely, come and join me. Please, Edie. I must have slipped into sleep.

# CHAPTER TWO

## THE ILFORD MURDER CASE ADJOURNED FOR NEW EVIDENCE

BROTHER SAYS DECEASED AND HIS WIFE WERE NOT ON HAPPY TERMS

A great crowd gathered by the Police Court at Stratford on Tuesday when the case against Frederick Bywaters (21) a ship's store keeper and Mrs Edith Thompson (28), whose husband they are alleged to have murdered, was resumed. But few were able to obtain admission, only a sufficient number being allowed in to fill the seats available. The crowd outside remained throughout the hearing, a police cordon being drawn in the road.

Further evidence was given, and at one point in the medical statement Mrs Thompson collapsed in a fainting fit, but soon revived under attention. Bywaters maintained an unaffected attitude in the dock, until the end, when on an application on his behalf, permission was granted for an interview with his mother. The case was further adjourned with the intimation from Mr William Lewis, prosecuting counsel, that new information had reached him the previous day which he desired to consider before he called evidence upon it.

Mr F. A. Stern appeared for the defence of Mrs Thompson and Mr Barrington Matthews was for Bywaters.

After formal evidence, Mr Percy Edward Cleveley, Corn Merchant, of Mayfair-avenue, Ilford, and Mr John Webber, sales manager, of De Vere-gardens, Ilford, were called and described what happened when they were attracted to the scene of the tragedy, soon after midnight on October 4th.

Mr Webber said he was about to retire to bed when he heard a woman scream. He heard her cry, 'Don't, oh! don't!' and when he went out he saw three persons coming along. One of them was a woman whom he knew as Mrs Thompson. She was sobbing and running hard. The other two were Mr Cleveley and another witness, Miss Pittard. He stood back until they passed. He looked in the direction they were running and afterwards saw a match struck and held low to the ground. He went to the spot and then saw a man sitting on the pavement. Mrs Thompson was by his side. He asked her if he had fallen but she was hysterical and cried, 'Yes; no; I don't know.' He asked if he could do anything for him and Mrs Thompson cried, 'Don't touch him; a lady and gentleman have gone for a doctor.'

Dr Maudsley, of Portland Avenue, Ilford, said when he arrived at about 12.30 a.m. Thompson was dead, and he formed the opinion that he had been dead for about ten minutes.

*East Ham Echo,* Friday 20th October, 1922

\*　　　\*　　　\*

I have formed the opinion that Percy is dead. It came to me late last night, when he appeared to me again, just as I was climbing into bed. He looked hideous as usual, stone blank eyes, the odd expression caused by the glistening red-black tongue drooling from his mouth and with his shoulders folded in that same position of resigned disapproval. You want too much, my girl, he said. I said it would get you into trouble and now look . . .

I said: Oh go to hell, Percy, you're dead, you know.

And I wasn't afraid. I wasn't afraid at all.

*Friday 20th October, 1922*

Darlint,
I am sorry I haven't written for a few days. It has been so difficult to take in all that has happened and to find myself here again, when I had worked so hard (and it was *work*, Freddy) to believe that I would be out by now. Stern had convinced me that my letters would not be admissible evidence but I am beginning to understand that he may not be able to keep them from the courts and the thought of this— of my letters being read and heard by Mother and Father and all and sundry!—Oh, a wave of sickness flows over me whenever the thought occurs.

I paused there, drank some water and paced a little. Now my heart is beating calmly again. I don't like to write to you in a spirit of admonishment—I know how frightened you really are, despite all appearances to the contrary. Stern tells me (and don't you think he is well named, Freddy, now you have seen him in action?) that your plea will be manslaughter and your good conduct in your years at sea will stand you in good stead, so I have the strongest of hopes for you.

This is an aside, really, but I just wanted to say how handsome you looked on Tuesday. Because I am afraid to glance up at you in court I don't want you to imagine that I don't know, that I'm not aware, that you are constantly watching me, your big blue eyes fixed steadily on my cheek. I gazed only one time at you, just enough to take in your neatly polished shoes and the crispness of the crease in your good wool suit. Then I had the strangest rush of jealousy and pride, knowing that I have held you, unloosened that jacket, unbuttoned your shirt, ruffled the crease and the crispness and the sharp polishedness of you, made you rumpled and desperate and utterly, utterly without your smart suit, your demeanour. Freddy, I know that I shouldn't write this and how sick I am of knowing all my letters to you from here are read, because surely it is the thought of that very thing, that *unbuttoning* which went on between us, which dominates the minds of most of those who jostle for a place in the court-room. I am not so stupid that I don't know this and know too that they express disgust and they shake their heads to one another, but they can't keep from imagining it, it runs in front of their eyes like those images at the peep-show, the jerky pictures of the lady with the huge behind and the rose bush, do you remember her?

I refuse to believe that I am the only woman in the world who has longed to travel the globe the way men do, tasting, experiencing all along the way. I know in the beginning you found it 'coarse' when I asked you for details, especially about Molly, but in the end you liked my frankness, didn't you, darlint, you were relieved to know that women were interested in such things, that we are not the mysterious laundered creatures of stiff carbolic and black boiled wool that Lily has led you to believe we are!

Eve says we are causing a sensation. This morning Eve and Clara were on duty in the exercise yard with another wardress—Wardress Jones it says on her badge but they call her Sarah. This yard is a very sorry affair, with a square of the most pitiful soil in the centre, with only a solitary bulb visible, which might or might not be a hyacinth, and high walls etc. The prisoners walk in silence, round and round and the wardresses smoke in the corners and are supposed to prevent us from talking. In reality, they are not in the least concerned to. They are just like women in any other situation, unguarded in their sharing and swopping of horror stories and gossip.

> *You ought to be ashamed, I said, to look so*
>   *antique.*
> *(And her only thirty-one.)*
> *I can't help it, she said, pulling a long face,*
> *It's them pills I took, to bring it off, she*
>   *said.*
> *(She's had five already, and nearly died of*
>   *young George.)*
> *The chemist said it would be all right, but*

*I've never been the same.*
*You are a proper fool, I said*
*Well if Albert won't leave you alone, there it*
*    is, I said,*
*What you get married for if you don't want*
*    children?*

I gather that Eve is in some sort of trouble, her being a widow and so quick to judge everyone else, it is particularly embarrassing for her. When she is nervous she pushes her cap onto her greasy hair in a funny anxious little movement. It is quite comical because, honestly Freddy, she couldn't possibly look any worse!

Of course, I pretended not to hear, as it isn't my place to say anything. I trust I haven't shocked you, it's hard to remember sometimes that so few men realise how freely women talk to one another about these matters, especially women of a certain class who don't have the sensibilities of ladies like myself! I have no fellow feeling for Eve so I don't even care if the Governor reads this and she loses her job.

Actually, I think I have decided not to even try passing these to the Governor. I have decided to hoard them for when I am released. Then I can send you the whole lot, and you will see that I never stopped writing to you, keeping faith with you, not for one moment. So I will not need to censor myself quite as much as I have, although on one or two matters it would still be prudent to be restrained.

I confess to being a little nervous about Stratford court again on the 24th. It is strenuous to maintain the confidence that I had last time that all will be well. However, I am trying.

Yours,
Peidi.

PS Oh and Freddy, I don't think it is helpful of you to laugh in court like that. Naturally, I know *why* you laughed when Percy's brother made that remark about you, but others would not understand. They won't understand the situation and they don't know you or Percy's brother as I do and it will reflect badly on you.

*　　　*　　　*

He used to say, You're sure you want to hear this?

Her name is Molly. She's pretty, yes, for sure, but not in the way you are, of course. She is . . . she wore rouge and some dark stuff round her eyes and—well, you know I've never been one for describing people.

The first time we docked in Sydney and we piled into the nearest bar and it was hot, hot and we were drinking gin and whisky and it was cheaper than water. So some girls came into the bar and they could only have been one sort of girl to enter a place like that and one of them was dark, with dark eyes and heavy eyebrows and small but well built and definitely the more *forward* of the bunch. So she sat down next to me and Jack said, Offer the lady a cigarette then and this girl said, The lady's name is Molly, and the others laughed and I stared them out. You know me, Edie, I stared defiantly because there was no way I would let them know I was new to this or shy, or any of that.

So. Sydney is a funny place so hot and light for so long and the girls were giggling and drinking with us and the atmosphere when a ship's new in, well, everyone's happy because there's money around for the bar man and the girls and we're on playtime aren't we, with two days shore leave. Molly has this nice laugh, a bit like hiccups, once she started she couldn't stop and her mouth was small and pink and only one of her teeth was missing. I knew she was poor because why else would she be doing this but I was surprised when she said that at sixteen she already had a baby at home with her mother and that on account of the size of her chest, men had always been getting the wrong idea about her and that was her downfall. So she said all this to me in private, out of the hearing of the others, giggling into my ear. I could feel her breath tickling at me, and the warmth of her and the gin, Edie, just enough to stiffen me and not enough to make me useless . . . I hope you're sure you want to

47

hear this . . .

And the others, Jack and the others, they stuffed some money into Molly's hands and said, It's his birthday, be gentle with him, and they were hooting and hollering as she promised to be. She took me by the hand and we stood up and the room span a little, so that the others fell into a navy and white blur and all I could hear was Molly's giggling. She giggled all the way up the stairs but when we got in the back room with the sun falling across the bed and lighting up the dust motes she fell silent and fell to chewing on her nails.

She slipped her top off and sat on the bed in all her glory and said, Have you got another ciggy then? and, Edie, I'd never seen a girl without her slip on in all my life and if the truth be told I was scared to blazes, but what a fine girl too, she looked just like a pointed figure-head on the ship's prow, so I fell to kissing her. I tried to kiss her in all the places she pointed at me but she held my head away and said, Pour me another gin, there's a good boy and she nodded her head to a beaker on a dresser and the rest of the bottle she'd brought up with her. So I lit her cigarette and tried to keep my hands off her while she smoked it and poured her the gin like she asked and she knocked it back fast and then she pulled down the bloomers she was wearing—only I don't think you call them bloomers Edie, they were short, a peachy colour, with buttons at the side and lace at the bottom, not long and white . . .

You're sure you want me to go on, you want to hear all of this?

Well she put her hands round my head and got me to kiss her—not on her mouth—but she held me there so tightly that I couldn't breathe and then she rolled over and she was drunk you know but she wasn't sad like she'd been a moment before, she had been staring at me when she was sitting on the bed and I reckon she was thinking about me and wondering if it was true, if it was my first time. She made me take my trousers off and she laughed when she saw me and said, Lord Jesus above, in that Australian accent of hers and she laughed her funny hiccup laugh and I laughed too because lord, I'd never seen myself so—so swollen I wasn't hardly recognisable. She wanted me to wear a Spanish Skin but we had trouble getting it on me because I hardly knew myself what to do with this great burning thing and it made her laugh again trying to get me to calm down, to wait a little, but the sweat was breaking on my brow and I tried to do what I was told, Edie, because I liked her and I was grateful to her and I didn't think she disliked me, not the way I'd thought such women would, and I was burning by this time—*you're sure you really want to hear this?*

No, I think you can guess the rest because you might say you do, but afterwards,

afterwards you'll hate me . . . and you have to remember I was only barely sixteen and I'd told them all I was eighteen and that was before I was found out, too, and you can imagine a lad of sixteen, well it was all over in just a second, in the fastest second, I mean I tried to angle myself where she directed me and I grabbed her and just pushed . . . she shrieked this one tiny bit and I was about to say to her, Did I hurt you? but then before I knew it I was off, just like that. I didn't mean to, I thought I'd get my money's worth but no—I had no more control over myself than a gun with the safety catch off.

So. Then she sat up and said, Lord, let's have another cigarette then, and I staggered over to the corner of the bed to get them, with this stupid great rubber thing dangling in front of me. It was only through the alcohol that I wasn't ashamed of it.

Suddenly there was banging on the door and I knew Jack and Ray and the others were passing and I felt embarrassed. I jumped under the sheet and pulled the covers up. Molly grinned at me and got in beside me and soon she was taking hold of me to try and get me in working order again. She told me she liked me and I wasn't like all the others and did I have any more money and she knocked back another beaker of gin and then rolled herself onto me and that did the trick, the minute I got a smell of her with her hot skin and her great mounds of flesh—well the next time was a bit more leisurely and—well nothing like it is with us, you know, it was just friendly and fast and funny—and soon the sweat between us made this slapping noise and I could feel myself well up inside her and she started to get this dazed look in her face like she was simple or something, with her mouth hanging open so I just thought I'd better push right on and I did. I pushed and pushed and she took hold of my hand and put it at the front of her and then she began quietly groaning to herself and then she was yelling, this big deep scary drunken yelling and I didn't know why or what it was but she soon pulled me off again, she was hot inside and she drew me on, she moved so fast that the tip of my cock felt like it was on fire.

She said to me that once a girl had learnt such things and learnt not to care about her honour or any of that then it was possible to enjoy it but she didn't think other women did, she was pretty damn sure her mother didn't for instance or her sisters, and from conversations with the other girls she'd never heard any describe it the way she felt it. She said she just took to it like riding a horse and then tried to choose men who weren't too dirty and had most of their own teeth and young ones she liked but I was her favourite now and I could visit her any time I was in Sydney and if I'd roll on my back she'd show me something else she liked to do.

*You're sure you want to hear this?*

*Saturday 21st October, 1922*

Dear Freddy,

Good morning to you, darlint, I am writing this at 10 a.m., sitting on my bed, trying to curl up into some semblance of a relaxed position to write this, but it is difficult when everything in the room is sharp corners, angles and not a single plump cushion or curve or even a shaft of clean light.

What I long for (you might think this is a little strange, Freddy) is to visit the Powder Room at the Cafe Royal. I sometimes have an image of myself floating on that soft carpet, sliding down those shiny handrails, wafting on clouds of pink. All light and puffy and unreal and nothing can touch me there.

When I get out that is what I will do. Sit in the Powder Room and stay there on the carpet, smelling the ladies' perfume as they sail in and out, refuse to move for an entire day. Odd how safe it feels, the Ladies' Power Room. No men in there, nothing grey or sharp and it's only the mirrors which glint.

Darlint, I've been to see the Doctor, because I might as well tell you I have been a little upset these last few days and sleeping has been impossible. The women here *want* to escape to the infirmary and will come up with any amount of symptoms to permit them a stay. I gather Dr Lynch is wise to this and highly cynical. Personally I can't see why anyone would want to be in the infirmary with its terrible vinegary smells and the occasional screaming baby. Can you imagine it . . . babies, in a prison! (They are allowed to stay in the prison creche until they are nine months old.) A more horrible discovery I couldn't wish to make.

The Doctor says I have been a vain and silly woman. You seem, Mrs Thompson, not to have accepted the reality of your husband's death . . . and the predicament you find yourself in . . .

I wonder, when he says such things, how I could *demon*strate that I have accepted the reality and the predicament I find myself in? Would he be satisfied with more emotion from me, or less? That is, if I fainted and took to wailing more often would he be convinced of my innocence and that I am a loving bereaved wife or would he find me *over*-emotional, even more vain and silly? Does he really require more composure? Would that persuade him of the authenticity of my distress?

It is truly so hard to know, Freddy. I hope *you* at least are getting it right. I think it must be easier to be a man in prison, it is so much more commonplace amongst men, if you see what I mean. You will be judged well for behaving in the way it is easiest in the world for you to behave—for being upright and firm, never faltering or weeping or snapping. All will assume, in any case, great torrents of emotion underneath. How women express things, our emotions, I mean, seem always to be quite wrong. Fainting, weeping, Stern has advised me against all of these. Yet, if I control my pounding heart and stand straight and tall at the wrong moment, will the court find me heartless and cold, doubt my innocence or even my qualities as a *woman*?

I am particularly concerned to get this right as I suspect the Doctor is not the only one who considers me vain and silly, and on the 24th it may be very important indeed that this is not the opinion of certain people. Is it such a terrible thing to be vain? I don't have a dictionary in here so I'm struggling to remember the definition but I suppose it must be two-fold; both futile, pointless or worthless—*in vain*—and then narcissistic, arrogant, conceited, taking too much pleasure in one's own appearance. Of course it is the latter that the Doctor meant, but isn't it connected to the former? That is, if you follow my train of thought, isn't it worse for me to be conceited when he believes me worthless? If I was some great lady, Lady Di, for instance (did you see she is to play the part of Queen Elizabeth in a new British natural colour film, Freddy—Clara mentioned this although she

54

wouldn't let me see the picture of her in the *Daily Sketch*), would it be fine for her to be conceited, or say, Bonar Law, because others, too, are convinced of his worth?

I'm running on. I have too much time to think here and not enough time to converse with others. I am thinking in a way that I never ever have before—my head literally aches with the effort of it sometimes! I had no idea that thinking was an activity, darlint, until now, that it was like exercise, it can exhaust me or enliven me, but it frustrates me, too. I have ordered more novels and more cigarettes and next time I visit the library I will look for a simple dictionary, as I have discovered a new pleasure in examining words, looking in them for cracks, for little slips where the meaning nestles.

I must finish here.

Love, as ever,

Your Peidi.

*     *     *

He is paper-thin and in his white coat insubstantial; he wavers a little in the light in the medical room, which is electric, and powerful. Just jump up here and loosen your things for me he says, as if I am nine years old. I know men talk this way to save themselves from embarrassment, when they are poking around inside women's bodies. They feel easier if they think of us as little girls, I've come across such things before. But then when Dr Lynch has me lying on the bench and helpless (feeling my stomach the way Mother primps the edges of pastry) his tone towards me alters. His beard is inches from my face, I almost feel the bristles rasp along my stomach and the words brush me (now like Mother brushing milk on a raw pie crust, I can't keep the thought from my mind that I am pastry, grey an flabby, ready to be cooked). Now what have we here? Let me see . . . as if he had really never seen one before, never seen a woman.

He takes one sly glance at Clara, who is tactfully gazing into the middle distance. He's close enough that I can smell a faint trace of shag tobacco; eerily, he smells like Percy. You have been a silly and vain woman, Mrs Thompson. It is hardly any wonder that you find yourself unable to sleep.

But he doesn't examine me properly. He skims over me with some distaste and doesn't even ask me to undress. He must think he is Jesus—that he can detect everything with his hands without the engagement of his intellect at all!

Oddly refreshing, my trip to see Dr Lynch. The chance to hate someone—truly, *that* is refreshing; the finding of a place to lodge some powerful dislike, let it take root there, watch it grow tough and fast as bindweed, choking everything in its path.

*Vain*: a. (F., from the Latin vanus). Empty, worthless; having no substance, value or importance.

*Silly*: (sile) a. (O. English Seely). Weak in intellect.

# SENSATIONAL LETTERS

### RESUMED HEARING AT STRATFORD

On Tuesday, at Stratford Police Court, Frederick Edward Bywaters, 21, a ship's laundry steward, of Wiston-street, Upper Norwood and Edith Thompson, 28, of 41 Kensington-gardens, Ilford, were again brought up on the remanded charge of wilfully murdering Percy Thompson, a shipping clerk, and husband of the female prisoner.

Crowds gathered in the vicinity of the court to witness the arrival of the accused, but no demonstration was made.

Bywaters, when now placed in the dock, nodded genially to his solicitor and then took his seat in the dock beside a warder. Mrs Thompson when she entered the dock, certainly looked more cheerful than on any of her previous appearances before the magistrates. Indeed, she nodded and smiled at quite a number of female acquaintances in court.

Mr William Lewis prosecuted. Mr F.A.S. Stern represented Mrs Thompson, and Bywaters was again defended by Mr Barrington Matthews.

At the last hearing there was a query as to the reliability of a plan of the district where the stabbing took place, and Detective Taylor now produced a revised one.

Mr Lewis said that that day he intended to call a large number of witnesses as to certain letters which had been found. These were found after the crime, a number of letters, one lot being on the steamship 'Morea', upon which Bywaters held a position, and these were from the female prisoner. These letters had been very carefully considered, as also had letters which had been found at his address at Norwood. There were some further letters in Bywaters' possession when he was arrested and a fourth lot was found in the woman's box at her place of business—these had been written by Bywaters. Mr Lewis added that the letters had been addressed by the woman to Bywaters at various ports of call.

Mr Stern, who objected successfully to the letters being read at the inquest, again raised his points and added that there was not a shred of evidence of guilt against his client, and therefore the letters could not be read.

Mr Eliot Howard: She must have known perfectly well who did it, and again and again in the course of that night's detention she told different stories.

Mr Stern: She told lies admittedly, but that does not make her guilty.

Mr Eliot Howard remarked that he appreciated the seriousness but he held that there was a prima facie case and the letters could be read.

Mr Stern asked that a note should be made of his objection.

Detective Inspector Shules, D.I.A. Police, deposed that on October 12th, he removed from the ss 'Morea' a box belonging to Bywaters. In the box was a photograph of the female prisoner, and a number of letters.

The evidence given by Detective Inspector Hall was read over, and when the woman's statement at the police station was read she bowed her head and became very agitated, although Bywaters remained quite self-possessed. The inspector added with regard to three letters sent by Bywaters to the female prisoner, that one was dated December 21st, 1921, and that the others were undated.

James Herbert Carlton, millinery manufacturer, of 168 Aldersgate-street, EC said that the female prisoner had been in his employ for over 10 years, her maiden name being Miss Graydon. She had gone by that name ever since. Witness knew that she was married and also knew her late husband. She was a book-keeper and manageress at £6 a week and a bonus of £30 per annum. Witness saw Bywaters in his showroom about 18 months ago. Mrs Thompson was then with him and Witness was not introduced. He next saw Bywaters on September 20th last. This was about a quarter to five at night and he was standing in the porch of Witness's premises. A few moments later Mrs Thompson left, but Witness couldn't *say* if the couple met. On the following day Mrs Thompson was away from business. He had granted permission for this at her request, although she did not explain the reason. On the following Monday she was there from 9 a.m. to 5 p.m. attending to her business, and also on the Tuesday, the day preceding the tragedy; she left at her usual time, and he next saw her in custody. Witness added that he had received registered letters addressed to the female prisoner in her maiden name. Witness had been shown letters sent to

Bywaters and they were in Mrs Thompson's writing.

Detective Sergeant Hancock stated that all the letters that had been found were handed to him, and also certain newspaper cuttings, which were found in envelopes. The first letter was dated August 20th, 1921.

Mr Stern: 'I hope you will put on the deposition that I make a formal objection to these letters.'

The Clerk: 'That will be done.'

The sergeant read the letter as follows: 'Come and see me Monday. He suspects.—Peidi.' Another letter, in an envelope, dated January 3rd, 1922, was next produced by the witness. This was addressed to Bywaters at Plymouth and it contained this passage: 'Of course, he knows you are due in on the 7th and he will be very suspicious of you after that date. I suppose I shall not be able to see you . . . To be careful I must be cruel to myself.' She added that she destroyed all letters she received except this one commencing, 'Dear Edie'. This was read, but it contained nothing material to the issue.

Another letter contained the following to Bywaters: 'I surrender to him unconditionally now. Do you understand? It is the best way to disarm suspicion. He has several times asked me if I am happy now and I have said, "Yes, quite", but you know that is not the truth, don't you?'

Another read contained the passage: 'Do something this time—opportunities come and go by . . . On Wednesday we had some words in bed. You know, darlint, the same old subject.'

She added in the letter that her husband had blamed him for making her alter towards him and she told him if he repeated it she would leave the house immediately.

The female prisoner, whilst this letter was being read, collapsed and had to be taken out of court, the chairman remarking: 'Take her out into the open.'

*Ilford Recorder,* Friday 27th October, 1922.


*Tuesday 24th October, 1922*
*About 9 p.m.*


Darlingest boy I know,
I thought that Wednesday the 4th of October had been the hardest day of my life so far but nothing up until now has quite matched today.

My pencil is nearly blunt and this letter must be faint, plus I am exhausted and my eyes feel sticky with my desperate need to sleep.

Lights will be out in exactly five minutes time but I must put some words down, words of comfort, I must let you know that I forgive you for keeping my letters. I know from your face today—as I was carried past you I caught that glimpse—that you are in anguish whenever I am, and that since I collapsed you have collapsed inside with guilt and shame and since you did what you did for me anyway, out of loyalty and love and a foolish, *foolish* (I must say it, Freddy, it was DEEPLY FOOLISH) desire to rescue me, or at least, this is what I believe, without talking to you it is what I cling to but how I long to talk to you, to understand what you did because, Freddy, it has brought us to this and I feel skinned alive, skinned alive—to have my letters read like that, to have everyone in that room—Mr Carlton, Agnes, Avis, Mother, Father, *your* Mother— the list goes on and on—to *have everyone hear my innermost heart beating on paper—Oh God, Freddy, Oh God . . .*

\*　　　\*　　　\*

A blistering afternoon, the office girls wearing their dresses without cardigans, revealing their pastry-white forearms, fanning themselves with newspapers, when Mr Carlton comes by, tooting the horn on his brand new Ford, bought that morning from London and Essex Motors on Ilford High Road.

Agnes and I, but not Miss Prior, come to the door of Carlton & Prior all giggles and excitement to admire the shiny beast and Mr Carlton honks the horn again and opens and closes the door for us in demonstration, and several passersby are smiling and admiring the car also. I'm sure it is I, not Mr Carlton, who suggests I should come for a ride and Agnes, of course, flapping and simpering and saying no she couldn't possibly and as he is opening the door for me and I'm slipping onto the hard leather seat. Miss Prior comes to the shop doorway, holding a new hat, a delicious ivory felt hat and she simply stands there and stares at us.

Of course, we create quite a stir, driving down Aldersgate and then passing St Paul's and I have never been so close to Mr Carlton before and certainly not when he is in this mood of pride and elation, continually honking the horn of the car for no reason at all, making pedestrians jump out of their skins. He points out to me the dials on the dashboard and the stick for changing gears and other features and then offers me a cigarette—he usually heartily disapproves of ladies smoking!—and shows me how to use a nifty little gadget for the ashtray.

Once, when he reaches for the gear-stick his hand brushes my knee but we both act as if this is nothing and fix our eyes in front of us.

How d'you like it then, Miss Graydon—

Edie? he bellows. (It is noisy, the sound of the engine rattles over our voices and judders and shakes our bones.) Mr Carlton hasn't quite got the hang of things and has had to stop a few times rather suddenly to avoid running into a horse or a bicycle. He smiles at me as best he can, with his pipe dangling from the side of his mouth and gives me a look which I know very well. A slow look. It never ceases to surprise me that men don't realise that women who have been married understand certain of their feelings perfectly well. The slackness at the sides of the mouth, the teeth biting down on the pipe and the slackness in the watery-blue eyes, too, roaming over my face with too much freedom, too much liberty. The inside of the car is filling up with the smoke of his plum tobacco. (A manly smell I've always enjoyed. When I step into the shop in the mornings this is the smell that greets me, it swims around the hats and pervades the felt and feathers, soaks into the tissue paper in the boxes.)

Of course, one could never say (and certainly not to one's employer) Oh, for God's sake, Mr Carlton, can't you do a better job of disguising what you're thinking? Or even: yes we think such things too sometimes but we have the decency to compose our faces properly and keep our eyes from sliding all over the place.

And there he stood in court, as if he'd never brought me that box of Turkish Delight, never taken me for that drive, never stopped the car near Charterhouse Square and run those thoughts all over me, like a child might run its hand through the fur on a dog, until I could feel my skin prickle and respond a little and had to clear my throat and say: Shall we be driving back, Mr Carlton, as the lunchtime rush will be starting soon? So that when he saw Freddy waiting for me all those months ago, when he saw us walking together, our heads inclining together like sugar tongs being squeezed at the bottom, walking into the Holborn Restaurant; he knew what was going on and resented it, I know he did. He resented it bitterly, that I, a married woman should give Freddy what I wouldn't give him, even though he and I never discussed it, he didn't even openly dare to ask.

I've found that it's often the case that what others most hate you for is that very thing in themselves they are most afraid of wanting. How dare you want what they dare not even admit they want? A fury can be directed at you then, which will snatch you in its blast, leave scorch marks on your skin. I've known that but not minded too much, because why should I mind, until now?

\*　　　\*　　　\*

James Herbert Carlton, millinery manufacturer, of 168 Aldersgate-street, EC said that the female prisoner had been in his employ for over 10 years, her maiden name being Miss Graydon . . . Witness knew that she was married and also knew her late husband. She was a book-keeper and a manageress at £6 a week and a bonus of about £30 per annum. Witness saw Bywaters in his showroom about 18 months ago. Mrs Thompson was then with him and Witness was not introduced. He next saw Bywaters on September 20th last . . . Witness saw. Witness said. Witness knew— nothing, what does he think he knows?

*      *      *

Our garden at number 41, thinking of the hyacinths again, the ones I planted there on my own in the autumn of 1920 and how droopy they were, spring the following year when the flowers were full grown; how they bent to one side with the weight of fragrance and blooms. That was just before Freddy moved in.

Picturing them, trying to recover every detail. Green, some buds still green, tight as a baby's closed fist: then the arrows of blossom, eyelid-pink, darkening to deepest red at the centre, and the leaves shiny and long and fat and waxy and smelling like grass, like silky, milky, succulent grass.

I could eat those flowers. I want to eat them, to fill up my mouth with things green, things alive, things which keep growing and dying and growing again. I want to fill myself up and keep out the grey in here, the fine dust, the thinness and coldness, the bloodless drinks of tea, the empty corners of the room where even light, even air is absent and only absence is present like a grey crushing blanket, a suffocating weight.

Just occasionally a simple task will float into my mind, perhaps turning down the crisp sheet on my bed, slipping the old pillow into a fresh envelope of linen, and I can't help myself, it's like the slicing pain of a cut from paper—an unexpected sliver of pain—and in a matter of seconds it's all too late and I've brought blood to the surface. *Will it bloom this year? Or has the sudden frost disturbed its bed?*

\*       \*       \*

No, I don't think it was the first moment that I *saw* Freddy. For if I had seen him but thought little more about it . . . Perhaps the first moment that I *responded* to him. And how far back do I have to go before I come to that?

Portsmouth and the weather has altered, with the heatwave suddenly giving way to an oppressive blanket of dark clouds. There's time for a quick walk, before the storm breaks, so the four of us march along the front with coats flapping, gulls squealing above them, and then Freddy points out where his ship the SS *Morea* is usually docked and remarks that he has just returned from Australia and I blurt out: Oh yes, you're a sailor! and I'm thinking How odd to be a child who refuses to enter water and to end up a sailor . . .

The others look at me and laugh. I pull the collar of my peach sports coat up to my chin and stare at the cuffs, as the first few specks of dark rain land on the pale coat in large splashes.

I'm not a sailor, Freddy replies cheerfully, I'm a laundry clerk on the ship. I sort the laundry. I take care of the sheets, the uniforms, all the linen from the kitchen. And I'm the writer. I keep the log-book.

Avis titters and a gull squawks back at her in reply. She is hoping for more than a laundry clerk, I know that. She wants to do well for herself, the way she thinks I have with Percy. A big house in Ilford like mine. That would do nicely.

She takes Freddy's arm in hers as they begin to hurry away from the sea-front.

Come on, Edie, it's about to sheet down, Percy calls to me. I'm staring out to sea, at the rain beginning to pit the surface of the water, raising silver patterns, like the wrong side of a cheese grater. When the rain is pelting in earnest, a sound I adore, I reluctantly join the others, hastening back towards the town. Avis is shrieking and I can't help laughing as the rain smacks at our faces and drowns the feathers on our hats.

By the time we reach the ferry, in time for the last crossing, the sky is calm again and it is as if the rain never happened. I declare myself disappointed—How much more exciting to cross in a storm! but Freddy answers that I might not think so if I was holding my head over the side to be sick. To which Avis says, with proprietorial delight, Oh Freddy, don't be disgusting!

The boat is crowded and the crossing choppier and speedier than either Avis or I expect. We link arms together on the deck, watching gulls follow the boat. We're jammed between a woman with an American accent and a fearfully overweight child. Percy prefers to be below deck, where he can be sure, he says, to get a seat. Avis is trying to whisper, but the wind snatches at her words and she's forced to raise her voice a little.

So, what do you think, Edie?

What do I think?

You know what I mean!

Oh darling, he's—

As I'm speaking I see Freddy approaching, bustling his way through the crowd on the deck. I raise my voice above the sound of the sea and the gulls.

What do I think of Freddy? I think he's very handsome, a very fine catch, and not at all the boy I remembered!

Freddy gives no sign of whether he heard me.

We decide that first night in Shanklin that we will take dinner at the hotel, Osborne House, which is rather grander than Avis expected and suitably close to the sea for my taste. I have paid half towards the cost of her room—there's no way she could afford it otherwise and the place she had picked out was—well, from the photograph it looked shabby and didn't even have a sea view. Anyway, I earned a huge bonus this year and it never feels right unless I share it with Avis.

Avis and I excitedly examine our rooms—hers is down a corridor on its own, with electric lighting and pretty curtains in a rich mahogany-coloured velvet, although no view of the sea. Percy and mine is sea-facing and we have plenty of cupboard space. It's very modern in design; peacock feathers in a vase on the mantelpiece, the wallpaper busy with cranes and storks. Avis sits on the bed and watches me unpack my things. When I've finished I suggest that we sneak next door for a look at Freddy's room, but Avis is horrified. We can just knock on the door and invite ourselves in for a moment, I venture, innocently. She giggles, as if the idea is too absurd to take seriously.

We join the men eventually in the lounge of Osborne House, where they are drinking a beer before dinner. Avis admires a huge aspidistra in a gold-painted pot in the corner. I order a Guinness and port and stretch out my legs luxuriously. Avis's gaze follows mine and travels down to my feet.

Ooh, new shoes, Edie! They're lovely!

Yes, they are aren't they? They're glacé kid leather. I love the patent toe-cap. I bought them from Debenham & Freebody on Friday.

Oh, were the sales on?

No, not in Debenhams. But we had a hat sale this week. Some beautiful new hats came in. Now you can't escape having a bob, Avis, because these hats absolutely will not fit on your head with all that hair—it's as simple as that.

Percy sucks on his pipe. I can tell he is trying to think of something to say to Freddy. He's worried that we might suddenly direct a remark at him and then he will be required to say something about women's shoes or hats or fashions or the latest book or film. He coughs, tapping the pipe on the ashtray first and strikes a relaxed pose, one leg folded over the other.

So, I imagine you were too young to see service, Frederick?

Avis and I groan.

Oh not the war!

A smile appears for a moment on Freddy's face.

That's right, sir, I was too young to see

service. My father did though. He—he was killed at Ypres. Chlorine gas.

Freddy says this plainly and without emotion, but everyone appears embarrassed.

Now, see what you've done? I nudge Percy, who glares at me in surprise. Luckily, there is a brief diversion when my Guinness and port arrives and the waiter confirms that we have a table booked for eight in the restaurant next door.

And you, sir, Freddy continues boldly, did you serve in France?

Percy takes a deep breath, about to embark on a very long tale. Avis and I exchange glances.

No, I didn't as a matter of fact. I have certain health problems and in the first instance . . . I mean I was in the London Scottish but I—I had my first inclination that all was not as it should be—

Percy has a weak heart. He had a doctor's note. I drain my glass with speed, clinking it down on the table with a bang. Freddy's look—the way he looks at Percy—startles me. He makes no attempt to disguise it. *Your tongue's so sharp, you'll cut yourself one of these days.* Something that Mother used to say to me. I might say to Freddy the same thing about the glance he gives. A glance so sharp . . .

So you didn't see service at all? The entire war? Freddy asks, managing to sound

73

incredulous, although it's perfectly clear that this is what Percy has just said.

Percy coughs. My heart—it was—it is quite a serious condition . . .

Freddy's neck looks rather pink, his adam's apple suddenly prominent, as if he is straining to swallow it down again. He opens his mouth to say something more but Avis seems not to notice. Surely it's eight o'clock now? she interrupts. I'm starving. She stands up and the two men jump to their feet. Percy's expression is grateful; like someone who feels rescued from something. Leaving half-finished glasses the men follow Avis and me into the dining room.

It is clearly the grandest dining room Avis has ever been in and she tries not to giggle as the waiter pulls out her seat for her at the same time as Freddy retrieves her napkin from the floor. The room is almost empty; which adds to Avis's self-consciousness. When I go to look at the marvellous view of the oil-black sea from the window she hisses: Edie, come back here!

Percy is 'doing the honours' and choosing the wine. Freddy stares into the middle distance, trying to look like someone who could equally well choose a good wine if he wanted to. In profile he is not really at his best; his high brow and the pushed-up way he wears his hair giving him an exaggerated silhouette, like that of a puppet. (Avis, I'd wager, longs to

74

sit facing him, so that she can stare without embarrassment into the deep blue pools of his eyes, bask in one of his sudden dazzling smiles.)

He is talking about one of his mates at the P&O Office. Arnie. How he lost five pounds to Arnie in a ridiculous bet. Impossible to resist responding to that.

Five pounds! I can't believe it. That's what I earn in a week . . . What on earth are you doing, throwing away that kind of money!

Freddy laughs.

Well, of course, I didn't intend to throw it away. I intended to *double* it!

Avis stares stonily at me. Her look says you *mentioned how much you earn a week just to impress Freddy!* She would never say so, of course. I can see it is exactly the kind of thing that *would* impress Freddy, for which I can hardly be blamed.

The waiter sidles up to the table and refills all the glasses and Avis makes a remark about the Derby this year, to which no one responds. And then Freddy is laughing again at something else that I've just said and tucking into his steak and spooning cheese sauce onto his cauliflower and suddenly he looks up and all eyes are on him. He pauses, the spoon quavering over the bowl like a tuning fork. He glances deliberately from Avis to me.

I'm sorry! Am I taking too much sauce?

Everyone begins talking at once, with both

me and Avis saying, No, no that's fine, don't worry and hastily returning our attention to our own food. Percy suggests loftily that the Duchesse potatoes are the best he's ever eaten. There is the sound of cutlery clinking on china and no one disagrees with him.

*     *     *

Day two at Osborne House, Shanklin. Breakfast is heart-shaped poached eggs and bread and fresh butter, all served on blue and white porcelain. Avis and Freddy appear from opposite sides of the great dining room to join Percy and me, already seated at the breakfast table. Avis's face lights up as Freddy approaches the table. She looks rumpled and still half asleep, with powder hastily applied and hair gathered up in a handful of mother-of-pearl pins at the back. I find myself wondering if Freddy has kissed Avis, or touched her and if so, where. In which places.

After breakfast, we decide on a walk along Shanklin Chine; that is, I decide and the others agree, so soon we are ambling, with the trees overhanging and the scent of wet soil and wet leaves, wet wool; the sound of the rushing falls beside us. There isn't room on the steep path to the falls to walk two-abreast, so Avis is in front, I'm walking behind Freddy; eyes fixed on the back of his heels (newly polished), the hem of his trousers (neatly pressed), the leather belt (worn, soft leather), the rolled up shirt sleeves (carefully, equally, rolled on each side), the cotton shirt (the sleeves brushed with pine needles). Finally from the sharp points of his elbows, to the back of his neck. His hair is neatly shorn, and the back of his ears sticking out, a little pink in the tingling damp air next to the falls. Like two pale rose petals. I'm surprised at this thought. If ever I've considered ears before—which I can't say I have—they were only cauliflowers or scrunched-up paper. Now I'm thinking shells for the first time. Young, curled-up ferns.

At the base of the Chine the sea-front, with a milky green sea, is quiet as a sleeping dog. Squawking gulls perch on the top of the lined-up rows of changing huts. We stop at a fisherman's cottage for cigarettes, with Freddy cupping his hands round Avis's to help her light it. Really, since there is no wind or spray from an utterly calm sea, there is no need for him to do this.

What a glorious day! Scarcely a breeze, I state vigorously.

Percy is the only one to respond, with a dutiful yes, following the direction of my gaze. Freddy and Avis link arms, each drawing on their cigarettes in a comfortable silence, continuing to walk along the beach, in the direction of Sandown, picking their way between the groups of families and strolling couples.

About a hundred yards down the beach, Freddy stops at a makeshift tent. I can't see what might be the attraction of the tent, so I grab Percy's arm and try to hurry him along. Percy has been ambling at a peaceful pace but now my shoes are crunching the sand and I'm almost at a trot. But the figures of Freddy and Avis are disappearing inside the tent! I let go of Percy's arm to dash after them.

I stop short outside the tent, facing a newly painted wooden sign in blood red letters. *Madame Sosostris. Famous Clairvoyant. What Does Your Future Hold?*

Percy catches up with me, panting a little, his pipe hastily doused and sticking out of his jacket pocket. That irritating cough again, the sound of something shifting down his windpipe. He reaches for the pipe and refills it with Shag tobacco, making a study of not paying any attention to me, not having had to run to catch up with me. I'm chewing my nails and pacing outside the tent.

Do you have a cigarette, Percy?

You know I hate it when you smoke.

That fact notwithstanding, do you have a cigarette?

He reaches in his jacket pocket and offers me the last in a squashed packet of Players. He tries to catch my eyes as I lean forward for him to light it but the instant he shakes the match out, I stride a few steps away from him, staring out to the cliffs, then to the flat thin sea, to the shadowy boats, bobbing on the horizon.

Have yours told, Edith. You go in next. Percy is reaching into his pockets and then opening his palm to show a handful of coins.

I can hear Madame Sosostris's tones, low and babbling, but not what she is saying. Percy shifts slightly, at a polite distance from the tent. I move closer. I'm kicking at a piece of bladder-wrack, flicking it up on the toe of my shoes.

You're scuffing your new shoes, he says.

I continue scraping up seaweed, then shells; balancing them on the toe of the shoe, then lightly kicking them up into the air. The shells fly up, smack back down among the others. A satisfying sound. Then Freddy's voice bursts out from the folds of the tent, followed by Avis's giggles and the two of them spill out, laughing and chattering.

She says another war is coming, Freddy whispers to Percy, in a tone of mock-seriousness.

Silly old bitch! Percy explodes. *His* tone is not mocking at all, but venomous.

Freddy and Avis are already walking off, so I hesitate, but Percy has not forgotten his offer, and pushes the money into my hand.

We'll catch you up! He calls to the others, nodding his head towards Madame Sosostris.

I close my fingers over the coins. Just my misfortune—he'll undoubtedly choose to come in with me. Then he smiles and I realise how foolish that idea is: Percy considers such superstitious nonsense silly in the extreme. The fact that he is offering to pay is a gesture of great indulgence. Sensing my mood, but not the cause of it, he simply wishes to cheer me up. He naturally has a preference for his wife in a good mood; what husband doesn't want his wife to be sunny and contented, especially on holiday? He intends to wait outside.

I push my way into the tent and stand blinking while my eyes adjust to the semi-dark.

It looks to me like Madame Sosostris has taken the day off sick and left her baby sister in her place. A girl of no more than seventeen sits at a table, which she's draped with green velvet; a scarf around her head and a candle placed in front of her, balanced precariously in a saucer. A pack of cards, a cup of tea and a large book make up the rest of the contents of the table. The girl smiles at me and I see at once that Freddy would like her—the smile is bold and self-assured.

The place stinks—an animal smell, like the inside of a stables and the whiff of wax and strong perfume on top of that. I wrinkle my nose and Madame Sosostris or Missy Sosostris as I've privately named her says: Won't you sit down, ma'am. She indicates a rickety wooden stool at the other side of the table, onto which I plant myself without much grace.

She is compulsively shuffling the cards in front of her, at the same time as running her eyes up and down me, as one might examine a horse or cow for its breeding properties. I see that she takes in the wedding ring, the haircut, the handbag, the gloves, the lilac costume . . . yes, I imagine she's reasonably good at her job, even if she is the junior substitute.

Now, ma'am, is there anything in particular you'd like to ask the cards? She has a strong Portsmouth accent. Again, I think of Freddy, of the girls he meets on shore-leave there and I'm stung with dislike of this young woman. I'm sure she's wearing rouge.

I hear Percy cough outside and wonder how much he can hear of this conversation.

Oh, just tell me my future, that'll be plenty, I reply.

She hands the cards to me. Give them a shuffle, dear.

Dear. A young woman trying to be an old gypsy. I shuffle the cards, clumsily. She takes them from me after scarcely a moment and begins laying them out on the table in front of us, moving her cold cup of tea to one side. I feel a shift in her concentration; she falls silent. When the cards are all laid out in the oddest of patterns she begins turning them over.

She tuts and 'hmmms' until I can barely sit still.

You're a married lady, and . . . let me see . . . no children yet?

I nod. That's easy enough. If I had children,

wouldn't they be chattering outside, with my husband?

You've had a happy life so far, and you . . . (she seems to wait for clues, wait for me to nod or give a sign of encouragement so I'm determined to do neither) you enjoy good health, although . . . perhaps you would like children and they have been slow to arrive?

I hold my head very still, avoiding the temptation to nod or shake it.

Well, have no fear, for they will surely arrive soon, she blunders on. Now. Let me see. This card, see, this is you: the Page of Pentacles and this is where you are right now in your life: the Hierophant, which represents the present, now the hierophant stands for the power of the keys (see these keys at his feet?), all things which are sacred and righteous, and this card represents outer influences—

I fear she can hear Percy outside and thinks he is another customer. She is racing through the reading at the speed of knots and it's well-nigh impossible to make sense of any of it, nor even keep up with her.

That's the Knight of Swords, he's riding see, with his sword held aloft and he represents, well, death, in some senses, but not to be alarmed, ma'am, it is not a worldly death, oh no, it's reversed, you see, that means imprudence, incapacity . . .

I'm wondering what Freddy asked her. How they got onto the subject of the war. He probably said: well, what's your hot tip for the Derby? Or maybe he asked outright, will there be another war and she said . . .

Now, this one, this is your outcome, see, the Devil. I'm not always sure, I'm not so sure of this card . . .

She turns to the book beside her.

You have to look it up in a book? Now I know she is definitely Madame Sosostris's stand-in.

She's not in the least perturbed. Well, the cards never lie, ma'am but sometimes I—I don't know everything.

She turns to the page on the Devil. We both stare at the card on the velvet in front of us. The candle splutters as the pages of the book flap air towards it. The card is particularly gruesome—a great horned, winged creature with taloned feet and chained to its feet, two naked people—a man and a woman. No, on closer inspection, not chained to the Devil's feet. Chained to each other.

The Horned Goat of Mendes, she reads, with wings like those of a bat, is standing on an altar. A reversed pentagram is on the forehead. The right hand is upraised and extended, being the reverse of the benediction which is given by the Hierophant in the fifth card. In the left hand is a great flaming torch, inverted towards the earth.

She is muttering, rushing still, trying to get to the interesting part.

The figures at his feet are tailed, to signify their animal nature, but there is human intelligence in their faces and he who is exalted above them is not to be their master for ever.

But what does it mean? I say.

She closes the book, glances at her watch.

The Devil signifies the dweller on the threshold without the Mystical Garden, when those are driven forth, having eaten the forbidden fruit.

Oh.

I stand up. She smiles again, obviously thinking she's done a good job. I put the coins down on the table. They chink against the saucer of her cup.

A long and happy life, lots of children and good health, be careful not to be imprudent and don't give in to the fruit of temptation. That's probably it, she offers.

Thank you.

As I'm standing up she knocks a couple of cards from the pack onto the floor. She bends to pick them up and her scarf slips slightly, away from her forehead. I notice she has an ugly scar at the scalp, which she quickly covers up. She picks up the cards and I back out of the tent. As I leave, she is staring at the cards fanned in her hand and the saucy smile has gone from her face.

I emerge from the tent blinking, to find Percy waiting a discreet few yards away.

Difficult to tell, from his back, whether he was listening. Even his discreetness, his attempt to indulge me, is irritating. But as I draw level with him, I realise it's not that; he's watching Freddy and Avis, now two distant figures weaving their way down the beach; Avis occasionally stopping to examine a shell, Freddy skimming a stone towards the sea. Avis in her plum-coloured hat, inclining her head towards Freddy, like a purple tulip bending towards the light.

Do you think she'll marry him? My voice is dull and flat.

Bywaters? I should think the question is: Will he marry her? Percy says.

What do you mean?

Well, I get the impression that young Freddy has set his sights on . . .

I wait, but the cliché I expect, the phrase 'higher things', doesn't follow. Percy seems to lose his train of thought and instead asks: What did old Madame Sosostris say?

Oh, the usual nonsense.

Well why didn't you ask her?

Ask about my sister? Why should I? That's for Avis to ask.

I imagine she told them they'd marry anyway. What clairvoyant worth her salt wouldn't tell a young couple all would end happily?

Yes. *A long and happy life*. That was my promise, much like anyone else's.

We catch up with Fred and Avis in a penny arcade. Freddy is looking into a What the Butler Saw and Avis is yanking at his arm to pull him away and telling him he's shaming her in public. When this produces no reaction from Freddy she announces that she needs to find a cigarette machine and abruptly leaves. Rummaging in his pockets for another coin, Freddy straightens up, and then he spies me and grins.

Percy is at the change window, exchanging notes for coins. Freddy's glance takes this in, and without speaking he holds out a hand to me with a penny in it. My heart starts a faint jumping, as if a moth were caught in my chest. I glance slowly over towards Percy.

I pick the coin from Freddy's hand, in the same movement I made a few moments earlier, accepting a coin from Percy. I'm conscious of an odd, pointed significance. As if I don't have money of my own! More than both of them put together. But they like to offer me money.

So I slip the penny into the slot above the box. Freddy stands behind me and as the machine whirrs into life, he lifts the black cloth and we both duck our heads under it. Our faces two inches apart. I can feel the brush of Freddy's hair on my skin, the muscle in his shoulders through the thin cotton shirt.

The first picture is a woman in a garden, smiling. My mouth is dry and I'm afraid to swallow, afraid the noise would be deafening in such close quarters and too intimate. The pictures flick speedily past, the woman turning jerkily this way and that, still smiling, placing her head to one side and then pulling at her scarf and gloves and then her blouse and then turning away coyly once in her underclothes but then quickly turning back again. The flickering pictures give her movements an uncertainty which is quite comical—her behaviour inexplicable, sudden, changeable.

Freddy has watched it before. Keep your eyes on the rose bush! he whispers. One minute the semi-naked girl is sniffing at the flowers and throwing her arms about like flapping wings and the next she is darting behind the rose bush, tearing at the buttons on the sides of her knickers. Next she springs out from behind the roses, her hands holding up her breasts in front of her, unsure who to point them at. She settles on pointing them at the camera, whirling them this way and that, at the same time as pouting her mouth and raising her eyebrows. Then a quick twirl to show off her behind, pale as the moon and bigger than any I've ever seen, and then the black slot drops and the pictures abruptly end.

We pull our heads out from beneath the dark cloth, glance at one another and burst out laughing. I know I must be flushed and—over my shoulder—I see that Percy is on his way over to us.

What a large behind that girl had. I was nearly blinded by the light! Freddy whispers and I shriek then stifle it, just as Percy approaches, announcing himself with a cough.

Oh! Did you get some change then? I ask him, holding my hands out for more pennies. I can tell that my cheeks are still hot and so I keep my eyes fixed on the coins. Freddy struggles not to smirk.

I'm glad when Avis joins us and presses on everyone some melting french almonds she's bought from a stall.

*       *       *

The next day is 27th June, Freddy's birthday. I don't see Freddy or Avis in the morning for breakfast, but we meet up with them both on the promenade later, sitting on a bench amongst a crowd watching a Punch and Judy show. Avis is holding Freddy's arm and when I ask playfully, Did you buy Fred a present? she moves his sleeve to show the watch she bought him. (A cheap one, nothing special.) But the movement, the way Avis is holding his arm, the way she lifts his sleeve!

Avis is whispering to Percy, in a stage whisper, easily overheard, as he cranes towards her over the back of their seat.

His mother sent him a parcel. Can you imagine? From Norwood all the way to Osborne House! It was addressed to 'The Birthday Boy' . . .

They both laugh and I smile for a moment, too, hearing about the socks and handkerchiefs it contained—and then I see Freddy's face. His eyes are fixed straight ahead and he seems to be intent on the Punch and Judy show. But he has gently untangled his arm from Avis's grip and he is drawing deep on his cigarette, his eyes narrowing . . . He looks as if he's about to cry.

Then it strikes me: The parcel is like something you'd send to a soldier. How many years is it since Freddy's father died? He mentioned Ypres, so that was only five. Freddy ran away to sea when he was under-age, at fifteen, he told us earlier, getting his sister Florrie to sign the consent form in place of his mother. He indicated with a wry laugh, that Lily, his Mum, was not well pleased about this.

Somewhere in Norwood, a woman I've never met has a photo of Freddy in his sailor's uniform on her mantelpiece, and a newly starched uniform hanging above the ironing board. A young—somehow I imagine she must still be quite young—widow has to wait for her son to return from three-month stretches at sea. Such a long, long time, to wait for someone you love. I edge closer to Freddy, as close as I dare. I can't think of a gesture, a single gesture that it would be permissible to make, which would tell him that I'm sorry we laughed at his mother's present. That I don't think he's hen-pecked. Just sensitive. So I simply stand there, beside his bench, gazing at the top of his head.

Freddy seems to glitter, his blue eyes fierce in the bright sunlight, the pupils retreating into tiny dots, as if he is withdrawing them by force of will. His ears move as he swallows hard, several times. He finishes his cigarette and grinds it under his heel.

Finally he becomes aware of me standing beside him and flustered, stands up at once to offer me his seat. Mrs Thompson! I'm sorry. What am I thinking of . . .

Avis smiles, patting his arm approvingly. Edith, silly. You must call my sister Edith.

Yes, I'm sorry.

Freddy stands expectantly and there is nothing for it but to move into the warm seat he's just vacated. I sit down, feeling self-conscious now that the situation has reversed. Now he's behind me. My hand flies up to the back of my neck, to the place where the skin is beginning to burn, suddenly realising I've forgotten my hat. I must have been rushing this morning, to leave the hotel and get to the beach. I can't think otherwise how I could have forgotten it. Now that my hair is shorter my neck feels as raw as a stick of celery.

I sense rather than see Freddy put his hands

into his pockets, relax a little. The Professor is Gus Wood, his name in gold embroidery on the blue and white tent. Percy announces loudly: He's from Dalston. We've seen him before.

Freddy likes the boxers best, guffawing noisily when they come on and have a round of fisticuffs for no good reason whatsoever. Whether he finds it genuinely funny or is laughing for spite, or nervousness, is hard to tell, since he laughs loudly too when the ghost of Judy comes to awaken Punch's conscience and when Master Marwood the Executioner comes to carry Punch off and when the Black Man and the Crocodile come on stage. I am thinking about this, thinking about Freddy. How polished he is. All about him seems to shine; the pearly buttons on his shirt, his black shoes, his eyes. Just the same, he gives me the feeling of something fragile, highly breakable. Like a clean-blown egg shell, something you could crumble in your hand with the lightest of touches.

I always find the executioner a hideous puppet and this one is a particularly ugly specimen with nasty staring eyes and a down-turned mouth and a little wooden gallows in one hand. He has a pink tennis ball for a face, a bald patch painted yellow on the middle of his brown head. He wears a grubby black dress and the white collar at his throat gives him the option of doubling up as a priest. For this scene he carries a miniature gallows with a swinging rope that flops around with him, occasionally thumping on the stage and making the audience jump. Whilst everyone else boos Master Marwood, Freddy is laughing.

A gallows, a tiny wooden gallows, to entertain a crowd.

Avis and Percy enjoy it well enough and begin talking excitedly about Gus Wood, who is now packing the puppets back into his suitcase, while Bimbo the skinny monkey-boy of an assistant is harassing the children sitting on the pebbles, blowing his squeaky whistle in their faces and insisting that they 'cough up'. Already their parents are moving away to avoid paying. Freddy throws a shilling into the hat and Percy, after some shuffling and scrambling in his trousers pockets, finds a penny and does the same.

\*       \*       \*

Evenings at Shanklin are mostly passed in the lounge of the hotel, where Avis declares she feels 'at the heart of things', able to note with satisfaction the comings and goings of a fashionable crowd, whilst at the same time keeping one eye on a game of Brer Fox and Brer Rabbit, which Freddy and Percy play in earnest.

It's an old copy of the game that Percy has

kept from before the war. I can't resist pointing this out at every opportunity. Why is it Lloyd George's face instead of Brer Fox? I ask, picking up the Brer Fox card.

He was the Chancellor of the Exchequer, wasn't he. Percy examines the box lid. Nineteen thirteen, he muses. Yes, he was.

Freddy would have been eleven in 1913. Three years after that and I was married. A sneaked glance at Freddy, sitting opposite me on the leather sofa, his shirt unbuttoned at the collar and a cigarette between his fingers, to see whether he is making this calculation. The worst thing about age is that faces set like plaster: nothing else—no one else—is possible. A person of nineteen—I'm pretty sure Freddy is nineteen, isn't that what Avis wrote on his birthday card?—might look like a man, but the line of his jaw, his profile, his nose even, still have a soft, fluid quality, as if they might still be able to alter, the way a child's face does. Then again, some people—glancing at Avis, squashed on the sofa beside Freddy, holding her cards against her chest and squealing excitedly whenever she draws a good one— some people seem 'set' very young, with the face they will always have. Like that childhood taunt: *if the wind changes, you'll stay like that.* At some point in Avis's childhood, a northerly wind must have shifted east, right when Avis was day-dreaming, when she was busy being blank and absenting herself; not thinking

93

about anything at all. Absence. Bewilderment. That's what her expression says to me. As if she's been dragged back from somewhere greener and more pleasant, to take on the messy task of being here in the world. Deciding she can just about cope, as long as most of what goes on remains a mystery to her. People think we look alike—Percy always says it, which infuriates me. Avis, of course, resembles Mother.

It's your turn, Freddy, buck up! giggles Avis, whenever Freddy deliberates too long over his cards. Freddy leans forward and picks a Luxury card.

A week's window-smashing in the Suffragette Ward of Dottyville Lunatic Asylum, he reads out.

Ha! Don't suppose you remember those days, Frederick . . . Percy pours himself an extra glass of port from the decanter on the table, without remembering to offer it to anyone else.

Window-smashing? I can't say I do, says Freddy mildly and then without looking up from the board, Did you go in for that then, Mrs Thompson? I mean, Edith?

Percy takes his turn to throw the dice, landing on Lord Tom Noddy's Grouse Moor and paying up his fine, before I realise that Freddy is actually waiting for an answer. He *has* worked out my age then. This is not entirely bad. It means he has been thinking about me.

I pick up the dice and hold them in my hand, saying lightly: No, I didn't go in for chaining myself to the railings or smashing any shop windows. All very silly, if you ask me. Why should women want to enter politics and all that dreadful boring rigmarole when they could work in a hat shop or go to dances and wear wonderful furs . . .

Edie, that's not what you said at the time! Avis pipes up. Why, I remember terrible arguments between you and Father at the dinner table about giving the vote to women and I was just a child of ten or so—

I glance at my sister and then at Freddy. Avis, darling, I was being sarcastic. My voice is quiet. I really don't want to start all those arguments up again, do I? You know how Percy feels about such things. Percy appears not to be listening, instead tipping his head back, draining his glass.

Freddy flicks his eyes from me to Percy, whilst I try not to notice his appraisal of us. I feel sure that his sharp glimpse is taking in the fact that we sit next to one another without touching and that I do not trouble to refill Percy's glass for him. In fact I have pointedly moved the decanter to the other end of the table. Percy is now sitting with an unreadable expression, his arms folded across his chest, staring at Avis, whose turn it is to play.

The silence is uncomfortable so I jump back

in: Yes, I did think women should have the vote, that seems fair enough but . . . but those women! Throwing themselves in front of the king's horse, and for what? It hasn't made a hap'worth of difference to my life . . . I mean I don't have the vote and Avis doesn't and none of our friends do . . . The only difference I can think is that women are now blamed for everything in a way that they didn't used to be . . .

Percy snorts and I stop quickly to see what it was that he wants to say. But he only wants Avis to pass the port to him.

Well I don't know about the vote, I mean you're too young—it'll be a few years, but the principle is there . . .

I concede that this is true. Freddy's youth now strikes me as more apparent by the minute, with his hot tone of voice, his earnest desire to discuss politics, while the three of us seem cool and dull and already decided, only half-heartedly listening to Freddy's sermon.

Look at my sister, Florrie. Working as a typist and out dancing all weekend with her friends . . . she smokes, she answers back; my mother would says she doesn't give two hoots what anybody thinks of her. She expects much more than Mum ever did and—and that's a good thing, surely?

Avis is looking from Freddy to me and tapping one finger in some agitation on the stopper of the decanter. She seems to register at last that Percy has asked her to pass it down the table and she does so rather showily. She can't have noticed me moving it, or if she did, she granted no significance to the gesture.

Perhaps we should call it a day, Avis says, cheerily. No one replies so she gathers the dice up in her hand and squeezes her fingers around them. That way you will have won, Fred, won't you? She smiles at him, eyes wide, head coquettishly on one side. Her hand rests on Freddy's arm, lightly, while she waits for his reply.

The moment is awkward; Freddy shakes his head, a tiny imperceptible, involuntary shake, as if to shake her off. He doesn't appreciate being interrupted. I stand up. Yes, I think we should probably retire. Percy?

Freddy and Avis begin clearing the board. Avis sighs. Freddy's so good at these kind of games. All those long voyages, the card games he plays on ship, she murmurs, smiling admiringly at Freddy. A long string of fake pearls swung from her neck, tapping against the table. She slips the lid onto the box and hands it to Percy, who has remained seated, unaware that the ladies have risen. Avis's cheeks are flushed, she wobbles ever so slightly on her feet.

I'm sure that whatever my sister says, ladies these days just want the same things they always did. A nice husband and children, a lovely home, and to be happy. Isn't that right,

Edie?

Freddy is politely standing, arms at his sides, as if waiting for something. Percy stands up, rather belatedly. All eyes are on me.

Yes. I suppose so, I say finally.

Freddy smiles faintly and in the quietest of voices, remarks: That could mean anything . . .

\*      \*      \*

He climbs into bed and I smell the beer and port on his breath. Despite the heat, Percy still manages to have ice-blocks for feet, which he places up against my warm calves, so that I shriek out loud. His hand shoots across my mouth, covering it.

I'm surprised by this gesture and lie still for a moment, pondering it. It must be that Percy is conscious of Freddy sleeping next door. Percy is embarrassed—a highly amusing thought. He presses himself closer to me and I'm aware—as any married woman is—of his intentions. I begin to unlace the ties at the front of my cotton nightdress, knowing that Percy, with his large fingers, labours over such fiddly tasks.

He is impatient however and, instead of allowing me to undress, pushes the nightdress up my body and launches himself on top of me. Percy's weight can be burdensome, squeezing the breath out of my lungs and this is a discomfort, but more so is the partially rucked-up nightdress, which is a new one and cotton, rather than silk, with more folds of material than usual. It becomes caught between us, and the folded material is rubbing on me, captured in a rough roll between our bodies. I am suddenly intensely aware of this part of my body and intensely conscious of the rubbing and aware that I am concentrating on it and for some reason want it to continue. The bed is creaking slightly (as beds are wont to do) and I become aware also of Freddy's proximity just next door, and all in a fever with the shyness and yet excitement at Freddy right next door, a young man who has travelled and experienced the world, and him knowing—no doubt—what we are up to.

Now Percy is becoming more urgent and again, to my surprise, he is less clumsy than usual and (as I always imagine) frantic to get his husbandly duties over with. He is breathing heavily and moaning a little and the weight of him pressing on me in a quite different way than normal and my heart is pounding and has jumped up a little towards my mouth. I endeavour to keep very, very still and contain my own fluttering, spiralling feeling but I can't. It is very strange indeed.

My nightdress is by now soaked in perspiration and there is no occasion to order myself better and no time to think of anything else or to wonder at the noise we are possibly making, because the giddiness of the port in my blood and the strangely different endeavours of Percy, labouring on me and building himself into such a lather and the noise our union is making on the bed springs, all rises and fills my head with a great loud thundering and then my blood rises to meet that, too, and before I can stop myself I am moaning also—I cover my mouth with my hands and try to disguise my sounds as sighs of pain—but I know my mouth is open and this is very odd indeed and my mouth will not shut of its own accord and my spine wishes to snap back and forth like a fish snatched on a hook, and I am rocking also, rocking from the waist down, drawing Percy further and further into me, without knowing why, or why I can't stop; a great thundering rhythm is starting up in me, until the whole of this rocking and pounding possesses my body and shakes it hard—I feel like a doll that someone is holding by the hair and shaking roughly—and then suddenly a wave of shame flushes over me and the rocking is over.

Percy rolls away, patting me lightly, as you might pat a child on its bottom, and I know he is embarrassed and possibly shocked. He couldn't fail to have noticed that my response was quite different to usual. All the same, the port, his labourings and the long day spent in the sun combine to draw him into sleep, lying on his back with his profile jutting up in the darkness like a rock-face. I lie sleepless.

Stunned, even.

I read a book once. I got it from the library and I was shy, I stood queuing at the counter with the book clamped to my side, in case anyone should read the title. The cover said *For Married Couples Only. Not to be Left About. Dedicated to Young Husbands, and all those who are betrothed in love.* I remember great chunks of it. It felt as if the words were written in light, or flames, they leapt from the page and seared into my brain. I didn't dare take the book home in the end, waited in the queue and then turned around, hid myself in a corner of the library, reading in secret with one arm in front of the page, ready to place another book on top of it if anyone were to come close to me.

*The truly monogamous couple, where the man and the woman go chaste to the marriage bed, and go through life in mutual love and respect, those feelings growing stronger as the years go by, finding full satisfaction in each other, without any desire for any other man or woman—what nobler, what more appealing ideal can one conjure up . . .*

*Though in some instances the woman may have one or more crises before the man achieves his, it is perhaps not an exaggeration to say that 70 or 80 percent of married women (in the middle and intellectual classes) are deprived of the full orgasm through excessive speed of the husband's reactions, i.e., through premature*

101

*ejaculation (ejaculatio precox) or through some maladjustment of the relative shapes and positions of the organs. So complex, so profound are women's sex instincts that in rousing them the man is rousing her whole body and soul. And this takes time. More time indeed than the average husband dreams of spending upon it.*

Eventually I fall asleep, but in the early hours of the morning I wake to find that Percy is out of bed, standing in his nightshirt, gawking at me. He has a glass in one hand and a bottle of port in another. The bottle is a large one, almost full, I recognise it from home. It must have been in his luggage. My first thought is: intruders! and I catch my breath and sit up with my heart racing, saying, My God, what is it? Percy sways for a moment—a ridiculous moment—while I wait for his explanation. But none is forthcoming. He has not lit the lamp and his figure in the moonlight filtering through the thin muslin, is grey and tremulous. Finally, feeling sleep stealing over me again and aching to close my eyes, I simply murmur: What is it, Percy? with no expectation of a reply and place my head down on the pillow.

Edie, he says in a croaky whisper, a voice slack with drink. He sits on the bed, not noticing that he is half-sitting on my arm and I wince and tug the arm from under him. Edie, he whispers again, his face close to mine, one hand under the covers, feeling for me.

I'm tired, Percy, what is it? If you can't sleep, take one of your pills.

He tries to get into bed on my side and, although he has put the bottle down, the glass of port is still in his hand. There is no room for both of us, so in a surge of exhaustion and irritation I move right over, allowing him my space. He glugs the last of the port and puts the glass down noisily on the table beside the bed. And still he doesn't relax and go to sleep but instead keeps whispering, Edie, Edie, in a quite absurd way. I keep my eyes tightly shut and repel all hands—as firmly as I dare—and I know at last what is wrong and bitterly regret it. Percy's discovery of a response in me he'd been hitherto ignorant of has triggered a beast in him.

Edie, he whispers again, and this time he is lying beside me, his face close and his eyes wide and glassy. Foolishly I push him, forcefully, towards his side of the bed. The second I touch him, I regret it. Percy pushes me right back; a hard shove, too, so that my nose mashes up against the wall and tears smart in my eyes. Wide awake now, I sit up and cover my nose with my hands, where they are immediately drenched. In the moonlight, the tears appear black and startling.

I think my nose is bleeding! I wail, a nasal voice, my hands over my face. Percy groans. He gets out of bed and fumbles to light the lamp and when the room is filled with wavering light, we both look in horror at the blood on my hands and the nightdress and the sheets.

Put your head back Percy says gruffly. He staggers to the jug in the comer of the room, pours some water onto a towel, trots back and flops the towel over my nose. The gesture is neither caring nor measured—water splashing everywhere and the sodden lump of stained towel threatening to make the mess worse. Percy stands in confusion, his nightshirt floating around him, water dripping onto the counterpane, like a hopeless child.

Oh, let me do it, I say, pulling the towel away from my face and noting how pink it now is. But the bleeding seems to have stopped. Percy climbs slowly into his side of the bed and I wait for him to say he is sorry. I don't want to climb over him so I wriggled to the end of the bed, to fetch a bowl to wring the towel into. Then I slip the pillow out of its stained case, leaving it in the bowl to rinse through. When I'm sure that my nose has stopped bleeding I extinguish the lamp and in the semi-dark hide Percy's glass and bottle under the bed, hoping he'll forget about it in the morning. Then I lie down myself.

We are both lying on our backs, staring at the ceiling, inches apart, waiting for the other to speak.

*That's it. If you ever strike me again, I'll divorce you,* I mouth into the darkness.

Quietly. Coldly. Percy's rolling snores tell me he is safely sealed in sleep.

*     *     *

The ride on the charabanc is the first occasion for me to be alone with Freddy and it is Avis who arranges it. It's our last day here and she says she wants to speak to Percy about 'something'; giggling and clutching Percy's arm as she says this, and then she suggests that we swop partners. She and Percy set off from Daish's corner on a shiny black charabanc packed with shrieking school children, and every one of them waving to us and laughing. Freddy and I wait at the same spot for the next one.

A shy silence descends on us. I stare down at my beautiful red shoes, then peer in at the window of Daish's Wool and Fancy Goods. Freddy whistles tunelessly. Our driver soon turns up, tooting the horn and by now a small queue has formed, so Freddy and I are obliged to squash together in the narrowest of seats at the back. The driver comes round, doffing his cap and taking our fares—three and six for Shanklin and Sandown only, which is what we plump for.

The coach sets off down the hilly paths at a fair speed, flinging us first one way and then the other. I have the feeling that Freddy is doing his utmost to distance himself from me,

105

stiffening his body the way a child does if it doesn't want you to pick it up, or just in some private, inexplicable way. His shoulders are held high and stiff and his face is stiff, too; his silence feels deliberate, an effort, like something held in. Finally, as we are passing the Parade Kinema and my comment on the picture showing has received no response at all from Freddy, I can't bear the silence a moment longer.

Is something wrong?

This feels an extraordinarily intimate thing to say and my shyness increases the moment the words are out. I'd hoped to make it an incidental, casual kind of question, quite suited to the sister of a young man's sweetheart. Instead it comes out sounding pinched and concerned. Anxious. And Freddy's reply does nothing to alter the mood.

You know what's wrong!

He says this with some force. Astonished, I turn to look at him and discover that he is glaring at me. His eyes ice-blue, the pupils tiny dots, the way they were the other day, when Avis teased him about his birthday.

No, I—I don't think I do . . .

Edie, I'm in love with you.

The driver chooses this moment to screech to a sudden halt, cursing loudly the elderly bicyclist in his path. We are thrown forward and I'm glad of the confusion, even glad of the hard bump my elbow receives, banging against the side of the charabanc. It gives me time. It allows the shock, the colour in my cheeks, to subside a little.

Oh . . .

He is staring, expecting a reply, searching my face, I suppose, for signs that I'm going to reject him or scold him or tease him. Or something. I feel as if a sharp jab just punctured my lungs and not from the jolt in the charabanc either. From the headlong, bald statement Freddy just launched at me: impossible to step away from. I'm gathering up my response and whatever it's to be, it feels false. Frenzied gulls are squawking overhead. The dramatic shaven cliffs slice into view as we pass the Rylstone Gardens and, in the silence while Freddy waits for my response, I hear the sea, whispering in the distance, and know without seeing it how flat and green and shallow it will appear, from up here. As if it has no depth at all. As if it never swallowed ships, men; holds no savage, murky green secrets at all.

Freddy agitates a speck of dust on his creased jacket, ferociously rubbing at it. Finally he asks in almost a splutter: Surely you knew?

Yes!

My voice, too, comes out wrongly. I'm struggling to summon up my old self; a smile, a dimple, something coy and flirtatious to rise to the occasion and fend off—fend off whatever it is that Freddy is presenting me with. But fright has subdued all these proper responses and I can't find them; only this—an unbridled tone, high-pitched, which leaps too quickly into intimacy.

But I'm married and you're—as I begin this sentence, the queerest thing happens. The charabanc with Avis and Percy in it and the gaggle of screeching children passes us on the road, honking its horn and carrying a boisterously waving Avis within a few inches of our seats. I jump away from Freddy—as much as I'm able in the cramped conditions—as if he is on fire. Freddy turns to me with an expression so odd—I suppose I must look nearly crazed with panic. As he looks at me, the tension in his face crumbles. He starts laughing. We put our heads together and giggle like children.

So that's as much as is said, and of course, it's far too much. My response ought to have been flirtatious; I did not play the role properly: the offended wife spurning the naughty young seducer. I know that in my face, Freddy saw all the wrong things. And as we step out of the charabanc at Regent Street, as he is holding out his hand to help me down the step, he says, out of the blue: I know you are unhappy.

And it's this which finally undoes me. It is this simple statement that makes my head reel. I feel giddy, unpeeled. I take his hand graciously, I allow him to help me step to the pavement, I make no sign that I've heard him even, and yet everything in me quakes, disintegrates. *It is as if no one has ever spoken to me before.* As if I have been asleep for twenty-seven years and am now waking up and those around me saying: *Oh there you are!*

A dizzying feeling. I have a desire to run away from it. But also mesmerising, tantalising. As if the sleeping girl has always been here—odd and ugly and not restful at all—a girl who lies at the bottom of everything, like a pebble at the bottom of a clean, glittering pond, but no one, up until now, has actually seen her.

Avis and Percy's return is noisy, chattering. They burst in on us.

We have some news! Avis announces. We're standing outside Abell's Jewellers on Regent Street, making an obstruction on the pavement. I'm trying to steer the others towards a tea-room. Avis is carrying her hat in her hand, I think because the band makes an unsightly red mark on her forehead in this heat, and I'm noticing this and feeling sorry for her and not wanting to, all at the same time.

I've solved your lodger problem, Edie. Aren't I the clever one? She links one arm in Percy's and one in Freddy's and they begin walking together, with me trotting to keep up.

Now I can see you all the time, Fred, whenever I want, and all on the pretext of visiting my sister . . .

A bold remark for Avis—the perfect excuse for the expression on my face as what she is saying sinks in.

You could move in next Monday if that suits you, Percy adds. How does 25 shillings a week sound? On a trial basis of course.

The three of them are slightly ahead of me and I really am practically running to keep up. I feel like a puppy dog, or a child chasing adults. Something has been decided, I might even say 'cooked up', without my participation at all and yet I'm the one to be most affected. How odd that they are excluding me in this. The strangest sensation. My husband, my sister and her—paramour—setting a great trap for me.

It's easy to see Percy's logic. The money—since our lodger Mrs Wright left—has been something of an issue with us. And perhaps in some recess of his mind he believes that the astonishing transportation which occurred to me last night will be repeated, if my blood is again disturbed by the presence of a strange young man in our home.

Avis, too, I can see why she would be pleased with herself. Now when Freddy is on shore, between trips to sea, he will be away from the influence of his powerful mother and, instead of being in Upper Norwood, he will be just a skip and a jump away from her, at Kensington Gardens, a place she can legitimately visit any time she likes. Her big sister's in Ilford.

A bell jangles on the door as the four of us burst into a tea-room, Avis still chattering excitedly. Percy steers everyone towards a window table. Freddy and I sit opposite one another and Avis places her hat on the table between us, picks up the menu. I'm so ravenous I could eat a horse! she announces firmly. I keep my eyes fixed to the menu, reading *Special Creamy Ices, the Best on the Island.* Over and over. Freddy, too, seems afraid to catch my eyes, but without looking up I can tell somehow that he is smiling, a broad smile; the sort one might describe as stretching from ear to ear.

\*      \*      \*

After dinner that evening we go to the Rivoli cinema. A spectacular evening, the sky unrolled above us like a parched paper canopy, the air spiked with the smell of so many men wearing Gentleman's Lime. The picture is *The Midnight Sun* with Laura La Plante. And Freddy buys icecreams for all of us, and the taste of the wooden spoon and the sweet vanilla melts on my tongue, as we wait in the queue; with Avis and I examining the outfits of the other women—she the dresses and shoes and I the hats—while Percy sucks on his pipe and Freddy . . . what is Freddy doing?

I know he is behind me, whistling. Maybe he is studying the women in the queue, too, although not their outfits. That sounds like Freddy. That's what I'd guess Freddy is doing, without actually turning around and observing him.

The film is a great romance and dramatic, too, with the terrible bloody ending and Laura La Plante marvellous and tragic as the sumptuous siren of Czarist Russia. Avis passes me her handkerchief when the Czarina's son trembles in her arms, suffering his terrible fits; and she and I end up sniffling and giggling all at once, until a woman in a dreadful black pillbox taps Freddy—stuck between us—on the shoulder and tells *him* to ssssh! I'm sure Percy is glad she did, I know he is secretly enjoying the picture and our snuffles and hiccups are distracting him.

A grand picture, we all agree, once outside again, although Freddy laughs and assures us that it was 'hopelessly inaccurate'. He remarks loudly that he hasn't been to Russia but to a great many countries just like it and *some people* who have never been outside of Shanklin hold rather childish ideas of what foreign climes look like or of the overly barbaric nature of foreign lovers towards their wives and paramours.

Avis takes his arm, saying, Oh Freddy has been to a great many exciting places, you should ask him about them, Edie, I'm sure he's bored of telling me . . .

A stream of people are piling out of the picture house and most drifting in the direction of the promenade, so we follow aimlessly, pulled by the crowd and the chatter and momentum. Avis and Freddy walk in front, their arms linked easily—it strikes me that it is they who seem like the long-married couple. Percy makes a great show of emptying and refilling his pipe and needing both his hands for this. I walk beside him, hands by my sides.

What did Madame Sosostris say to you, Edie? Avis asks, out of the blue. The question surprises me, so she explains: I looked back after we came out. I saw you going into the tent.

Oh, you know. The usual poppycock.

A little pause. We stop walking for a moment, hesitating at the steps down to the beach, staring at the top of the bathing machines, lit by the lamps on the promenade, the moonlit foam glinting on the waves.

What did she say to you? I ask, finally.

Freddy says: Well there is to be a dark stranger coming into Avis's life . . .

We all laugh, lightly.

Avis lets go of Freddy's arm, comes around to my side: Freddy asked her something. He whispered to her. Very mysterious it was. For answer she turned over that horrible card—which is it? The Death card? No, not that but another one. I can't remember now which it was. I know the girl said it was nothing to fear, despite the ugliness, it was a Pisces card, a card of the 'ocean'. I remember that much. It means something to do with surrender, she said. Being 'suspended in a sea of emotion and irrationality'. She was odd, didn't you think?

Yes, I reply absently; I am picturing Freddy, leaning forward and whispering to the girl, his mouth brushing against the scarf she wore around her head, as he whispers his request; Avis sitting right beside him! What could he possibly have asked her? Avis, no doubt, hands folded in her lap, no hint of impatience, was fully confident that he enquired about *their* future.

It strikes me now as curious that Avis didn't remember which card she turned over for reply. Avis, so concerned to know that she was going to make a good match for the future, that the man she married would be more than a ship's laundry clerk *one day*. Curious, too, that I didn't push her to remember it, or ask Freddy. As she whispered to me, her mouth warm on my ear, I caught a whiff of her perfume, Crown Rose, and I knew then that she was in love with Freddy.

Which card *could* it have been? What did she say, ugly like the Death card, but not the Death card; a card meaning surrender, suspension, losing oneself? I have never been sincerely superstitious, not the way Freddy is.

114

But right now, such things have become vital. I really would like to know.

## CHAPTER THREE

When the case was resumed, Mrs Thompson again took her seat in the dock with bowed head, while Bywaters sat with his arms resting on the dock-rail, looking steadily at Mr Lewis, who continued the reading of various letters.

A passage in one of them asked: 'What is aromatic tincture of opium?' and another said: 'I was glad you don't think and feel the same way as I do about the New Forest. I don't think we are failures in other things, and we won't be in this . . . Darlint, fate can't always turn against us, and if it is, we must fight it. You and I are strong now. We must be stronger. We must learn to be patient. We'll wait on, darling, and you can try and get some money and we can go away together and not worry about anybody or anything. You said it was enough for an elephant. Perhaps it was. But you don't allow for the taste. Only a small quantity can be taken. It sounded like a reproach. Was it meant to be? Darlint—I tried hard. You won't know how hard. I can't tell you all,

115

but I did. I do want you to believe I did, for both of us . . . I was buoyed up by the hope of the light bulb and I used a lot—big pieces too, not powdered, but it had no effect. I quite expected to be able to cable, but no, nothing has happened from it and now your letter tells me about the bitter taste again. Oh, darlint, I do feel so down and unhappy. Wouldn't the stuff make small pills, coated with soap and dipped in liquorice powder, like Beechams? Try while you're away . . . but I suppose, as you say, he is not normal. I know I shall never get him to take a sufficient quantity of anything bitter. If we ever are lucky enough to be happy, darling, I will love you such a lot. I always show you how much I love you for all you do for me . . . All that lying and scheming and subterfuge to obtain one little hour in each day—when by right of nature and our love we should be together for all the twenty-four in each day.'

Mrs Thompson, who had been brought back to court, again collapsed and eventually Mr Stern asked that she should be kept out. He said that he represented her and didn't object.

The clerk pointed out that in an indictable offence the prisoner must be in court.

*Tuesday—very late*

Darlint,
Mother came to visit me this evening, Freddy. Again, Father wasn't with her. She has the darkest of shadows under her eyes and the way she stares at me I know I can't be looking any better. But I try to be cheery. The moment Clara stood aside, placing the cigarettes I'm permitted on the table between us, Mother's face dropped and her hands fell onto the table, too, with a lifeless thud. All the breath went out of her. Edie, how could you write such things?

I simply answered, No one knows the letters he was writing to me.

Of course, I am not angry with you, darlint. I really do not blame you for the letters you wrote me. You may trust me that they are well and truly destroyed. The ones mentioned in court, the notes found at Carlton & Prior—honestly, Fred, I think there can only be three in total, merely that note wishing Percy and me a Happy Christmas, the one asking whether Avis liked chocolates, something else incidental and innocent enough.

There are ones I remember though, I remember every word.

Still. However many times I might wish you

had destroyed *my* letters, wishing is not going to help us. Stern says matters are really quite grave and now it seems unlikely that we can keep the letters out of a court case at the Old Bailey. Naturally, I can't help but be dismayed and a little alarmed by the complexion that the reading of my letters has put on matters. From Mother's face, from her howling at me and her beaten, despairing manner. *Well.* One can see that if she, my own mother, feels such doubts about us now, feels that there is no way to understand my letters other than to presume they are unambiguous proof of our evil plotting, I am going to have a troublesome task persuading others of any other possible interpretation. If only they had chosen some other ones, some letters of love, some letters which show my sense of humour, which show the kind of things we wrote to one another about, and that all between us was not *serious* and beastly in the way they suspect!

I could feel a ripple when I walked through the corridor back to my room, with Eve and the Governor beside me. It was quite different from two or three days ago. Listening to those details, the part about the light globe and the herbs. How damning it all sounds, even I know that. How it reminds me of my own mood back then, of the things I dreamed of, of what I longed for. Of course I have to be careful what I write here but it made me think of things again. The part about the herbs. I'm sure you know what I'm talking about.

Oh, I feel sad tonight, Freddy, I will stop writing here. It's hard to keep my spirits up when others have begun to speak of the worst possible things, the worst possible fate for us. I refuse to countenance their suggestions but I am tired, and I must go to sleep.

All my love to you, I'll see you in court tomorrow.

Peidi.

*     *     *

Violet and Pearl. Their blonde heads in sharp curls like the heads of two hyacinths, running, scattering, playing hide and seek in Valentine's Park, with the sun on their dresses and shining into their big dark eyes . . . Two little girls, never boys. Boys would be . . . too difficult. Boys might have heart-stopping blue eyes, or those vulnerable little knees; they might look like Percy or Freddy, force me to decide. To know things I couldn't possibly know, then or now. Destiny again, fate. What might be. What might have been.

Sometimes it's as if I see the future—the alternative future, the one I didn't pick, the one that I didn't plant, over a dark hill somewhere, somewhere else, running alongside this one, like a track. Here I am on a train and it's right beside me, the children in their green cotton dresses waving to me, as if

119

they see me, too.

Then I'm picturing that train journey back from Shanklin and I realise I *did* see girls, blonde, sunny-haired girls, waving handkerchiefs at the train. Girls who might have been Violet and Pearl. Girls who bore a faint resemblance to Avis and me.

And I think of us all travelling back from Shanklin and the train thundering towards something, towards *this*! And Avis and Percy and Freddy and I silent and contained within it. Flying past trees, hedgerows, chimney tops, and those children, those girls who were there for a moment waving but then would never be there again. The sun blinking at me through the window. Light feathering through a web of trees. Sadness and excitement roaring in my blood.

And I was thinking, *I will do such things, what they shall be, yet I know not,* and staring out at other lives; tiny lives glimpsed at gateways, in shop doorways, playgrounds, school-yards, tiny fleeting lives all to be snuffed out one day and feeling both terribly important and terribly unimportant to be alive, this one beating engine of a heart . . . and then this word struck me, this peculiar word, quite from nowhere, this word *exist*. A stupid word, too mundane to describe what I want it to, but there it is, it lodged and started drumming in time with the rhythm of the train and then it grew bigger and began beating on me until all

120

I could hear was this: *I exist, I exist, I exist.* Blood pounding in me, that's all I knew, I could cry with joy and delight and wondered why I didn't know such a thing long ago, why it struck me now for the first time. The horizon furring into the distance, a soft fringe on a faded rug, my heart as full of fire as this round descending sun, saying to myself: no one knows what I am thinking, what decisions I have made, what it is that I am about to do, but I do, I know, I know this: *I exist.*

Every day a thought, some seemingly trifling, passing thought, opens a door. So was it then, was it the train journey, was it allowing my thoughts to roam a little, to make a decision without having acted at all? And not even a decision to act, only a decision to be open. But at the time I made it, I felt so much more powerful, more alive than at any other time before or since.

I can see that it has brought us to this. It felt already too late, even before anything had happened, before anyone was aware of my thoughts. A door opened and I jumped inside the carriage and then the train started rolling and speeding along and kept going and gathering speed and after that I might say it was Fate, because there was never a moment— never one I spotted—where I might have called Stop! or Turn back!

## Wednesday October 25th, 1922

Finally I manage to see Father and it is in a court-room!

I kept wanting to run to him from behind the dock, and fling my arms around Father's stout chest, and bury my head there. I know exactly how he would smell—the wool of the sweater, the pipe tobacco, the smoky smell that always hung about him and that I came to think of as the way *all* men smelled, and I knew he would feel rough and soft in equal measure, as he always did. Hugging him was never quite a comfortable experience, always his stubble would rub my skin like sandpaper or a button on his coat would dig into me; something would jar and leave an imprint on my cheek, a sharp red spot where I had pressed my skin too hard against it . . .

He looked old, old, and sunken, as if the flesh holding out his cheeks and giving him that distinct, proud expression he wore for all those years, has been sucked out from under him and the face is collapsing in on itself. Nothing to be proud of, any more, I thought. No reason to hold his head up. No reason for his fine arched cheekbones to arch like that.

I'm sorry I broke down like that, Freddy. Later, I realised how painful for you it must have been to see me like that and not be allowed to comfort me and I know I increased Father's pain, too. Such a simple question, really, after all the other difficult ones we have had to answer. Did your daughter have any children?

None, Father answered and—again, the overwhelming shame and humiliation and pain came to the surface again, and all the things I'm not allowed to mention—no respectable woman is allowed to mention—and I wished to get hold of Percy and shake him and scream at him and say: See, see what you have done and it's all your fault, you should have let me go years ago!

No, there were no children of the marriage, my father said, quietly, in his proud, formal voice and he kept his eyes down, down on his hands and away from me.

I noticed how polished and shiny his shoes were and it was the same feeling as when I observed *your* shoes. They are making an effort, I thought, as if such things matter.

Now it is snowy and my tears have dried up and I am writing only to tell you that I am recovered from my outburst, so you are not to worry about me. Clara came in just then. Snow falling now, Mrs Thompson, imagine that and it's not even November. And she has brought me a book I ordered, Robert Hitchens' *The Fruitful Vine*. I'm sure you'll remember reading this book, Freddy, and the irony of the subject matter—Dolores' barrenness and the decision she makes about it—is painful, as if someone is stabbing at me with a sharp stick. Someone who takes pleasure in my misery, in my punishment. But then I've had that feeling throughout the last month and am becoming used to it.

When I'd drunk my milk and eaten my stirabout and had allowed Clara to settle me a little with her gossip and her tart remarks about the prison Doctor—You'd think the man was born in a bloody glass phial and no contact with a mother's body. Why a man like that chooses a job like this, I bloody don't know—I picked *The Fruitful Vine* up again and started to read a passage.

The problem is, of course (and I'm sure you have the same problem, darlint), that it was lights out before I really had time to lose myself in it. In any case, a strange remoteness interrupted my pleasure. I read the passage when Dolores' husband describes how he first fell in love with her: 'Her long eyelashes showed against the beautiful pallor of her face. Her husband noticed them, and remembered how he had delighted in them when he first fell in love with Dolores. It had perhaps been very absurd, but he believed that he had first fallen in love with those long and curling eyelashes. They had seemed to mean—what? a whole world of delicious, sensitive, shrinking, promising womanliness as they showed against the soft cheeks. They had touched him, he remembered, in the innermost part of his nature; had stirred within him a protective instinct that was acquisitive and not wholly without brutality; they had filled him with the mysterious longings of a complete man, longings that came surely from God, and reach out towards God, and that make a man glow with a splendid wonder at himself, at the stirring of the strange living force which is his essence.'

And I remembered, I used to love that passage! What was I thinking of? How did I manage to read such a passage and not think of Percy, lumbering into bed with the customary breaking wind that he did outside the covers to 'keep the sheets sweet'. Never, not even before I met you, did Percy feel that way about me and how could I for one moment not question this? I don't mean question Percy—since I don't think he was particularly unusual, judging from remarks Florrie and others made to me—I mean, question my belief that this is how men feel about their wives? The 'mysterious longings of a complete man'!! How Clara would laugh if I read her this remark. I can imagine her now: Nothing mysterious in most men's longings! Plain as bloody day if you ask me . . .

Strange to think of London being quietly iced with snow tonight. My pencil is worn down and my fingers have developed a bulge on the knuckle from so much writing but the oddest mood is on me as I write. Freddy, I'm suddenly, surprisingly, almost gay! Perhaps it is exhaustion, or the effects of so much weeping, but suddenly, here in my thin grey room on my thin grey blanket, I'm finding it cosy and safe. The muffled sounds of steps outside my door, of others settling down for the night, the usual mingled smell of carbolic and boiled cabbage now mixed with something else, something damp and fresh that hints at the clean white snow outside. It's like I'm living in a giant pillow. In here is the site of new discoveries, of a cleaner, cooler, different way of thinking. Out there—out there is where all the ugliness and dirtiness lives, where the thoughts of others crowd in on me and cover me and rub up against me. I feel . . . almost cosseted, protected, knowing that there is a damp cold London world out there but I can't see it or touch it.

I suppose this is a dangerous feeling. Maybe I will become afraid to leave the prison? Already I find it far more painful to get in the van, to be marched past the other prisoners, than to sit in here, alone with my pencil and my books.

Writing and reading and thinking of you. Those are the only companions I want right now.

Goodnight, Darlint Boy,
Peidi.

\* \* \*

My little girls, my little girls are running

everywhere, covering their ears with their hands and screaming as those big male voices drone on and on and the dark wooden chairs in the courtroom heave and squeak, while all lean forward to hear more, more of my shame.

Percy snuggling up to me, saying: Don't you want a baby, Edie? A child to love, a child of our own . . .

Trying not to sigh, wondering yet again why it is that so few men ever realise that they might have something to do with whether children come along or not. Surreptitiously doing up my nightdress, knowing that to suggest this is impossible, will be seen as a slight on his manhood, produce the most fearful of rages . . .

Yes, I do, I suppose. In time. I mean, when the time is right—

When the time is right! Anger flaring in him again. As if someone had struck a match on his side of the bed.

Edith, I swear you are doing something to stop us having a baby! Something, I don't know what, and anyway God knows, you are hardly helping the odds: most nights I have to beg you to give me what you used to give willingly enough before we were married . . .

I have no reply to that. Only to consider in amazement how mysterious my husband really does find me; how magical and beyond reasoning must I be, if Percy really has no idea whether or not a woman might be able to prevent a baby.

*     *     *

*It becomes the sexologist's most sacred duty to do everything in his power to make the monogamous relationship as pleasant as possible, to remove as far as possible all removable causes of friction, to steer the frail matrimonial bark in safe channels, to guard it from being wrecked on the Scylla of asceticism or the Charybdis of excess; in short to help the Man and Woman to go through life in mutual love and respect, finding full satisfaction in each other, without any desire for another man or woman.*

*     *     *

If I try to remember the early days of meeting Percy, it's as if those three years existed in a constant fog. I can pick out some details, the way you can hold out a hand in front of you and manage to see that, although the trees and buildings disappear into mists. The splash of the red roses Percy bought me at the first dance he took me to. His large hands with their clean, neat nails, slipping inside my coat as we waited at Fenchurch Street for the last train home. Such a long time it took me to remove them; first feeling a paralysing shyness, then curiosity, holding my breath, waiting to see how much they might dare, where they might roam. But the train came then and we had a shared carriage.

Percy tipping his hat to me at the bottom of the road, me waiting on the step to wave goodnight to him. That image a little sharper than the others. It has edges, outlines. We had been dancing all night and I remember my insteps were aching. A delicious kind of ache, the ache after a party, after exhausting yourself by not noticing how excited and hectic you were being. I felt like a tiny girl, standing on her tiptoes to wave to her father. It was an image we saw a lot in those days. Women, daughters, wives, mothers, on doorsteps, in bare feet, waving goodbye to men who were walking away from them, men who wore coats, and hats and uniforms.

It was probably then that I said yes to Percy.

## MRS THOMPSON IN TEARS

Mr and Mrs Graydon (right and left), the parents of Mrs Thompson (inset) leaving Stratford police court yesterday with Mr Carlton (centre), of the firm who employed Mrs Thompson. Along with Frederick Bywaters, Mrs Thompson is being charged with being concerned in the murder of her husband at Ilford.

When her father went into the witness box she burst into tears. (See News Page)

*Daily Sketch*, Thursday October 26th, 1922

\*  \*  \*

*A strongly built but graceful man of about thirty was coming quietly towards them, with the complete ease and lack of self-consciousness characteristic of well-bred Italians. Neither tall nor short he was intensely masculine in appearance. Some men seem far more male than others, as some women seem far more female than other women. An atmosphere of sex surrounds them. Cesare Careli was one of these almost violently male men. Yet he often looked gentle and kind, was what Italians call very 'simpatico' and had not a trace of 'swagger' or of conscious conceit. His complexion was clear and colourless. He had a round white forehead, a splendidly shaped and small head, covered with black and curly hair which, though cut very short, was so thick that it looked almost unnatural, dense black eyebrows and a pair of the shining and intense black eyes which are seen so often in Rome; eyes which cannot look dull, cannot look inexpressive, but which, perhaps, often seem to mean more than they really do mean, more of passion, of melancholy, of violence or of reverie. He had a rather splendid mouth closely shut when his face was in repose, with splendid, not small, teeth and a firmly modelled chin with a cleft down the middle. In the shape of his forehead and in his eyes there was something that suggested intellectuality, yet his face as a whole was the face of a man of action, who was intelligent, rather than a thinker, or a student He could look very gay, even impudent, but often looked calm, with intensity behind the calm. His figure was that of a very supple and athletic man, and he wore clothes that had certainly been cut in London.*

*The Fruitful Vine,* Robert Hitchens

\*　　　\*　　　\*

I used to think that description sounded just like you, Fred. I read it again last night and the problem was that certain phrases jumped out and then would not climb back into their rightful place. *Man of action. Intensity behind the calm. Eyes . . . which seem to mean more than they really do mean.* These phrases trouble me now.

And that *firmly modelled chin with a cleft down the middle.* It reminds me—I keep thinking—of you as that boy of seven at the lake. Such a chin looks something like a child's fat backside! But that would be unglamorous. I shouldn't have said it, I'm sorry, it ruins the description entirely. And now I've thought of it, I've spoiled everything. I can't help

131

laughing, guffawing silently into my pillow, the way I used to do sometimes when I had hilarious dreams. I used to wake with the pillow wet, with my mouth open, hearing someone giggling and thinking it was Avis in the bed beside me, then realising it was me.

Well, here there is no one. No one to hear me and no harm in laughing into my pillow, should I so desire.

Peidi.

*     *     *

The footsteps of a wardress hesitate outside the door. I think she heard me laughing. It's late and she's doing her rounds. Then she even knocks at my door before entering! At first I assume it must be Clara, and I don't turn to her but hear her breathing in the darkness and then clearing her throat. But instead it is Eve's voice, low and kind of crackling.

I used to think things like that about my Bert sometimes. Those things you wrote in your letters . . . poison. Ground glass. Oh yes, I thought of that. Knocked me around something terrible, he did. I probably said it to him an' all. More than once. I wish you were bloody dead and in your grave. But I never would of touched him. Can't hang a woman for hating her husband, can they? Half the country'd be in prison. I never would of touched him.

132

And she just keeps hovering there, as if I am accusing her of something. I take no notice of her. I continue quietly laughing, snuffling, and thinking how I've never made such a noise before; exactly the noise a kitten makes, or perhaps a young pig.

And then I remember a dream I had two nights ago, of a great struggling bundle of squalling kittens in a sack, with a rope around the top, being flung, flung wide, right into the Thames. I don't like that dream, not one bit, and tomorrow I must pluck up my courage and go to Dr Lynch, ask again about the pills he can give me, what pills there might be, to stop me laughing like this and dreaming of these terrifying bags of squalling creatures.

## CHAPTER FOUR

A summer evening in late June, the smell of honeysuckle mixing oddly with the powerful scent of onions from the hawkers just down the street. They call from door to door at around this time of year, this time of the evening. Six fifteen, precisely.

Opening the door to him, shyly, knowing Percy to be in the back kitchen smoking his pipe. Freddy standing on the doorstep with his one small bag and that shiny, polished, *new* appearance he has, like a beautiful new conker. Shining, *shining,* something is shining, as I open the door and we smile at each other.

You travel light, I say and he steps over the threshold.

Freddy steps into our hallway, clutching at the small bag. I feel without turning round Percy stepping into the hall behind me, a shadow crossing our path. Freddy holds out his hand to shake and Percy barges forward. Awkward, suddenly—he seems too big and male to be standing in my hallway, squashed into a space so small and feminine.

I'll just show—Fred to his room, I tell Percy, discovering that I'm afraid to use Freddy's name in front of him.

So I trot upstairs, conscious of Freddy behind me, his step, unhurried. If we'd never had that conversation at Rylstone Gardens, he wouldn't feel able to follow me at such close quarters. Each moment permitting the next, as stitches chase one another on cloth.

I hope you don't find it too small . . . stepping back towards the window to give myself some breathing space.

Having spent the afternoon cleaning from top to bottom, now I'm feeling dreadfully self-conscious about it. There are fresh sheets on the bed—the most expensive, exquisite French linen from Harrison Gibson's, bought this morning; hidden from Percy in a brown paper package and smuggled upstairs. The room smells of lavender, sewn into a cotton bag

134

under the pillow. Today I put a vase of violets on the table beside the bed and then fearing I was overdoing it, threw them on the compost heap.

Freddy smiles at me and embarrassment crackles between us like hot starch.

Well, I'll put the kettle on and let you unpack . . . come downstairs when you're comfortable, won't you . . .

He looks as if he is about to say something but already I'm scuttling out, meaning to close the door carefully behind me. Instead the door catches a non-existent breeze and slams with some force. I'm sure as I turn on my heel, I hear Freddy chuckling to himself.

We have tea together; cold chicken and salad and Freddy loves cucumber but not radishes and he likes his tea with one sugar and he shakes too much salt onto everything. Then later that evening he meets our neighbour, Mrs Hester, and he is characteristically charming to her, tipping his hat and generally overdoing it. Freddy and Percy go to the Angel Hotel without me, while I spend an hour or two on my own, sitting in my sewing chair, trying to control the slippery needle and the stubborn lace in my hand. Percy comes back loud and boisterous and happy to have male company and we are all happy, that evening, the first evening, when it looks like summer will be extended, the green sea and icecream world of Shanklin might go on forever.

Mornings begin to shape themselves into a pattern. I get up while Percy is still asleep, his body beside me hot and softly snoring, like an apple pie baking, bubbling softly in the stove. I put my slippers on and pad downstairs to the kitchen.

The first morning I receive a shock. There is Freddy, fully dressed, smoking a cigarette with the back door open, shoes shined, shirt crisp, kettle boiling on the stove and him looking as if he hasn't been to bed at all.

I say the most stupid thing, the first thing that comes into my head. Your shirts, does your mother starch them like that?

He pulls on his cigarette before replying, but treats it as the most normal question in the world: Yes, Mum's very particular.

I send Percy's shirts to the laundry on Ley Street. Maybe I could do the same for you?

That would be kind. Thank you.

Ridiculous. I'm not his mother, I say to myself, turning my back on him to lift the kettle from the stove.

You don't have to make my breakfast, Edie, he says, from behind me, seeing me bring out the bacon and pan from the cupboard.

Edie. I feel the same shock I felt in Shanklin when he said my name. The same quiver of danger. Still.

It's no trouble, I'm making Percy's breakfast anyway, I reply evenly, pouring him a cup of

136

tea. I turn back to the stove, busying myself with frying bacon.

Freddy taps his shoes on the linoleum.

It's nice in here. You have things really nice.

Thank you. A little glow of pride, knowing he thinks me posh, or fashionable, or whichever word he might use.

Edie, I—

A weak cough, something like the bark of a small dog, interrupts Freddy, as Percy stumbles into the kitchen, sleepily rubbing his eyes.

Good morning, Freddy says, his voice fresh and undisturbed.

Percy sits at the kitchen table and Freddy moves his legs over to give him room. Not for the first time I have the annoying sensation of being excluded by them, as if they are about to begin their important talk about work or the racing and fill the kitchen with their smoke and dark suits and smell of wool and shaving soap, while I run around serving bacon and pots of tea. So I ask Freddy for a cigarette.

I'm running late, I say, a little testily, as if anyone had asked me. I plaster four fat strips of bacon onto two separate plates and butter some bread to put with it. Then I push the salt towards Freddy.

The two men tuck in and I drink my own tea, standing in the open doorway smoking.

Edie, don't you eat breakfast? Most important meal of the day, Freddy says cheerfully, speaking with his mouth full.

Odd to have someone commenting on me, on my habits; the little details that make up a person.

Oh, she usually does.

Percy states this with confidence although it is untrue I turn around in time to see that Percy is observing Freddy with an expression of satisfaction on his face. I know that for him, the idea of having Freddy provides a companionable kind of pleasure, male company, extra money, someone to ask the racing results. Not to mention the brush with youth that he enjoyed so much on holiday. Avis is transparent enough in inviting Freddy. She simply wants to see more of him. And me?

I fetch my hat and my light-weight peach coat.

Are you off to work, Edie? I'll walk with you to the station. I'm off to the P&O offices and then I think I'll go to Mum's to pick up a few more things.

Freddy pushes back his chair. His plate is clean and Percy has scarcely begun, so there seems no argument there. Anyway, Percy always leaves a full forty minutes later than me in the mornings. I can't remember one occasion when we walked to the station together for work.

Outside, Freddy and I walk quickly up Kensington Gardens, and I nod to our neighbour, Mrs Hester, who is pulling up the blind in her front room as we pass.

Then Freddy is at my side, speaking in a lowered voice.

Is this how it's to be between us? Frost and ice and never a moment to talk to you alone?

So my heart starts thumping and I know that I have been hoping for this. My eyes straight ahead, but my voice higher-pitched than usual, hotter.

I don't know if this is how it's to be. I don't know at all!

We clip along Belgrave Road. Others pass us but we could be having the most normal conversation in the world.

Edie, don't pretend. Don't pretend you don't know how I feel about you. I told you in Shanklin and you didn't reject me—

I didn't reject you, no, but that doesn't mean I return your feelings!

He stops in his tracks and grabs my arm. So you don't? You don't return them at all?

And suddenly I think, I'll lose him. If I say, point blank, I don't have any feelings for him, then he won't stay and it will be me and Percy again, thrown back on ourselves. We are about to cross York Road and a man on a bicycle nearly crashes into me and instead of being angry I'm saying to him, Sorry, I'm so sorry! while my mind is elsewhere; a picture of Percy at night, undoing the belt of his dressing gown and the way the bed groans as he climbs into it, flashing into my head. Percy at the breakfast table, as we left him, wiping around his plate

139

with the thick slice of bread, mopping up bacon fat.

I'm . . . sorry . . .

No other phrase will come out of my mouth.

We've reached the station and a bustle of people are swarming around us, hurrying down the steps, going about their business, oblivious to this conversation we are having, this most immodest of conversations, conducted on the street. I make a move to follow the crowd, but Freddy draws me back, pulling me towards the Coal Order office beside the station entrance.

Stand here. Let's have a cigarette.

He pulls out a packet of Players and offers me one, offers to light it for me. This gives him an excuse to put his face close to mine for a moment, but over his shoulder I can see Mr Bedford, trundling his milk cart on the other side of the road and instead of enjoying Freddy's hands, cupping mine, I'm thinking, he's bound to say something to Father or Avis . . .

I know you're afraid, Edie. But if I didn't think you had feelings for me, too, I wouldn't persist. I don't want to bully you. I think you've had enough of bullying to last a lifetime.

I hold the cigarette to my mouth but I can't inhale; my bottom lip is dissolving. Tears drum at my eyelids, a hammering in my head has started up. It's that new feeling again, the same one I had at Shanklin, the entirely unfamiliar sense of being *seen* by Freddy. As if no one ever has seen me before, not even my family. I can't abide the thought of crying in front of Freddy. I hand him back the damp cigarette in daze, murmuring: My train. I'll be late if I don't go now.

I'll come with you. Where do you get off? Liverpool Street? I can get a bus from there . . .

I make no protest, and the reason is clear: I wish to continue talking to Freddy. The thought of him taking off now in a different direction and of not seeing him until this evening makes my heart dip, my shoulders slump.

We run to the steps, hearing a train approaching, and for the millionth time I read the hand-written sign which says *Please don't run. We'd rather you missed your train than broke your ankle.* Freddy has his hand under my elbow and steers me, skilfully, dodging the other passengers to install us in a seat in record time. Several others are standing, a couple of them frown at me above their newspapers. But I'm the only woman amongst the suited men so courtesy dictates that the seat be given up to me.

It is impossible to continue our earlier conversation, which helps. We gossip about a multitude of other things—rumours of a new super cinema to be built in Ilford, Freddy's first trip to sea when he was fifteen, Freddy's brush with scarlet fever when he was five. As he is telling me this story I'm busy calculating how old I would have been, and for once the difference between us doesn't seem remarkable. I would have been twelve. Nearly thirteen, but still a child. We were both children at the same time, just as the memory of Freddy swimming in Valentine's Lake attests. I don't mention this to him. But it comforts me.

He is impressed with Carlton & Prior, with the shop front (Agnes is in the window, brushing the dust from a dove-grey velvet hat), but he doesn't follow me inside. He is off to the P&O office to see his mates there and to ask about more work. We pause a few doors down at the bank and again I have the sensation that he might leave and the day will turn dull again and the giddy feeling in my stomach, the quickened heartbeat simply turn to nausea.

You could meet me at lunchtime, I say. My voice comes out a little breathlessly. There's a park near here—in the middle of Charterhouse Square. Why don't you meet me there at one?

The smile that breaks across his face makes me blush. I'm caught in a beam which shines from Freddy, and the beam is intense; no wonder I feel hot.

Fine, he says, I'll see you at one.

I'm expecting—what, I don't know, a peck on the cheek, a touch of my hand, but Freddy turns around smoothly on his heel and starts walking away. He has been swallowed up by the office workers on Aldersgate before I have time to wonder why I said it; to wonder why, instead of the giddy anticipation of a few moments earlier, I now have a sensation of flatness, of defeat.

It is a busy morning, the sort I like, with customers one after the other and boxes of new hats arriving from Paris, and the rustle of tissue paper and the constant ring of the shop bell and the *trring whirr* of the drawer to the till; the click of shoe heels on tiled floors and Agnes saying *yes ma'am* and *no ma'am* and *that looks lovely on you ma'am* with so little feeling that I have to stifle a laugh whenever I hear it.

At 11.30 Agnes makes me a cup of tea, which is a first. I ponder what might be coming next.

Saw your new friend, Edie. Isn't that him again?

She nods out towards the door to the street opposite and there is Freddy. I leap off the chair.

Oh! Freddy! He's—my sister's new boyfriend.

Agnes is making no attempt to hide her curiosity craning her neck over the wooden counter to get a better look at Freddy.

Avis's! Tell him to come in the shop, why don't you? Then I can get a look at him.

No, no, I should go . . . we . . . we're going to

choose Avis a present.

I'm putting on the peach coat, hoping that Mr Carlton isn't about to re-emerge from the office at the back, and see me leave early.

I'll be back at 12.30 Agnes and then I'll cover your lunch break, OK?

She is pushing her hair behind her ears and staring at me rather insolently, for someone nearly ten years younger than me.

Handsome, isn't he, your sister's boyfriend . . .?

I let the shop door slam and hurry over the road.

At the park, Freddy has brought sandwiches and bottles of lemonade. He's undone the buttons on his shirt and left his jacket somewhere, and he looks relaxed, with his dark hair springing up from his forehead, ungreased, and his smile freer now, now that he knows I'm willing to meet him—nearly two hours earlier than planned!

Why don't you have any kids then, you and old Percy?

I laugh at the 'old Percy' and the directness of the question. I take my peach coat off and fold it carefully on the bench. Sit down beside him, with the coat between us.

How serious are you about my sister?

Freddy begins tucking into his sandwich, talking between mouthfuls.

Avis. I like Avis well enough. Avis is sweet and pretty and . . . She's not like you, Edie.

You must know that. You're something else.

I know I want this line of talk to continue, but somewhere in the back of my mind a drawer opens at the words: something else. Something remembered and stale with a salty taste. I take a bite of my sandwich, bite into the sharp clean taste of cucumber.

What do you mean? I make my tone playful, only a little interested in his reply.

Freddy is looking straight into my eyes, earnestly, sitting very close on the bench. One more inch and I'd feel his knees touch mine. My mouth is curiously dry and the sandwich hard to swallow.

Well there are some women . . . men can tell at a glance sometimes, Edie, if a girl is . . . well she might be a respectable married woman just like yourself and it's through no fault of her own, but something just . . . a quality of—oh, I don't know—I've noticed it particularly in redheads . . .

I burst out laughing and he scowls, pouting slightly, pretending to be wounded. I'm enjoying his discomfort—him suddenly the ardent young man, myself the cool sophisticate. He smells of beer and must have been drinking with his mates at the P&O, loosening his tongue.

Oh, don't tease, Edie. You don't want me to insult you. You're a married woman and you must know exactly what I mean.

And Avis? She has the same hair colour as

me. Does she possess this quality?

You know she doesn't. You—your—it's not just your hair. It's other things about you. What they are, I don't know But a man can tell, a man like myself—

This time I endeavour not to laugh, sensing that he might be genuinely offended. The way he refers to himself as a man makes me realise I think of him as a boy. But his words are making me feel warm, creeping over me like fingertips drumming. And still at the back of my mind there's that other feeling, from the past, some occasion just out of reach but murky, unsettling.

It's a while since a man flattered me. Makes me realise how much I miss it.

I'm not trying to flatter you! It's the truth. I couldn't help but notice, from the first time I saw you, how you wear your clothes differently from Avis, how you move differently, a different kind of womanliness . . .

He has taken my hand firmly in his and I make no move to release it. He must know that every woman in the world longs to be told how she is different from other women, how she is special, desirable. How this image of herself arouses her, makes her skin glow. He is after all, a seaman, and I don't doubt he is well practised at such conversations. His large fingers are smooth and his grip strong. The drumming quickens and a feeling like an air pocket in my lungs grows a little bigger, constricting my breathing.

A different kind of womanliness! You talk as if you've tried all the tea in China. How many girlfriends have you had? Freddy, I hope you're not stringing my sister along?

He tugs his hands away and tilts his body slightly away from me in a sulk.

When I want to be serious, you tease me. I told you in Shanklin and I told you this morning, I think I'm in love with you. And I'm pretty sure you return some, if not all of my feelings.

His tone is serious. His eyes are lowered and his lashes long and an expression of unguardedness in his face made me lean forward and do the most extraordinary thing. I kiss him, full on the mouth.

My God. Now I think I might suffer a heart-attack, my heart is smashing against my rib-cage with such savagery. A surge of warmth floods up over my body as we draw away from each other and Freddy stares at me in astonishment. My own daring pricks at every pore, raising blood to the surface. I love the sensation of surprising him, after he has been confidently telling me what kind of woman I am.

Two office-workers passing by didn't even quicken their step, although I'm sure that the delirious sensations going through my flesh must be visible for all to see.

Ah, Freddy says.

We sit in silence for a moment. Then I gather up the paper with the sandwich crumbs on it and walk towards the nearest bin. As I stand up pigeons scatter in a flurry, as if a frozen moment has been restarted. I look back at the bench, at the way Freddy is sitting. He has folded his arms behind his head, leaning back against an imaginary pillow, smoking. And then the memory floats up again and I have some irresistible desire to tell him about it.

I do know what you mean, I begin, cautiously. Red-headedness! I've never heard it called that. But men have told me. The first time I was told I was just a child. Thirteen or so. An Irish man came to Mother's house. selling something, pegs I think. And while she was in the back getting her purse I was standing half behind the door, looking at him. He had a big beard and—hair on his chest that was curly and fascinating to me. Come over here, he said, so I stepped out. Come to the doorway, let's have a look at you. So I did, because I was curious. And he said—well I won't tell you exactly what he said, because it was coarse. But the thrust of it, was. That men could tell. What kind of girl I was and that I'd better watch out or I'd be discovered. It made me feel—well, sick I suppose. It was a horrible feeling.

I glance at Freddy to see what he was making of this. His expression is not shocked, so I carry on.

And something else. Sick. And—excited. I mean, if men could tell, well I would be discovered, wouldn't I? I wouldn't be able to hide it. Does this make sense to you, Freddy?

He smiles at me. He brushes crumbs away from his mouth and his eyes are on my mouth again.

Men say anything when they want to seduce a girl.

This is a shattering remark, not what I'd expected at all. Here am I, confiding something I've never told a soul and Freddy's interpretation is completely out of the blue, completely at odds with our conversation earlier.

Are you laughing at me? I've never told anyone about that Irish man before. It was— horrible. Frightening.

But you believed him. You didn't think he was just talking about his own feelings and trying to blame them on you? Or simply sweet-talking you to steal a kiss?

Oh, I don't know. Is that what you were doing then? Just flattering me? A moment ago you swore you weren't . . .

Freddy stands up.

No, I wasn't. But *he* might have been, he states firmly. The clearest of demarcations between other men and himself, I notice. Mother would say: Pride comes before a fall. But I like it. I recognise it.

149

He offers me the cigarette that I returned earlier and we laugh at the fact that it is a little bent at the end. He lights it for me and we begin walking. Despite the pique in my words earlier, the atmosphere between us is different. Talking flows naturally and it is hard to tear myself away to go back to the shop. I feel as if I'm leaving something with Freddy. Something important that I'm not finished with yet.

He helps me on with my coat and I love the sensation of slipping my bare arms into sleeves that Freddy holds out for me. They slide in so much more easily, with none of the awkwardness of Percy making the same gesture, or of Mr Carlton. The skin of my arms feels hot against the cool fabric. I keep thinking of that movement, the sliding arms, the dark tunnels of the sleeves. My breath quickens. My throat constricts and my eyes must look as wide as golf balls.

*     *     *

All day at the shop my heart is beating differently. Or not my heart really, but the whole of my body is turned into a clock, ticking, humming, marking time. Some beautiful hats come in and it's my job to unpack them. I'm doing this with my eyes wide open but turned inwards. The different textures of the hats float up to me, through my

150

fingertips, as if I were a blind person; I feel the fine squeak of velvet, the faintly rough woven straw of a black hat, particularly lovely, with its fluttering, egg-coloured ostrich feathers, the soft murmuring of a beige felt cloche, and the cool bite of a huge broad-brimmed grey silk, with the palest of pink silk flowers. Agnes is chatting as she works beside me, displaying the hats on their wooden stands, whilst I log them and make notes in the ledger of the prices and dates of arrival.

She picks out a hat pin from a box under the counter, silver tortoiseshell, and holds it up against her hair. That's what I'm after. We get paid Friday! I've been saving. What did you and Freddy choose for your sister's birthday?

Avis's birthday! It's in a fortnight. Freddy has been invited to Shakespeare Crescent, which will be the first time the four of us will have been together since Shanklin, since Freddy's moving in.

Oh, there's plenty of time. We couldn't decide. I might choose something from Bodgers in Ilford. We have shops there as good as the West End, you know.

Always Agnes provokes this in me. This showing off. I refuse to look up from the ledger. I note that my handwriting is wobbly and the ink has left two blots, as if I had been shaking the pen above the page.

Turning my back on Agnes for a minute, I step towards the storeroom, acutely aware of my feet moving in front of me, one in front of the other, the beige stockings, the tip-tapping of the heels on the tiles. I carry out a new box of summer hats. This will be the last display of flower colours, transparent tulle in the green of an English lawn. Soon it will be all furs and gorgeous winter colours.

Agnes and I begin unpacking and she picks a butter coloured straw toque to twirl in one hand admiringly. Usually this would be the task I most enjoy—logging the new hats—but today I'm still hearing echoes of the conversation with Freddy. *A different kind of womanliness!* The archness of the sentence makes me smile. It's just as I told him. Others have commented on it and it only frees me into thinking: it can't be helped then! How swift Freddy was to distance himself from other men. He didn't want me to think that was the only shape his desire for me took, he didn't want me to be shocked and reject him for coarseness, the way I recoiled from the Irish man, from others in the past.

But I was a child. And even then, curious. Six years of marriage hasn't made me any less so. How sweet Freddy makes himself to me, by struggling to disguise the very thought which is drawing me towards him. Struggling to be such a man of the world and seeming oddly more and more childlike as a result. He is still stuck, as stuck as any other man, in the idea that a decent married woman of a certain class

152

wouldn't know about the feelings of young men and would be disgusted by them if she did.

It's true that there's plenty I don't know about. Plenty I wish to learn about. And that I believe I am capable of more passion than others might appreciate. Than I have demonstrated to date. I feel my body tick with that knowledge. There is a warmth, a heatedness in my blood that lets me know that this is true. I can't remember when this knowledge started. But it was long before my marriage, long before that curly-haired Irish man came to the door. I think I have always known that I possessed an unusual gift, the same way another child might always have known that they were musical, long before the slim curve of the violin was placed in their hands.

All day I've felt as if someone is chasing me. Once, I jumped out of my skin when Agnes came up behind me and quietly asked if I'd put the ledger away as she had something to add to it. Don't creep about like that, Agnes! I shrieked.

At 5.30 I'm outside pulling down the wooden shutter of Carlton & Prior and there is Freddy, across the road, leaning against the bank opposite; now wearing his jacket again, with his hair dark and flattened down with oil. He is smoking, his body languid, one arm stretching along a window ledge, the other hanging limply by his side, holding a cigarette. I stare at him for a moment before he sees me. The oddest thought pops into my head. He looks like a clock standing there, still and fixed. His arms are in the position of half past three!

He gives the appearance of utter relaxation, smoking, watching the office girls go by, not waiting for anyone at all. But I can't shift the image of the clock. It corresponds perfectly with my heart ticking. I fetch my coat and hat, and wonder, in a nonsensical way, if Agnes can hear it too.

He persuades me, he insists there is time, for a drink in the White Horse before we go home. Five-thirty and I'm the only woman in here. I order a Guinness and port and we choose the darkest corner, to continue our hand-holding and whispering and the conversation is more of the same, more about Freddy and his knowledge of women, and more of my unhappiness with Percy and how he is, in Freddy's words, 'the wrong kind of fellow for me'. The lunchtime kiss hovers in the air between us. I can still taste the beer and smoke and the salt on his mouth. His blue eyes glitter in the lamp-light in the dark corner of the bar-room and my excitement, my daring in being there, a saloon bar in the middle of town, trills in my blood.

What are we to do, what are we to do? I wail, after the second Guinness and port. I do not really wish for a reply to this question. I wish to convey to Freddy the strength of my passion for him, the quandary that it throws me into, being a respectable married lady and all. I pat at my throat with my handkerchief, alarmed at the way I'm perspiring. Freddy lets his arm stray to my bare shoulders and his fingers make my skin tremble and my legs turn weak.

I've no idea how we get to the train. I've no idea how we arrive home. I only remember leaning on Freddy as we cross De Vere Road and I remember Percy's face, like a stony gargoyle as he opens the door and says, Your mother's here. She called in with the curtains you asked her to bring.

So then I have to talk to Mother and introduce her again to Freddy (unable to remember in my giddy state if she knows him or not) and knowing that quite possibly they are able to smell the Guinness on my breath and suddenly in the midst of making a pot of tea for all of us I shriek, far more loudly than is necessary: Oh my coat! I must have left it on the train!

Percy's eyes land on my bare shoulders and I wonder why he never remarked sooner that I seem unnecessarily underdressed. Freddy and I dare not meet each other's gaze. We both know I left it, not on the train, but in the White Horse. Still, emboldened, I insist that I remember the carriage I left it in.

Maybe someone handed it in to the station master. I'll run back there and find out, I announce, plonking the cups down noisily on their saucers.

Freddy shifts in his seat. He picks up a biscuit and nibbles at it.

I'm out of the door and hurrying down Belgrave Road before I hear his footsteps catch up with me. And then we're laughing, both of us, giddy, breathless, like children . . .

How did you get away? I ask.

I said I was off to the Angel with some mates. Percy said he might join me there later. Quick—come to the park, for five minutes. I know a spot where we won't be seen.

And the giddiness just bubbles over me and won't subside and with it the sense of misbehaving, but of a game, that it doesn't really matter. We walk to Valentine's Park, calculating that Percy will allow me time to ask the station master and perhaps fill out a lost property form and then walk back, so we have around—half an hour in total.

At the park Freddy takes me to a spot behind the boat-house and makes me giggle, telling me about the 'kneetremblers' the area is famous for and we manage at last to kiss fully and properly and it is as if my mouth, my whole self has waited for this since lunchtime and now vibrates like a gong struck hard, making the ground beneath my feet shake. Freddy's big hands smooth all over me and,

156

although I know I should stop him, I don't, because we only have these brief few moments and perhaps I think, even now, at this point, that it might go no further, that I might experience this much and no more, call a stop, close a door, whenever I wish to. He kisses my ear and my neck and runs hands over my waist and hip in the thin crepe de chine dress and says, Say no, Edie, say no to me . . .

But I say nothing at all, until the sound of children's voices looms up on us, approaching the boat-house, so we break away and smooth our clothes and begin walking in opposite directions.

*     *     *

After that, it is only a matter of waiting for an occasion. Routines are established; mornings it seems legitimate to Freddy to walk to work with me, lunchtimes to meet me without Percy knowing, evenings to travel home together. After tea, Percy and Freddy go out for drinks or a game of cards, evenings we drink cocoa together in the kitchen before retiring to our separate rooms. Rarely are Freddy and I free from the presence of strangers, but we continue our conversations, the source of everything, the elixir, the fan, the spoon which is stirring up our interest in one another—in a railway carriage, in the Holborn Restaurant or the Chapter House; waiting on the platform or

157

for a tram at Cobweb Corner.

Perhaps we might have continued indefinitely with this game, this flirtation, if Percy hadn't become more jealous, more unreasonable than usual. One evening we've been at 231, having dinner with the family and now walking home (Freddy having left earlier to go to the pub with Arnie) Perc puts his face close to mine—*too* close to mine—and remarks nastily: You and your sister. What a bloody pair you are.

I keep walking, acting as if he hasn't spoken. There no point arguing with Percy when he's been drinking and in such a mood.

The way you carry on, the pair of you . . .

It's no good: I can't keep up my silence.

What do we do that offends you so much? Laugh? Enjoy ourselves?

You fawn all over that damn Bywaters, that's what!

I try to control my voice, to sound calm. Oh, so that's the trouble is it—

He makes a ridiculous snorting sound. No, that's not the bloody trouble and don't start putting words in my mouth!

We reach our own front gate and he pushes it open and barges through, without holding it open for me. He fumbles with his key in the front door lock. I'm waiting for him to manage this, biting back a desire to ask politely: Do you want me to do that? After several minutes of jabbing and thrusting at the lock in the moonlight Percy wheels around and bellows at me:

A husband has rights, you know, and don't you forget it!

Instinctively I take a step backwards, but he is already backing down the path, repeating loudly: A man has bloody rights . . .

Mrs Hester's curtain next door opens for a second, and then the drape is quickly dropped. I reach in my handbag for my own key, watching Percy stumble down the street in the direction of the Angel. As the curtain next door flaps again I resist an urge to knock on Mrs Hester's window and shout: That's right, the Thompsons are having a scene in the street, again! Roll up, roll up! Tears are streaming down my cheeks as I push the front door open. The last thing I expect is to see Freddy, popping his head around the kitchen door to say good evening.

I rub at my face, duck my head, keep my eyes lowered. I thought you were out with Arnie?

Oh, he went chasing a girl. I thought I'd have an early night.

I mean to pass him, to go upstairs and wash my face and go straight to bed but acting as if nothing is wrong is not easy with Freddy.

I've just made a pot of tea, Freddy says. I hesitate at the kitchen door. Glance at the tray he's set out, the teapot with its knitted cosy, the strainer, the jug of milk. Two cups in two

159

saucers. My eyes meet his.

Did you hear us arguing? You heard Percy leave?

I couldn't help it. I—I wasn't snooping. I'm pushed to blazes sometimes, living here, hearing the way he talks to you . . .

And that phrase is enough. Sympathy. Freddy minding. That opens the flood gates. We sit and talk at the kitchen table, and when it gets to eleven and Percy is still not back, the possibility creeps into my thoughts, the knowledge of what so often happens if Percy goes to the Angel already drunk. He can rarely make it home and the landlord, a friend of Percy's brother Richard, lets Percy sleep it off in the downstairs bedroom. I am wondering how to mention this to Freddy. I should say, *whether* to mention this to Freddy.

Freddy looks at his watch, the cheap watch that Avis bought him, and announces he is going to hit the hay. He politely bids me goodnight and walks past me, past the back of my chair. His jacket brushes my hair. I link both hands around my tea cup. Swig the last of the cold tea. Take the cups and the jug to the sink and carefully wash them in the hottest water I can bear.

# CHAPTER FIVE

## ILFORD CRIME EXHUMATION GRAVEDIGGERS TASK BY MOONLIGHT

POST-MORTEM TODAY
POLICE VIGIL BY COFFIN
The body of Mr Percy Thompson, a shipping clerk of Ilford, Essex, who was stabbed in the street within a few yards of his home in the early hours of October 4th, was exhumed from his grave in the City of London Cemetery, Manor Park, last night.

The gravediggers began their work soon after 5 p.m. The grave, on which remained a few withered flowers, was 10ft deep, and the men digging by the light of the moon, it was three hours before the coffin was lifted to the surface. Superintendent Wensley, of Scotland Yard, and local detectives, watched the operations, which were carried out with great secrecy.

The coffin was taken to the crematorium in the cemetery. Two police constables were detailed to mount guard over it. This morning, Dr Bronte, the pathologist, will conduct a post-mortem and will remove certain organs which will be handed over to the Home Office experts, for examination.

Mr Thompson's wife, Edith Thompson, 27, and Frederick Edward Bywaters, 20, a ship's laundry steward, are under arrest, charged with his murder. The prisoners were remanded until next Wednesday.

A feature of the evidence has been the reading of the letters said to have been written by Mrs Thompson to Bywaters. Several of the letters contain references to poisons.

*Daily Mail,* 3rd November, 1922

\* \* \*

Percy's body exhumed at midnight, by the fur-grey light of the moon. Digging and digging, they are, the thump thump of the spade, then the thud and scatter of the earth over their shoulders, until finally the spade bats against wood, against the brass handles of the coffin, now scattered and soiled in mud, and then— how? How would they lift out the coffin, two men at midnight by the light of the moon? They use ropes and leverage, and Percy's body would be in there, slipping to one side, shuffling up to the white silky edges of the coffin, like a cat carried inside a lined basket.

And would he be light now, light or heavy? Well, heavy if you picture Percy, a big man with a scowl on his face and a wool coat and his arms crossed, but light, light if you picture a dead body, beginning to disintegrate, the flesh inside the clothes beginning to—what does it do? Turn green, like mould? Fall away from the bone like the rotten fruit of an apple? How strange that we dress them. Dress dead bodies. So that the flesh inside the clothes turns to the brown pulp of a peach, and a doll is there wearing a suit. Percy as a dummy, a shrivelled effigy inside the trappings of himself, his clothes, his job, his other time.

And we'll all do that, one day, even me. Especially me. Even this hand, fine veined, the long tendons down to the fingers, the freckles and the pale moons at the base of each nail and the tiny snips of skin that I bite sometimes, all of that . . . will start to turn bad, and melt away from the bones like the flesh of a peach from the stone. Can I imagine that, can I really? And then the bones will be clean and light brown, slender fine pieces of driftwood, washed up on a beach, floating on a white spume of wave. Yes, that will do nicely, that will be fine, floating out to sea, that's where I picture myself.

And then as I'm closing my eyes the driftwood floats up and the wave starts rising. That's not right, I want to go on floating; floating is fine, but instead there is turbulence beneath me, the water is foaming and frothing and the waves are churning and spitting and the driftwood, the bones, my bones, start twisting and turning in agony, and now the water is red, red hot, boiling heat is cooking up the bones in a big steaming stew and there is nothing peaceful, no nothing peaceful at all, I have never been so scared nor so hot, nor felt such blood-red heat beneath me and if only I could wake, wake up, this might all be over and I could be cool again and floating and Percy would still be here, still alive, sitting in his chair in the front room, the paper would say 1st October, 1922 and be lying across his knee, the tea-cup would be brimming with hot tea and back in its saucer.

Percy's body is being exhumed, Percy's body is being exhumed. I am an evil woman, going to burn in hell and Percy's body is being exhumed.


CEMETERY'S SEARCH
Following the announcement in The *Daily Mail* on Thursday that the body of Mr Percy Thompson, the murdered shipping clerk from Ilford, was to be exhumed, hundreds of people visited the cemetery during the day. At five o'clock the grounds were closed in the ordinary way, but detectives, watchmen and keepers made an unusually thorough

search for lingerers, and anyone found was escorted to the gates. Policemen in plain clothes and uniform in unusual numbers maintained a ceaseless patrol of the three mile circumference of the cemetery boundaries. The wreaths were removed and piled behind the stones of adjacent tombs, and then the diggers began their task. Working only by the light of the moon, while policemen kept guard, they removed the earth to within a few inches of the top of the coffin.

*Daily Mail,* 4th November, 1922

*Externally.*
*The body was that of a well nourished man. Putrefaction was advancing. There were incisions of previous post-mortem examination along the trunk and across the head. There were three stab wounds on the body, each a clean cut wound having a surface measurement of 1" to 2" wide. One wound was situated at the right side of the back of the neck: it penetrated to the spine. A second wound was situated on the right side of the neck and short distance below and behind the angle of the jaw. It passed upwards and inwards and penetrated into the floor of the mouth.*
    *Post-Mortem Report,* 5th November, 1922

*5th November, 1922*

Darlint,

I'm sorry I haven't written for a few days. I have not been well; in fact, I suppose it is truer to say that I have been heavily sedated and so don't really feel I have been here at all. I can only remember snippets—the constant presence of Dr Lynch looming out of every dream as if on a cloud, offering me this pill or that pill and always with the same expression, an expression I'd find impossible to name but which reminds me of Mrs Hester, regarding her little dog, whenever he had fouled the pavement.

Now, darlint, I don't want you to worry, so won't go on any further with that, except to say that I am feeling ever so slightly better and have managed to stop thinking about Percy and to put my mind to other things. Stern has been to visit, and he brought me that most marvellous of gifts—a clean new box of the freshest cigarettes!—each one slipping between my fingers gave me the purest sliver of joy, and although they have not relaxed the two a day rule, I've even found a delight in that . . . I have one in the morning and one before bed and never did a cigarette taste so exquisite and cool and satisfying, or the smoke linger for so long. I always think of you, Freddy, when I smoke, I imagine you doing the same in your cell over in Pentonville and I know just how you would look; narrowing your eyes so that they are darker and more scowly than ever! And I think of your wrists, fine and strong at the same time, and the way you sit when you smoke. (I picture you sitting on the edge of your bed, the way I used to imagine you at sea, sitting in your cabin, legs apart, staring into the middle distance.)

I've never *yearned* for anyone the way I yearn for you, Freddy, but I don't resent it. What is the point of living if we can't experience all that there is in the range of human feelings? I feel these days that I know so much more than I ever used to about human beings, through this experience. I know it's not quite the same and I hope you won't take this the wrong way, but I've even thought a lot about the men, the young men, fighting, away from home, steeped in their trenches, longing for cigarettes the way I long for them, longing for a letter, longing for their girlfriends and wives and longing for that thing that women are supposed not to think about; the union of one body inside another. Freddy, that would fill me up, that would make me feel complete and whole and I know that men think our desires don't take such a plain shape but God, how I long simply to have you penetrate me, over and over. I think of this, at night, when I can't sleep, when I am unsure if I am alive or not. To have you enter me, again and again, endlessly, that's what I think about, Freddy, and I know you, of all people, could accept this confession and not judge me harshly.

See how lax I'm becoming? I've long ceased to care whether the Governor reads this, or wonder if he will ever agree to let me send this growing bundle of letters to you. I write anyway because when I write I am communicating with you, talking, reaching you, and I need that feeling, wherever I can find it. Of course it is not as wonderful as what I have just described but it satisfies something in me, just the same.

Now to more mundane matters. Someone new came to see me this morning. He is a young chaplain. His name is Piper and he has the most ridiculous red hair and freckly skin you've ever seen. He reminds me of a boy in school we used to call Poxy! I don't suppose you remember that boy, he was my age, but if I tell you that his eyelashes were transparent and his face covered in spots, you might have a sense of what Piper looks like.

I wasn't impressed. He asked if I had anything I wished to discuss with him 'of a spiritual nature' and I practically laughed out loud. Clara was on her way out at that moment, taking the tray, and I caught her eye. That said plenty. Barely twenty-five, Piper is, I'd guess. Surprised he felt able to share a room with me after what's been said about me.

He wasn't unpleasant, he only looked shy and ridiculously young and I wondered why on earth he would choose such a job as prison chaplain. I must ask him, if I get a chance to, next time. Is he one of these men who want to save women? And if so, why? Father used to say, While you're about it, vicar, save one for me!

Piper. We'll see. At least he's somebody new to talk to.

Last time he was here, Stern was rather pessimistic, Freddy, and now I have recovered a little, I am determined not to be. What good can it do me to think the worst? I need all my energy, all the resources at my disposal for the trial ahead of us. There, I will have my chance to tell my story, and the other extracts and the other letters can be read and understood.

I really do believe that on account of your youth and high passion, your crime will be reduced to manslaughter and although this sounds terrible to us now, Freddy, that is because it is such early days and I believe you, like me, can't really quite believe what has happened in the last month or so.

Now, as ever, my hand is aching from writing and I will finish here and write again tomorrow.

All my love,
Peidi.

# SHOULD MARRIED WOMEN WORK?

## TEACHERS RESENT SUGGESTION THAT THEIR CHILDREN SUFFER AS A CONSEQUENCE. ECHO OF CORONER'S COMMENT

Women teachers bitterly resent the remarks of the Cardiff coroner on the case of a married woman teacher whose son died of lockjaw.

The mother had her school duties, said the coroner, but she would have realised the growing gravity of the symptoms if she had been home with the child the whole time. This pathetic case recalls Mr A.S.M. Hutchinson's much discussed novel, 'This Freedom', which raised controversy as to whether a married woman who went out to work could exert the proper maternal influence over her children.

*Daily Sketch,* 1st November, 1922

Freddy,

I'm sending the above cutting as I know you've read *This Freedom* and we had a long conversation about it. Eve sneaked in a newspaper for me today! This is quite a departure for her and I'm intrigued by it . . .

usually she does everything to the letter. (For instance, when we are prowling round the exercise yard like big cats in a circus, if it is Eve on duty she rebukes us quite fiercely if we chat, and makes us walk a certain distance apart, unlike the others, who usually smoke and natter and don't mind too much if we do the same.)

I read the paper avidly from cover to cover, not just the bits about us, of course, although they were fascinating and gave me a strange jolt. Now I know what Avis mean: when she says that each time she opens a newspaper she feels as if ants are crawling all over her skin . . .

Avis came this morning and I feel truly worried for her. How much weight she has lost! The beautiful peaches and cream costume she bought last year was hanging off her and I noticed her hands were trembling, although she tried to keep her face bright. I suppose I haven't thought enough of everyone on the outside. It's all been happening in my head. I've thought of you, of course, and Percy and myself. That is easily enough for me and actually feels quite crowded. Then Avis broke in with a shove.

It made me think of Shanklin again. Shanklin poured into the room, and I remembered Avis asking me to come. It'll be fun, Edie, and you and Percy are such old sticks on your own! You need us two to liven you up . . . She was laughing and linked her arm in mine; we were walking towards Lyons tea-shop on the Strand. A Saturday trip out. It wasn't that I needed much persuading either, only that my silence confused her and she thought I was resisting. She had already mentioned you—her new young man, and I was wondering idly, without *undue* interest you understand, what this new young man would be like and whether it might not be good sport indeed to have another male presence on holiday.

We clinked our tea-cups and leant our heads towards each other and giggled when a waitress we knew passed us with a huge black smut on the back of her white apron. That particular waitress was always a sour-face, so I voted we should tell her but Avis kept shrieking, No, Edie, and putting her hand over mine to restrain me as I tried to wave and catch the waitress's attention. Finally the girl stopped at our table and tilted her face enquiringly. Yes, Madam? (It was that ginger-haired girl, the one with the faint eyebrows and pointed chin and the pale eyelashes that I accused you later of flirting with. Remember that cutting I sent you, *Do men prefer Redheads?* and me insisting I'm a redhead but she was a ginger.)

Excuse me, miss, have you been sitting in something? I asked politely. The girl looked ready to return a tart remark at first and then understanding dawned and turning slowly round, she discovered the large black blot, scowled and glanced instantly in the direction of the head waiter, bowing obsequiously by the door.

Just trying to be helpful, I called after her as Avis stifled more giggles and then said, Edie! again, reprovingly, but with that mixture she always managed—disapproval and admiration rolled into one.

Fine, I said, putting down my spoon with a resounding clatter. A week in the sun will do nicely. And I'll put up half the money towards your room, Avis, then we can go somewhere really nice. Just what Percy needs—although he doesn't know it yet.

Percy was easily persuaded anyway. I don't know if I ever told you that. He liked holidays. He had what I thought of as a 'Holiday Personality' and I much preferred it to his workaday one. It consisted of him throwing caution to the wind and buying a penny icecream.

So I packed with care, and who can say why? A week by the sea, the Isle of Wight, early summer, gulls and charabancs and Guinness and port; Punch and Judy and sticks of candy-rock; that's what I was thinking as I picked out my loveliest items, my best silk camisoles and other things that women take pride in, and folded them carefully into the leather case.

I noticed as I did so that one set had a

button missing and set to sewing it just then, so all would be done. And the lace, some Chantilly lace on one very special slip, was torn just around the neckline and I sewed that too. I hesitated over the egg-shell blue cami-knickers, with the coffee coloured lace—part of my wedding trousseau and, of course, associated with that night—thinking I suppose, something like: well they'll never be worn otherwise, and who will see them?

I had a new hat of mushroom-coloured felt, neat, the first hat I'd had in the latest cloche shape with a coiled spiral of felt at the side, like the shell of a snail, and I remember myself pulling it down low, so that it squashed my fringe closer to my eyes, and I remember looking at myself in the mirror at my dressing-table.

What was I thinking, was I thinking about you, I mean you in the abstract—a new young man—that's what I wonder now? I honestly can't remember, no matter how hard I examine myself on this. Perhaps I was thinking of you, perhaps not. I finished sewing the button, cut the thread with my teeth, folded the soft silk lovingly, put it on top of some blouses and snapped the case shut with a satisfying click. If I *was* thinking of you it would have been in the role of *witness,* you understand—as an additional admirer! Because since I am an honest person I will admit that I may occasionally have thought something like this: *what is the point of turning heads the way I do, of having hair of dark copper and shiny in a new glossy cap around my face, if only Percy is here to admire it?*

You will laugh at that sentence, I know, Freddy. Accusing me not of the sin of vanity but of being too candid, not dissembling the way women ought! It pleases me to know that you love this quality in me and have never been shocked by it. So many things about me that you were the only man—no, the only *person*—to appreciate.

I must finish now. In ten more minutes we must suffer a 'room inspection' when a chief wardress comes around with Clara or Eve and takes us to task on whether our cleaning is up to scratch! I'm sure your room will be spotless, like your cabin always was. What a sad pang it gives me, to think of you, pacing that shiny square box, perhaps hearing the noise of traffic outside, or staring at a cloud as it floats past your window.

I try very hard, darlint, not to picture sad things. This will not help us, I've decided, and you must keep from such thoughts also and remember only that Peidi thinks of you every moment and sends all her love to you.

\*          \*          \*

Avis today, in her peaches and cream costume, her gloves, her brown coat. Her eyes down, staring into her lap. How dutifully she comes to visit, how little we talk. And this evening, before lights-out, I had another flash of Shanklin; this time, a conversation between Avis and me on the first day; in the Ladies Room at Osborne House, when I took off my hat and showed her my new hair cut.

I remember Avis gasping in surprise and then suddenly hugging me, in a gesture she hasn't made since we were very small children. I feel her heart beating beneath her thin cotton dress and pull away from her, straightening her collar.

So you like it then? I ask, gleefully. We stare at ourselves in the mirror, both of us with our hands at our hair. I adjust a buckle on my dress (also new, iridescent green and silver, shaped like interlocking diamonds) and take out a cigarette.

I offer Avis one of the Players but she shakes her head. She is holding up her long hair and I realise she is testing what she would look like with a bob.

Oh, but I don't have a nice long neck like yours, Edie I'd look like a bull-terrier.

She lets her hair drop and busies herself washing her hands. I pat my own hair and finish my cigarette, watching her.

*   *   *

I was Father's favourite. I say that not as a

boast, but as a simple statement of fact, and not necessarily a blessing either. I'm sure Avis knew it, or rather felt it, all through our childhood, the way I did.

He made me a doll's house. when I was six, just before Avis was born. A beautiful doll's house, a little replica of the new house at Manor Park, the dreamed-of house, bought when he was promoted to chief clerk at the tobacco factory, a huge promotion, after the poky terrace at Stamford Hill. The doll's house had a square of painted wooden garden at the front and back, and tiny, perfect furniture. Sometimes when I picture it, I get confused and instead of Manor Park it becomes a doll's house replica of our house, mine and Percy's, at 41 Kensington Gardens.

Double-fronted. Eight rooms and a scullery, a front drawing room, a back morning room, a front bedroom and the back bedroom, where Freddy slept. A grand sized house, on a clean-swept, broad street; warm and summery, with tiny doll people in their hats, walking up to the door, peeking in at the windows. In the bedroom a tiny jug and bowl, a feather bolster the size of a finger; in the kitchen a polished copper coffee pot; in the hallway a tiny stand with peacock feathers in it.

And then great big clumsy hands lifting muslin curtains, fingers knocking over a stand of fire irons, fingers flipping over a coconut mat, creeping like spiders up the stairs and

177

into the bedrooms, right into the back bedroom, the one where Freddy slept. Huge hands, rummaging, fingering, clambering. Peeling off leaves from the privet hedge outside, searching in drawers for a scrap of silk, a souvenir. And the house is now a hollow box, without any people. Wooden, rattling, all the furniture slipped to one side like furniture in a boat, lifted and floated on a stranger's shoulders and then put away somewhere.

Two small girls—very faint, very pale are floating into view, with doll-like faces, and there are hyacinths in the front garden, the Violet Pearl hyacinths, small and waxy.

If I close my eyes now I can still smell their scent, heady and plump; fat and lustrous and smelling like grass, like silky, milky, succulent grass.

*19th November, 1922*

Freddy, Freddy! A letter from you! I can't believe it. It was Eve who brought it, and she looked quite flushed when she came in the room and full of self-importance but then when she handed it over our eyes met and she pushed nervously at her cap and then broke into a grin. It's from him! she said, and hovered around me just like a sister. I think the drama of the whole situation had really started to get under her skin. She would have stayed too, while I read it, except that I didn't, straight away. I simply put it on my pillow and Eve stood there for a moment, with this expression of excitement and anticipation on her face and then she looked at me and the other expression, the sly, slow one slipped over her, like a mask.

I'll leave you then. A slightly annoyed remark, I thought. But surely she could understand I would want to be alone when I read it!! Clara would understand. Clara is less caught up in the drama, less enamoured with the fame, and more . . . human.

So, darlint, I read it a hundred times and it was so frustrating—so short!—and so exhilarating all at once. Obviously you haven't received any of the early letters I thought were reaching you. The few lines you write sound despondent and almost—but not quite—giving up hope of hearing from me. But, darlint, I have a great pile of letters, stacked up for you, under the bed. What shall I do with them? Shall I attempt to send them? I just don't know.

When I read, Peidi, darling, I am so worried about you, a great lump came into my throat. Always that care for me, that tenderness—the gift you gave me of *mattering* at all. Of course I know, Freddy, that you have told anyone who will listen that I am innocent, that I had nothing to do with your actions on that Tuesday evening, you don't have to assure me of that! I don't doubt for one instant that you are a loyal person, an honourable man. Isn't that what incensed you so in the first place? Please don't think you have to persuade me of that.

Your little note—how many times have I read it!—has revived my sense of talking to you, of nearness to you. Yesterday that was fading. Now it is revived all over again—the sight of your writing reminded me of some of the beautifully neat writing on the ship's log that you showed me one time, aboard the SS *Morea*. That was in Portsmouth, with Avis and Percy again, on the way back from Shanklin.

I have little hope of getting a letter to you. Yours is dated yesterday but it sounds as if you wrote others. How touched I am that you, like me, have kept faith with writing, despite not receiving a single reply. That you, like me, are continuing a conversation, as if it were never interrupted. I love this idea. And you too are thinking of our 'one little hour', although you of course express it differently.

It is only twenty-four hours now until we will see each other in court. I hope Lily has visited you often. I hope she has forgiven me for seducing her innocent darling (as she will surely think of it) by now. (Although knowing Lily, I doubt she has.)

In only a few hours this mess could all be cleared up. I can hardly contain the excitement I'm feeling about this!! I could be out—

outside—and then able to visit you, darlint. I never know what to write about this, aware as I am that your situation is not as certain as mine but a sentence for manslaughter could be greatly reduced and, remember, I am now a widow, a free woman! Enough said.

This has been a terrible terrible nightmare for us and I would still like to talk to you properly about the event (which I don't wish to discuss here) but now we must set our hearts and minds to the future and to concentrating on it all working out well for us in the end. Yes, yes, your Pal loves you madly, madly, no matter what.

Don't be downhearted. A boy was never loved as much as you are. No, I'm sorry, I meant to write there no man was ever loved as much as you are, darlint. Thank you, thank you, darlint, for the lifeline you sent me, for your letter! All will be fine, you'll see.

Your Peidi.

## CHAPTER SIX

## NEW CHARGES AGAINST MRS THOMPSON

ANALYST'S REPORT
MORPHINE IN EXHUMED BODY
WOMEN FAINT IN COURT

Three women fainted at Stratford Police Court yesterday when Frederick Bywaters, 20, ship's store-keeper, of Upper Norwood, and Mrs Edith Thompson, 28, were committed for trial at the Old Bailey on a charge of murdering the woman's husband, Percy Thompson, a shipping clerk, at Ilford, Essex, on October 4th. Mr and Mrs Thompson were in the street on the way home from a theatre when the husband was fatally stabbed.

Mrs Thompson fainted away at the end of the hearing, and her mother, a frail grey-haired little woman, ran up to the dock saying, 'My child, my child.' She clutched her daughter's dress but her hands were gently removed by the wardress, whereupon the little woman in black collapsed on the steps of the dock.

Mrs Bywaters—the mother of Frederick Bywaters—who had been present at every hearing of the case, also fainted in the passage outside the court.

In addition to the joint charge for murder there were further charges against Mrs Thompson. They were that between June 1st 1921 and October 4th 1922, she administered poison to her husband; that she unlawfully solicited and proposed to Bywaters to murder Thompson; and further incited Bywaters to conspire with her to murder her husband.

*Daily Mail,* 24th November, 1922

WOMEN JURORS: SOME HELPFUL
ADVICE
Many women when they receive a jury summons for the first time become quite agitated, especially if they are the home-keeping type.

There is no need for this as there will be plenty of officials to tell them exactly what they have to do. They have only to follow out instructions.

In their anxiety not to be late, some women get to the court more than an hour before the time named on the summons. This is a mistake, as there is seldom a room in which to wait, and the passages of the courts are often stuffy. A quarter of an hour before the time named is sufficient.
WEIGHING THE EVIDENCE
The judge in his address to the jury will have told them exactly what are their powers and functions. Similarly he will direct them with regard to the evidence. She will be an unusual woman who does not come away from the court with an increased respect for English justice and the conviction that prisoners are given

every chance.

*Daily Mail,* 24th November, 1922

*26th November, 1922*

Dear Freddy,
I'm writing this in the early hours. I've no idea
of the exact time. I'm not sure I even know
where I am any longer. The light at this
moment is a shade of joyless grey. I long to
feel light that can touch me; brilliant light, the
light at Valentine's Lake when we were
swimming, keen and pure and strong as a lick
from a dog's tongue. Or wobbly light, candle
light. If I concentrate I can smell the wax, see
the brass candle-holders in the back bedroom.
Why did we use candles, that first time? For
fear that if we shone a proper light on things
we might be too afraid to continue?

Intensely, I remember every step up to your
door. My knuckles rapping lightly on the
wood, my heart rapping lightly at my rib-cage.
The sound of you moving in there. A
breathless moment when I said to myself, *I've
made a dreadful mistake! He's asleep, he wasn't
expecting me at all.* And then you answered the
door and there you were, fully dressed, right
down to your shoes and I knew that you must
have been waiting, musing, perhaps trying to
pluck up courage to come back downstairs to

the clean washed pots and pans and me in the kitchen with my back to you and my apron on and perhaps start up the same conversation, the one we were having about Percy.

So you kissed me, approaching me with that skilful angling of the head, tilted enquiringly, like a bird, a question. You wrapped your arms around me. I smelt your light salt sea sweat and was reassured that you were nervous too. But you didn't rush. You carried on kissing and kissing me so that I could drink you in, all I wanted to, all I had longed to for many months.

You're sure about this, Edie?

And I said, Yes, yes, I'm sure! And you began kissing my neck and my collarbone, but tenderly, shyly, less forcefully than I would have liked and I was standing like a doll, floppy, not knowing what I was supposed to do in return and when you would progress.

I remember in perfect detail what I was wearing. The pale mauve voile with the embroidered bodice and sash and the buttons down the back. When I felt your hand finally reach for one of these buttons, the tension became too much, I was nearly bent in two, nearly broken by the trembling terrifying delight of it all and almost, almost feeling too awe-struck, too aghast at the danger, the frightful magnitude of what we were doing. But then that terror passed and I was wanting to shout *yes, yes, come on get on with it,* and of

185

course, darlint, I would say such things now but then I was struck dumb not knowing whether to help you or let you struggle like that with one hand and so just standing there arching my back to you, as hard as I could, trying with all my will to make it easier for you to get me out of that little voile dress and into my petticoat without interrupting our kissing and then finally it was done and I stood before you like a child and you still fully dressed and me thinking, *Oh, my God! Surely it is not my turn to undress him now?*

But, I remember you, thankfully, as rather businesslike at this point! How you undressed yourself hurriedly and stood awkwardly trying not to show that I had noticed how urgent you were, the sweat breaking out on the bridge of your nose, how you nearly knocked the candle over with your shoe, flicking it like that and then to see your shirt open and the dark forest of your chest with the hair growing in that V-shape it makes there like the pattern that geese make in the sky and your shirt so brilliant white and your eyes so pearl-pale blue and your grin so ridiculous and unstoppable and you practically panting now and forgetting to hide your impatience; not noticing that I am standing quite petrified, as another wave of panic hits me, another great flooding sense of trepidation, of disbelief at my own daring, until your kiss shoots flames and fire-crackers through my body, scorches every doubt into thin air, and you lift the tarantulle petticoat over my head and carry me onto the bed beside you (a little clumsily with our knees knocking together and your trousers not quite fully off at the ankle) and my teeth chattering and my skin breaking out in goose-pimples and every pore tingling with nerves and all sensation now concentrated in the hot numbness of my mouth kissing and kissing, then closing my eyes tight, unable to bear to see the expression in your eyes. Feeling your hands all over my body so freely, freely and you holding me while you slip yourself into me. Really not wanting to know, not wanting to check by looking if you are still you: *Freddy*, good and loving, or if you have become like Percy, like other men, taken over, glazed over, mesmerised by your own desire until you don't see me, don't know it is me at all. But then not able to resist opening my eyes and finding yours open too and it was just then that you gave a short sharp thrust that seemed to knock some breath out of my lungs and you smiled at me and said, Edie and I kept my gaze wide and kept looking and looking and searching and searching while you began to launch yourself into me with such abandon the way a child launches in a swing sometimes—wildly and wildly—and the bed creaking as beds do . . .

. . . and I was astonished, *astonished* at this slipperiness that my own body can produce and the absence of pain and the entirely

187

different, *different* drumming feeling everywhere inside and all around me and I was terrified, almost too terrified to enjoy it really but I held you, I felt the salty sweat slippery on your back and smelled your hair with the sandalwood pomade and I let you do all those things to me, those tender kisses and caresses that I was quite unused to and I remained *separate,* quite awake and watchful and reached . . . I was rocked and wild and holding you and saying to myself: *So this is it, this is it then, this is—oh my God, after nearly seven years of marriage!! This is it.*

*     *     *

Well, after that, after me coming to Freddy in the little back bedroom, after the awful daring of a moment's surrender, was there still a chance to turn things around, a chance to halt right there and then, for nothing more to occur: for him to go away to sea again and for me to continue as if nothing at all had altered? Toss the chalk again, jump back, land on another square?

I don't think so. I don't think there was ever a moment in my mind when I considered that this one transgression might be enough, might satisfy me. Freddy said in a letter later that he knew how much it had cost me to come to him like that, an act which an age of prudence could never retract. I believe it is true. He understood the cost, but he underestimated the prize.

The very next morning the knowledge of Freddy which my body holds, makes my skin tingle and my stomach turn somersalts, my blood spark inside me like fat spitting in a pan. Serving him his breakfast bacon and eggs I can't look him in the eyes and I feel pricked and tormented by physical sensations, like a wax doll with pins stuck in her. Freddy clatters his knife and fork. He shakes the salt with a huge gesture like a magician waving a wand over everything. Even with my own eyes fixed on the stove, the kettle, the pans I'm washing, I can feel that he is trying to catch my attention. It is an extraordinary feeling—being alone with Freddy, here in the house, for the first time, knowing that Percy might get back from the pub at any minute, chance upon us, surely spot or smell or sense in an instant, how different things now are.

When I go to clear Freddy's plate his hand snatches out, catches my wrist.

Edie. Don't act this way with me!

A whisper. His dramatic tone alarms me and I try to twist my hand away from him.

I'm not acting any way! I'm trying to get on with the breakfast things . . .

He releases my wrist and scrapes back his chair. Fetches his jacket and hat, makes towards the kitchen door.

I'm not sorry you know. I'm not going to act

sorry, either. The man treats you lower than a snake. He doesn't deserve you.

I start to laugh but the smile freezes on my lips, seeing Freddy's expression. I put the pans down, dry my hands, move as close to him as I dare.

No, I'm not sorry either. But we both will be if Percy finds out. You know what he's like. I told you about that time, didn't I, that time at Shoreditch Town Hall when he hit Gerald Marsdon, he hit him in the face—he was drunk, I know, but just the same—he hit him! And for nothing, nothing at all. I think Gerald looked at me, he asked me to dance—

I'm not afraid of him, Edie.

His voice, a scrubbed whisper, belies the sentiment. Percy can be heard outside, approaching the kitchen door.

Brightly, moving a little towards the stove I say: So, we'll see you this evening, Freddy, at Shakespeare Crescent, around eight, yes?

Avis's birthday. Freddy goes for the door, acknowledges Percy without a flinch, betraying no surprise at all. Percy steps aside to let Freddy pass. In the smoothest of gestures, Freddy tips his hat.

I tie the strings of my apron more tightly around my waist, reach for the milk and Percy's favourite porridge bowl, instinctively start humming; foolishly imagining it might drown out the sound of my heart thumping.

*　　　*　　　*

Avis sits next to Freddy, she shrieks and twitters at the present he has brought her—a long string of palest pink pearls and some Hindes hair-wavers, which she must have asked him for, unless possibly Florrie told him: I can't think otherwise, how men would know of such things. I'm stung, watching her unwrap the presents, as she puts her hand lightly on his arm, asks him to place the beads around her neck. I'm reminded of seeing her lift Freddy's sleeve to show me the watch she bought him, on the beach at Shanklin, and so much has changed since then, since four weeks ago, but for Avis it's as though nothing has. I asked him, I plucked up courage, and he says they scarcely even kissed. Chaste kisses. He has not promised himself to Avis. She knows it is little more than a friendship. Now I watch as Freddy gets up, stands behind her, holding the beads in a circle over her head, and I wonder. He lets them drop with a light rattle as they brush her bare neck, her throat, slip down inside the grey lace bodice of her dress, where she retrieves them with one hand, laughing.

I leave the table. Mother needs help with the dishes.

In the kitchen Mother whispers excitedly, Isn't he lovely, what a catch! smirking and simpering in an uncharacteristic way. What a catch. The exact phrase, I believe, she used about Percy when I first brought him home. I march back into the dining room, carrying the bowls for dessert.

Well, Freddy, you've certainly charmed Mother! I say, as I rejoin the dining table, placing the bowls down on the damask. They make a curious crashing sound. Everyone looks at me, and Freddy's expression is startled. I sit down and drain my glass of port and smile gaily at everyone.

Here's to Avis! Happy twenty-second birthday! Just think, I'd been married a year by the time I was your age . . .

Now it's Avis who looks surprised, her eyes darting to Percy and then back to me. A scarlet blush creeps up from her neck.

Now, Avis, no need to be embarrassed. Looks like you've found your prince at last, with charming young Frederick here . . .

Now she's blazing from neck to forehead and Percy has a restraining hand on mine as I go to refill my glass. He coughs, of course, before speaking.

*That's enough for you, my girl.*

He says it with a grin, as if it's a joke that all the family might like to share. He slides the bottle along the table cloth, out of reach. No one moves. The room has become very hot. I'm thinking Mother should keep the wooden shutters down in the daytime, keep the room cooler. There is a fly—a blue bottle—caught in a lamp shade and buzzing like something quite deranged. I think vaguely that I would like to swat it, really smash it into a pulp, but I can't unlock my eyes from Percy's, nor withdraw myself from the challenge that has just been thrown down to me.

My voice surprises me by sounding unsteady, even a little wobbly.

*So it's fine for you to have more port when you choose . . . but I'm to be treated like a child, is that it?*

The sentence rings in the room and no one answers. Freddy makes the faintest, smallest choking sound, muffled by his napkin.

After a second, a second in which even the fly seems to cease buzzing, I lean forward, pour the port noisily into my glass. It floods out quickly, almost spills over; several red drops splash the table cloth. Mother glances at the stained damask, then at Father, but says nothing.

I raise my glass to the table in general. Anyone else? Avis, go on it's your birthday. Let your hair down. Let yourself go, why don't you. You've started smoking now. What's wrong with a little social drinking?

You've taken up smoking, Avis?

This is Father, the first time he's spoken. He pauses with his dessert spoon halfway to his mouth, a great blob of cream and cherries wobbling an inch away from his moustache. Avis shoots a furious look at me.

Well, no, I only tried it, Father. On holiday.

I—I don't believe it will become a firm habit.

Oh, all the girls smoke now, Mr Graydon. The nice ones I mean. It hardly signifies a thing, these days, Freddy wades in, cheerfully.

Ha! Well, by your free admission then, it used to signify something! Father says, in his dourest tone of voice, setting the spoon down in the bowl, preparing himself, puffing out his chest a little. He directs a slow, appraising gaze at Freddy. Mother twitches somehow, I see her out of the corner of my eye, making movements with her hands like a squirrel, fussing with her trifle, dabbing at her mouth with a napkin.

You young men have only yourselves to blame if you find that the women you are chasing after have no more—morals—than a cat in an alley, because this racy, short-skirted, short-haired modern miss—she's your doing! And your un-doing, if you ask me.

Avis's face has been repossessed of its normal colour, but she is tapping her spoon around her empty trifle bowl, one thin muscle along the side of her neck standing out, fine and tremulous, like something that might easily snap. She pushes some hair back behind her ears, takes an audible breath.

Father! There is no need to exercise yourself. I gave smoking a try and now I've abandoned it. I hardly think this merits a lecture on the morals of the modern miss and I'm sure Freddy hasn't come here to hear one.

Father's mouth closes with a snap. It's the most I've ever heard Avis say to him in one go. Ever. I'm almost impressed. I sip the rest of the port, quickly, giddily; feeling the heat trickle down my throat and into my chest, and the danger of giggles rising into my mouth. Percy is making moves to go, to thank Mother, to fetch my coat, to hurry things along. I believe I'm sitting dead still, and staring. Staring at my sister.

Freddy might have said their kisses were chaste. But looking at Avis now, her eyes glittering, her skin pale, except for those two red spots on each cheek, her perfume of geranium and rose and undertones of smoky wood floating around her; her pearls now warmed and nestling into her bosom; I know she wishes with every bone in her body that they were otherwise.

\*     \*     \*

After that evening, I have the sense that I am not quite in control, that events are trembling, shimmering dangerously on the edge of a full scale explosion. Freddy and I meet every lunchtime, we kiss feverishly if we can find a spot in Charterhouse Square or the Holborn Restaurant when Agnes's beady eye won't spot us, but we can do no more than this. Frustration simmers and sizzles in our home life. Even Percy seems to feel it, although of course he doesn't appreciate the cause of it.

On Bank Holiday Monday, we're all sitting on a bench in the garden, Freddy reading the racing pages, Percy reading the shipping news and me—I'm sewing, taking up a hem on new dress, staring at the roses in the garden, thinking how big the petals are, how they droop, and flake away, how summer in this garden is like an overladen branch, weighted with foliage, exhausted; almost ready to snap.

Freddy's friend from the P&O office, Bill, pays a visit.

Fine garden you have here, Mrs Thompson. Fine house! You could fit two of ours in your scullery . . .

He's tall and pale, a round-shouldered young man, bendy as a stick of limp celery with his tufts of blond hair at the top and he reminds me that Freddy is young, very young, if he's the same age as Bill. He has a brand new Kodak camera and wants to take a photograph of us all; posing, me pointing to the rose bushes, Freddy with his hands in his pockets, Percy smoking his pipe. Rearranging my dress, I smooth the gold leaf-patterned skirt over my knees, cross my legs primly.

That's it, sit between Freddy and—Percy is it? That's it, and just give me a minute here, that's right, a nice smile, or well, that's fine if you prefer . . .

Bill is cheery and naive, oblivious to any kind of atmosphere.

196

The SS *Morea* sets sail for Port Said in two weeks time, know that don't you, Fred? Plan to be on it, do you? Bill says, looking through the camera lens at us.

Click. I drop the sewing I'm doing. Both Freddy and Bill rush to pick it up, Freddy getting there first. He places it on the bench beside me, avoiding my knees.

Well . . . Freddy says, seeing that Bill is still expecting an answer, I always need the money.

Click. That's it, let's have another one, maybe with you pointing Mrs Thompson, pointing at the flowers, Bill says.

I fix my eyes on my sewing; the material is tough suddenly, and I have to stab, stab forcefully to push the needle through.

I think I'll go in and lie down. I feel a headache starting. I believe it's through squinting in this sunshine.

My heels tap on the path, then pad softly on the parched grass. I fan myself with Percy's rolled up newspaper, hearing them still chattering behind me, Bill making his demands, Freddy and Percy awkwardly complying. Later, when Bill goes, Freddy comes into the living room, where I'm lying on the sofa with a folded towel over my forehead. My eyes are closed but I know it's Freddy from the scent of him, a mixture of sandalwood and something else—an indescribable, salty smell. His knees creak as he kneels beside me.

You knew I had to go away again . . . It's my

197

job.

When I say nothing, he asks: Are you all right? Can I get you anything?

I'm about to say, Where's Percy? when I hear his footsteps and know he has come into the room. I take the towel from my eyes, smooth down my dress, sit up clumsily, reach again for my sewing.

Some pins, thanks, Freddy. There is a box of pins in the kitchen, on the window ledge, would you mind fetching them for me?

I daren't look at Percy. I feel him standing there, I feel rather than see that he doesn't move, he doesn't say a word. A powerful glowering silence emanates from him. He stands in front of the doorway, barring Freddy's way to the kitchen.

Edith, don't make the boy run around after you.

In return, a fury—cold then hot, then searing hot—shoots through me.

I'm not making him do anything! He asked if I needed anything. He offered!

It's fine, Freddy says, quietly. It's no trouble at all . . .

Freddy shifts from foot to foot. He makes a slight move, a duck of the head, manages to slip past Percy into the kitchen. When he returns with the box of pins, he places them beside me on the sofa. Percy is silent, his arms crossed across his chest. Freddy's hand is shaking but he saunters out without a word,

Percy steps towards me, puts his face close to mine.

Yes, you like to have him fetch and carry for you don't you!

Well, if my husband is too selfish to do it, what's the harm in finding others who will?

Suddenly Percy lunges at me, grabbing my arm. I try to stand up, dropping the dress and pins to the floor with a rattle and a shriek, as Percy is pulling on me, fingers digging into the bare flesh of my arm.

His arm flies out, his fist, a great smack, a cracking sound; a pain splintering across my cheek and another scream and this one brings Freddy running. Then the two of them are scuffling, shouting. I'm not sure what is happening, as I'm half lying, half sitting in a crumpled heap, my back against the sofa, holding my cheek, my nose, feeling the aftershocks, the sting surge through my skin, the blackness in front of my eyes flood to red.

It's all over in an instant with me scarcely able to make sense of the words that fly between them or how much Percy knows or how much Freddy gives away but only to hear that Freddy is to leave—*You are by no means welcome in this house, young man!*—*I wouldn't stay a moment longer in a house with a man who treats his wife lower than a dog!*—and to wonder, wonder, just for a moment, if either of them is thinking of me at all.

I press the palms of my hands into my eyes

to block out the room, feel the sensation in my cheek which is surely the blue-print of a bruise already spreading just under the skin. I'm dimly listening to them, to Percy still shouting, to Freddy stomping up to his room to get his bags. I wonder why the scene feels familiar, why I have the sensation that it's nothing to do with me.

Instead it feels like part of some long-brewing feud; a spark ignited when they first met, that first awkward conversation about the war, smouldering since then; long before Freddy and I had even exchanged one illegitimate glance.

It is a long time before Freddy comes back downstairs. Percy has left with a great slam of the front door—for the Angel no doubt—and I have dabbed at my face with a cold flannel and managed to stop crying. I'm sitting on the sofa, my sewing beside me, almost as if nothing has happened when Freddy comes back downstairs and pauses in the doorway. I hear the sound of his bag being placed on the floor beside him, and turn my head towards him.

When he sits down beside me, puts his arm around me in a natural, unconstrained gesture tears start up, all over again. He offers me his handkerchief.

Edie, you must leave him. His voice is tender and wraps itself around me. I can't bear for him to treat you like this . . .

How can I leave him? It's not that easy, he's

said he'll never give me a divorce, I've told you that . . . and I'm not strong enough, I'm not brave enough . . . I don't know how I should cope . . . with Mother and Father and . . . the scandal . . .

But these are damn foolish reasons. Scandal! Is this Edie Thompson speaking? The man's a snake, when I think of him, of you, I—I—

Now Freddy is angry again and I cannot help but wonder why, when he speaks of Percy an animal of some sort always smuggles itself into his sentence; but then I remember a moment ago, how he spoke of me. The word 'dog' rings in my mind and I keep seeing myself, hunched by the sofa, with Percy's fist inches from my face, yes, exactly like a cowering dog. I know that Freddy meant it differently, he meant it in support of me, but the picture I have of myself now is ugly, I can't erase it. The last few glorious weeks; kissing in the park, the one candle-lit night in Freddy's room, all seem stupid and unreal, lit in a particular way, arranged in a particular way. This sordid, ugly, shameful scene—myself a crumpled heap by the sofa, my face a great blue-black blotch, Freddy and Percy grappling and stumbling and forgetting about me—only this is plain and without special lighting or arrangement. A sickness creeps over me when I replay this scene. And now Freddy is leaving and, despite my hints, he is not offering to marry me, or rescue me and it's going to be me and Percy again as it was before, as it was for years, almost seven years, since I realised my terrible mistake.

Oh don't, Freddy, what's the point? I say, finally, sniffing loudly, and handing him back his handkerchief. I suppose you had better go so that he doesn't find you here on his return.

Where am I supposed to go? Back to my mum's? Then we'll never have a chance to see one another!

A leap then, in my chest, startles me. My heart jumping. I had thought that was the end, but here is Freddy talking as if we have to find ways to carry on. His arm is along the back of my neck, his fingers curling with my hair.

Well, I can write to you. While you're away at sea. We can arrange to meet when you come back . . .

Possibilities start beating again, restaurants, parks, maybe even a hotel?

It's three months you know. It's a bloody long time! And all the while you here with him . . .

Freddy's voice sometimes is hot and petulant, he has a quality of obstinacy, a jealousy in some ways similar to Percy's. This has never struck me before. Why something that I find abhorrent in Percy would seem charming in Freddy.

I'll write every day. I—of course I—I'll refuse him! I'll only be thinking of you!

He takes my hands and his are warm, velvety; the fingers wide and firm as they close around mine, folding them so that they feel like the hands of a small girl. Just before he kisses me I'm thinking, all this trouble through kindness, through Freddy bringing me a pin, and remembering the old rhyme *For the want of a nail the shoe was lost, for the want of a shoe the horse was lost, for the want of a horse the rider was lost, for the want of a rider* . . . but I can't remember any more, and when Freddy kisses me all thoughts are driven from my head and only my body, my blood responds.

*       *       *

*Freddy will never sleep in this lovingly prepared bed again.* The scent of him is still on the sheets as I strip the bed. Monday morning and Percy has left for work. I claim that my headache is no better and I'm taking the day off from the shop. Of course the real reason is the bruise on my face. No amount of powder can disguise it. A bruise like this one won't fade quickly either and I may have to take the whole week off.

I peel the sheets and wrap myself in them, breathe deeper, imagine Freddy's arms wrapping themselves around me. Soon imagination mingles with memory and, rather than his arms, it is his legs, his naked skin I can feel and smell and remember, the soft rough feel of him, almost fur, the soft animal quality of his skin. How different it is to welcome skin, different from lying with Percy. Once welcomed, the rough-sweet softness is disturbing and I'm surprised to find my heart beating a little faster, my palms and the back of my neck and the place between my shoulder blades beginning to sweat, ever so faintly.

So I lie down on the bed, still with the sheets wrapped around me. I'm smelling Freddy and smelling my memories and allowing them to surface in a way that even in dreams I usually stifle and now heat is flowing over me, my tongue is sticking to the roof of my mouth, my thighs are sticking to each other and my body is flowing warmth and stickiness. I'm remembering how Freddy pinned me with his thighs, how he took each wrist and held it above my head and how I arched my back for him, how he held me there, suspended like a chicken trussed for the oven, dangling in someone's hands, while from the neck down our bodies smacked and thrust at each other without consciousness, without an ability to do otherwise.

I've waited all my life to discover this. To feel this power, this pleasure, this much alive. So long ago glimpsed, so, *so* long in arriving. There's no way I'm giving it up now. Not for anyone. Not for anything.

Percy can go hang himself.

You must have loved Percy once? Freddy asks, a week later; a question I've been expecting.

We are in the Cafe Royal, at lunchtime, the week before he leaves. Freddy stirs his tea with the daintiest of silver teaspoons, dropping cubes of sugar from a great height and watching them splash. (He loves to make a mess in fancy places.) The smell of cigars wafts over us.

Well, I was young, you have to remember. It was wartime. He was a little older than me, and impressive, I suppose, with that commanding manner that now I find so tiresome. I was—

How to tell Freddy that I've had this same quickening feeling all my life, practically since small girlhood and how I felt it driving me, urging me in a hungry, inexpressible way. Percy being four years older, tall, broad, grown-up, handsome even with his high forehead and his solid jaw and his hard, determined quality. In the early days—when we were courting—even his jealousy was gratifying to me, but more than that. Stimulating. In Percy I thought I'd found the mirror that would reflect me back not a girl from Stamford Hill but a sophisticated woman from Ilford; glittering, silver, as dazzling as these chandeliers swinging above us; so glorious that men everywhere would fall at my

205

feet, bedazzled.

To Freddy I say: I suppose I was easily flattered.

*        *        *

Freddy's ship leaves on the Friday; after work I buy paper and envelopes and a ditty box with a key and I go to sit at a table in a smoky corner of the Holborn to write to him.

*Darlint,*
*It's Friday today—that loose end sort of day (without you) preceding the inevitable weekend. I don't know what to do to just stop thinking, thinking very sad thoughts, darlint, they will come, I try to stifle them, but it's no use.*
*Last night I lay awake all night—thinking of you and of everything connected with you and me.*

The waitress glides up to my table, notebook poised, spotless white apron, stiff as a sheet of paper. I put my arm over my letter, smudging the ink slightly.

Oh, just a cup of tea, please.

I realise that she had been frowning at the cigarette glowing in my saucer. Glancing around I see that plenty of others are smoking and wonder what her expression meant. No smoking for *ladies* no doubt.

*Last night I booked seats for the Hippodrome—the show was good—not a variety, but a sort of pierrot entertainment and 2 men opened the show with singing 'Feather your Nest'. I wished we could, just you and I—but we will, yes, somehow we must. I enjoyed the show immensely—you understand me, don't you, darlint. I was dancing the hours, I was forgetting, but by myself in bed I was remembering.*

My hand flies across the page, with such ease, I'm delighted. I always liked writing compositions in school but it's a long time since I wrote letters, letters of this sort, letters where one pours out every odd thought that pops into one's head, without censorship or regard for style or decorum. A warm, comforting feeling steals over me. I take a sip of the good hot tea the waitress brings me, pour boiling water into the little pot she sets at my table. Now Freddy won't be lost to me—I know how lonely and bored he can be at sea and how he has told me he longs for the sense that someone is thinking of him, remembering his existence. I can provide him with that and more! I can entertain him, beguile him, keep me in his thoughts, hint at the further delights still to come . . .

*Yesterday I met a woman who had lost 3 husbands in eleven years, and not through the war, 2 were drowned and one committed suicide and some people I know can't lose one. How unfair everything is.*

A pause with the pen in the air, a blob of ink splashing to the table cloth in a perfect blue dot, which fans to a tiny flower. I slide my saucer over it. Looking around I see that the Holborn is filling up, that office girls and their older boyfriends in the city are chattering and laughing amidst the clattering of crockery and scraping of chairs on the wooden floor.

A man is heading towards my table. I fold the letter closed and lay my pen beside it.

Excuse me—

He is smart; silk lapels, a good suit, a cotton piqué tie. I smile in confusion, trying to slip the letter under my arm without looking ridiculous. I expect him to ask if he may take the spare chair at my table but to my astonishment he sits down at it.

Are you Romance?

Pardon?

You are—your name is Romance?

No—

He leaps up as if the chair was a spike, his urbane charm quite ruffled.

Oh, I'm terribly sorry, do forgive me.

When I smile again, bewildered but not unfriendly, he recovers himself a little. Backing politely away from the table he is muttering: I was looking for a—friend. Romance.

Romance! I watch him walk to a table at the other end of the long cafe, casting a glance towards another woman sitting at a table alone. Admittedly there are only the two of us. I wait to see if he will approach her, but he seems to be aware of me observing him; instead he leaves by the front door, without a backward glance. From the back of his head, the set of his shoulders, the way he tugs at his lapels; somehow I can tell that he is still embarrassed.

I hastily unfold the letter from its unsealed envelope.

*Freddy! The strangest thing just happened. I'm sitting in the Holborn and a gentleman approached me and asked if I was 'Romance'— a made-up name if ever I heard one! What do you think it means? Should I have been affronted? He had a red rose in his hand and I believe a box of marrons glacés in the other, half hidden behind his back—should I have said yes, just to find out what he would say next? I confess to being flattered—don't be cross with your Peidi—it amuses me so that since you and I began our Great Adventure I seem to be radiating some strange beams to all around me, so that your darling has become the most desirable girl in all of London!*

The pen hovers over the line about the red rose and the marrons glaces, while I wonder whether to cross them out. But the story seems so much better, funnier, with that detail in. It gives a sense of the kind of 'romance' the man was offering. How much more interesting life is when one has an occasion to write about it! (Or someone to describe it to.) I lick the envelope and the matter is sealed.

I'm wearing my favourite hat, recently acquired from the shop; the lilac crepe georgette toque with a 'ragged rain of ospreys' (Miss Prior crossed out my description in the log book, calling it overly poetic as usual) and as I readjust it to leave, I can see the waitress stare admiringly.

*You must have loved Percy once?* Freddy's question of a week ago. Hard to believe I did. Hard to remember. Surely I was always as I am now—dressed in a lilac crepe de chine dress, a carefully arranged curl sneaking over each cheek, a cigarette between my fingers; surrounded by chatter and tinkling silver and bobbed hair and skirts floating high above tender ankles; writing a secret letter to my lover, on a balmy Friday night; an evening perfectly melancholy, but perfect too, for dancing.

\*　　　\*　　　\*

Percy is waiting for me at home; I am over an hour late. As I turn my key in the lock, using the kitchen door, not the front, he springs up from the kitchen table where he's been sitting, nursing a cup of tea and a bag of cough sweets. When he opens his mouth the strong smell of the dire paragorics nearly chokes me.

You're late! Where've you been?

Mr Carlton asked me to stay behind and do a little extra paperwork . . .

I'm gently pushing past him, taking my hat off, putting my bag down, filling the kettle with water, keeping my back to him, while all the time conscious of him following me around the kitchen like a child.

I went over to Richard's house and telephoned the shop from there. So I know you weren't at Carlton's!

So then I turn around and face him, receive another blast of the strong medicinal cough drops on his breath.

Well, I didn't want to be disturbed, so I didn't answer the phone. In any case, it's only seven o'clock—

I was worried about you!

His voice a little subdued, mollified. He sits back down at the table, puts both hands around the cup of tea.

You've been with him, haven't you?

Him? Who?

You know who I mean.

If you are asking me about Freddy, the answer is no. His ship left today for Marseilles. You can check with Avis if you don't believe me. But even if I was with Freddy, I would be perfectly entitled to be. To have a drink after work with a friend. After the way you've treated me, you should be glad I came home at all.

All this delivered calmly, facing Percy, my back to the stove. Weariness, disappointment, making me bold. All the way home on the

211

train from Liverpool Street, my letter to
Freddy safely posted, buoyed up with silver
and lights and men who mistook me for
Romance, I have been dancing, dancing a
foxtrot at the Waldorf with some of the most
elegant dancers in England. And meanwhile,
this great sulky child of a man has been waiting
at home for me, sucking on cough drops.

He hunches his shoulders, rummages in the
white paper bag for another sweet. His eyes
are lowered and his expression is not one I can
read. I expected—no, wanted—him to be
angry with me, after what I just said. Instead,
he looks, or seems to look, contrite.

It won't happen again, Edie. Now that he's
left. I—I swear I won't touch you again.

Not until the next time you've been
drinking.

Well, it's only that! Many a man loses his
judgement on account of drink . . .

That's no excuse!

But I need to know, were you—have you
been carrying on with him, you know,
encouraging him—?

Oh, for God's sake! I won't stand here and
be accused like this in my own home. If you
say another word I'm going to leave right now
and spend the night at Shakespeare Crescent
. . .

All right, all right. I'll leave it at that. Only
that beloved shop of yours. The hours you
spend there. Many's a husband who'd find *that*

something to complain of—

Oh, don't start about the shop again!

I say this so sharply, he stops in mid-sentence. Rolls a cough drop round in his mouth, puffing his cheek in an ugly bulge.

I feel dreadful, he says, I have the flu coming on. I need a drink of honey and lemon . . .

His voice suddenly croaky in the most put-on way imaginable. I stare at him for a moment, struggling with a desire to pick up the kettle and pour the boiling water right over his head.

Well, if you're ill, Percy, I'll sleep in the back bedroom. I don't want to catch the flu. One of us needs to be fit and well and to bring home some bacon. And we both know that it makes more sense—financially—for you to be off work than me.

I have no trouble reading his expression this time. I whirl around, my back to him again, in real danger of laughing out loud. His face! Pure shocked defeat. As if someone just slapped him with a great wet fish and then snatched his chair from under him. Yes, I like this picture of Percy, tipped on the floor, floundering, the way I floundered when he hit me. I'll save it up. I must write and tell Freddy about it, later.

\*　　　\*　　　\*

I've had a funny sort of weekend, darlint. I want to tell you all about it and I don't know how. I am staying in this lunchtime, especially to write to you. First of all, on Sat at tea, we had words over getting a maid. He wants one, but he won't have Ethel, because 'my people won't like it', he said. I was fearfully strung up and feeling very morbid so you may guess this didn't improve things. However at night in bed the subject—or the object—the usual one, came up and I resisted, because I didn't want him to touch me for a month—do you understand me, darlint?

He asked me why I wasn't happy now— what caused the unhappiness and I said I didn't feel unhappy—just indifferent, and he said I used to feel happy once. Well, I suppose I did, I suppose even I might have called it happiness, because I was content just to let things jog along, and not think, but that was before I knew what real happiness could be like, before I loved you, darlint. Of course I did not tell him that but I did tell him I didn't love him and he seemed astounded. He wants me to forgive and forget anything he has said or done in the past and start afresh and try and be happy again and want just him. He wants me to try as well and so that when another year has passed, meaning the year that ends 15th January, 1922, we shall be just as happy and contented as we were on that day seven years ago. These are his words I am quoting.

I told him I didn't love him but that I would try to do my share and make him happy and contented. It was an easy way out of a lot of things to promise this, darlint. I hope you can understand.

*　　*　　*

If Percy hasn't been drinking, then it is easy enough to refuse him. But if he has, like tonight, if the whisky is strong on his breath, the stale sour smoky smell in his hair from drinking at the Angel, if his words are slurred and he doesn't bother to switch on the electric light, or attempt to take his shirt or socks off; then I know refusing him will be impossible.

He is heavy, heavy as a dead weight. I can scarcely breathe beneath him, as if my lungs are held and squeezed between two big hands. I stiffen my body, I turn my face to one side, I shove at him, but he uses his leg to brace mine, he lands his great stinking wet whisky mouth on mine, and even if I protest—I do protest sometimes and squirm beneath him, trying to roll myself from under him and I've dug my nails into his back before now—even if I do all of that, it only excites him. Drink makes him insensible, all he can feel is in his loins, and he has no sense of hurting me, of the searing shameful disgusting feeling of a body not admitting him at all, a doorway not opened but so rudely forced, with a shoulder, a battering ram; a shaking, pounding, dry and splintering smash.

\* \* \*

On the Saturday before Freddy's return I'm in our bedroom going through Percy's pockets, sorting clothes to take to the Steam Laundry on Ley Street. I don't feel well, I almost fainted on waking this morning, and my mind is on this; glancing at myself in the huge oak mirror behind my dressing table, noting that my skin is blanched like an almond and knowing full well what it might mean. My mind is not on the beads of fluff, the betting slips or packets of State Express in Percy's jacket pockets. But when my hand closes around a glass phial, I pull it out, turn it around in my palm, hold the slender shape to the light at the window, startled.

A glass phial of coloured sand in bands, stoppered with a cork. Obviously bought a few months ago in Shanklin. Scarlet, crimson, salmon, orange; the colours of dawn in stripes, with the purest, palest, whitest sand right at the top.

I had no idea Percy bought this souvenir, and the discovery stabs at me. A souvenir, a present for himself, a lucky charm. The thought of Percy going into a shop, selecting this particular tube of glass (and it is a pretty one, a good choice, because I remember them—there were hundreds to choose from, many fancier, but not such fine sand; or in bigger bottles, shaped like ships; but the colours not so well graded). The thought of him keeping it in his pocket to feel sometimes, to close his fingers around.

I'm surprised when tears slip over my cheeks, as I place the phial back in the pocket of his navy jacket, then hang the jacket back in his wardrobe with a feeling of stealth, of guilt, of terrible intrusion. Such an unlikely image . . . Percy buying himself a souvenir of his holiday. The idea that he believed he was happy, that he was having a good time! Why is it that he and I are always so much at odds? Even down to the detail that on the trip where I finally give up and permit myself to fall in love with another, Percy seems to have been having the happiest holiday of his life?

I sit on the bed with the bundle of laundry and put my hands over my stomach, feeling the pains grip. I've already written to Freddy, telling him that I've tried herbs and gin and bitter apple and that I sent away for some of Dr Patterson's pills, advertised at the back of the *Recorder*. It's these which must be working now. I know Freddy won't try to dissuade me. This is not the right time and I couldn't bear to have Percy crowing like a rooster for something that is not of his doing.

I should be excited about Freddy's return but instead I'm weary, weary, and frightened and it's the discovery of the tiny phial of glass that has done it, turned my mood around. Those bands of swirling sands, darkening in a vortex from white to deepest blood red; that's a perfect reminder of something, but not our holiday; something ugly and distasteful. I wish I'd never seen. That now I can't put out of sight.

Percy's happiness and how directly it runs counter to mine.

\*　　\*　　\*

By the time Freddy returns I'm feeling fine again. He manages to get a note to me from Bill to say that he'll wait outside the shop after work, 5.30 p.m. on Thursday. Agnes, with her special nose for intrigue, sticks to me like a burr all day in the most infuriating way, even answering the telephone once, when she is not authorised to do so. I have told Percy that I'll be working late, since we are approaching our Christmas season and that this is likely to be happening with regularity, now that Mr Carlton has given me a raise and more responsibility.

At five o'clock I catch a glimpse of the dark tall shape of Freddy, flitting past the window like a shadow, and smile to myself. He is early. *Five o'clock shadow.* The phrase doesn't make sense but it suggests routine, the future, and it's comforting. Part of me wishes he'd chosen

218

somewhere less prominent, away from Agnes's stare, to stand and wait, but another part recognises his logic. We've nothing to hide. He's Avis's boyfriend. A friend of the family. All above board, to use a phrase Agnes is fond of.

So the test of the last half hour is to keep my heart from leaping right out of the top of my dress, to keep my cheeks pale and my hand steady as I count the money from the till and slip the coins into their bags, counting the float out three times at least, to be certain of no errors.

I'll do the float for tomorrow and the takings, Agnes. You can leave now if you like, I tell her at 5.25 p.m., knowing that when Mr Carlton is absent (one of his many excursions to the garage to have some aspect or another of his new car looked at again) the unspoken understanding is that I'm next in charge. However this can't be acknowledged openly; as junior partner, Miss Prior, ought officially to be second in command.

So when Miss P re-emerges from the stock-room, a heavy ledger clasped to her bosom, a pen sticking out of her wispy bun, she looks surprised to see Agnes with her coat on.

It's five thirty, I offer, busying myself with locking the till.

Oh, well, run along then, Agnes, says Miss P, and then remembering, Who will do the float and the till?

It's almost done. I don't mind locking up, either, I tell her, keeping my eyes away from the glass at the front of the shop, not wanting to see if Agnes and Freddy greet one another as Agnes passes him.

Miss P takes an age to fetch her coat, to fix her bun with a pin under her hat, to put on her gloves; to consider whether it really does look as if it's about to rain cats and dogs, and whether Mr Carlton would mind terribly if she allowed me to do the locking up and the float and takings again, three nights in a row, she seems to remember . . . I busy myself with the coins again; counting, piling up, placing the velvet bags in the box safe under the counter, trying not to notice the minutes ticking away, or to watch Miss P waddle the length of the shop and close the door behind her.

Then Freddy is ringing the bell, insistently, ridiculously and banging on the glass. I go to let him in and his presence as he bursts into the shop is all noise and chaos and knocking me almost off my feet, knocking the breath out of me, making me laugh and fuss and shriek, squeezed in a huge embrace, showered in kisses and endearments. When I can catch my breath I break away a little, lock the door behind him, slide both bolts across.

Did Agnes see you?

What if she did? I just said Good Evening to her and here I am, about to walk my sister-in-law to the station . . .

Hardly a sister-in-law! I thought you had broken things off with Avis? Did you write to her?

I didn't. The message should be clear enough . . .

That's no way—

Edie! Not now!

He has one arm out of his jacket, wriggling with the other sleeve while he switches off the electric lamp, steering me in the dark towards the back of the shop, asking, How long do you have?

Only about an hour. I've told him I'm working late again. He's bound to telephone.

Freddy smells of smoke, and sea-salt and beer and the familiar pomade he uses in his hair and of Shanklin and the new linen in the back bedroom and a trillion other memories. We're giggling, our eyes becoming accustomed to the dark, shuffling blindly on the tiled floor; feeling our way along the counter-top, running our hands along dusty walls, our faces tickled by the occasional feather of a hat on a stand; Freddy running his hands along me in the same way, pushing me towards the sofa he knows we keep at the back of the shop for clients to wait on; sweeping the magazines to the floor with a splatter of glossy paper, tumbling me onto the hard smooth velvet beneath him.

Three months . . . Freddy murmurs, into my neck, three bloody months . . .

I don't like to say *not here! Not in the shop.*

He's unbuckling his belt, he's tugging at me, pushing up my dress, feeling for the silk beneath it and suddenly it's too fast and that 'three months' feels like an insult to me, it sounds like desperation. I sit up, with an effort, somehow managing to roll his head to the edge of the sofa. I stare into the grey-light, pick out the gleam of his eyes.

No, not here. I can't.

A groan. Freddy readjusts himself and I hear him breathing heavily, feel the shift in weight as he sits up.

No one can see us here—it's pitch black.

It's not that.

He feels on the floor for his abandoned jacket, finds it, produces a flask and slugs from it, then offers it to me. My lips close over cold metal and the taste of whisky. Sounds of Freddy doing up his belt, the buckle clanking.

You know, he says sulkily, it makes men ill if you do things like that.

Ill? What do you mean?

My voice is sharp and I sit up, too, begin smoothing down my dress, my stockings.

Blue balls. It bloody hurts, you know.

Panic flares up for a moment. I've never heard of it but Freddy knows about such things and the picture is fearful enough, hideous. Panic for another reason, too. *Please don't insist and press me, the way Percy does . . .*

But although he sounds disappointed, his

movements, stretching his legs on the sofa, putting his arm around me, slugging on the whisky again, suggest resignation and, after a hesitation, I snuggle into him again. The shop door is firmly locked. The street outside bustles with office workers going home, buses, horses, trams . . . but in here all is whisky-sealed, safe and warm and caught in its own bubble. One little hour. Freddy strokes my hair with one hand, asks gently: So how have you been? I lean my head against him, relief flooding through me. *Freddy is on my side.* That's the way the thought occurs. Knowing that he doesn't intend to press me, that he can—with an effort (and after all, every girl likes to feel that it should be *an effort)*—put his own needs to one side if necessary.

I fetch one small white candle from under the counter, light it, and place it on a magazine, on the floor beside the sofa. That way I can see Freddy's chest when I take off his shirt, run my hands over the soft tangle of dark hair. Wonder why it is that Freddy's chest-hair always makes me think of a sky with a sweep of birds flying in a shape, or the strange black patterns that iron filings make, when you pull with a magnet, towing all the dark lines towards you.

# CHAPTER SEVEN

*27th November, 1922*

Dear Freddy, Piper came to see me yesterday. He stood in a corner of the room, for a very long time. I began to wonder how long he could stand like that without speaking at all, and whether he really expected me to speak. My hair was uncombed. My dress has a stain from the disgusting porridgy-soup that they call stirabout. I didn't care about any of these things. I didn't care if I made Piper uncomfortable.

Would you like a cigarette, Mrs Thompson? he asked eventually. Of course, I said yes. I may even have shown flicker of pleasure as I reached out my hand for it.

Piper came quite close to me to light the cigarette. Just lately—yesterday I think it was when I first noticed this—at the furthest periphery of my eye I can see something dangling, a little like a hair, a strand. It annoys me—it is almost like having a shadow in the corner of the room which disappears when I turn to confront it. I wonder if my eyes are weakening in this dreary light? It worries me intensely—and also, knowing how vain I am, Freddy—I'm anxious that I might appear a little strange to other people, trying as I am to glance at it, to tug at it, to catch it out.

So I said to Piper, as he stepped back from me, Can you see something in the corner of the room? He looked startled, glanced in a dart at the direction of my gaze and without taking the time to register anything asked me: What is it that you see there?

I don't know. Something dangling. A thread. Something dark. I don't know.

I was inhaling the cigarette, sitting on my bed without shoes or stockings on bare legs which now appear to me to be as grey as the light in this room. How low I must have sunk, not to mind that a strange man stood only a few yards from my bed and I sat on it with bare legs and he not even a doctor!

You see someone on the other side of you? Is it troubling you?

Now I recognised the direction his questioning was going in and laughed, privately, silently, not out loud.

Not someone. *Something.* What do you think I see there then? Some devil or shadow or wicked reminder of my dark deed?

He said nothing to this. There was another silence which he broke with a cough and with a small movement towards the window. Then he turned back to me.

You know I am here to offer you solace, Mrs Thompson. That's my job. If you want to talk to me about anything—anything at all . . .

Piper's squeaky stupid little voice tailed off.

I finished the cigarette without enjoyment and looked around for the tin plate that Clara had provided me with to throw the stubs in.

You're afraid of me, aren't you, Chaplain?

I don't know where that question came from but it struck me with such force then, Freddy, staring at him, that the words were out at the same instant that the idea formed. And I watched him try to compose himself, ready to deny it, but the words had such suggestive power that then I began to feel frightened, really darlint, I felt a chill run through me, wondering what it was that Piper thought was in the room with us, what shadowy ill omen, that I could glimpse but not quite see.

He did do quite a good job of repositioning his features so as not to look so much like a frightened rabbit. His face—small for a man, and with tiny eyes, too (a little like a pig's eyes) and the pink patches that I explained to you before, Freddy—unfortunately for him is very expressive, rather like a child's. I imagine it is quite a trial for him to hide his repugnance for me, although he manages it tolerably well.

I looked towards the cell door to see if he would follow my stare.

More silence. Then, after another cough—dear me, the man is beginning to sound like Percy, if only he would take some tincture or something!

Perhaps we could begin again, Mrs Thompson? Your situation, clearly is rather bleak at the moment and you are understandably despondent ...

Ha! I interrupted. That stopped him. So when I had his full attention I asked bluntly:

Are you thinking of me doing it, Chaplain? Wondering what kind of woman ... Picturing me dropping poison int Percy's drinks and then chopping up the broken light globe to put in his porridge? And then when that failed, plotting and scheming together with my young lover (I enjoyed saying *lover*, Freddy, just to see him flinch) to murder him that night as we returned from the theatre together?

I was quite enjoying Piper's discomfort. I'm sure you will understand. As you mentioned in your own letter, the monotony is so onerous that anything at all is a diversion and, as such, mildly thrilling.

The cell was unnaturally quiet. I had a sudden mental image of everyone else in the prison outside the door listening. I often picture the other inmates and wardresses outside the door but I've found I can't get much further than that in my mind now. Do you have the same difficulty? The world outside has somehow shrivelled up. Here in this room we are a screwed-up little kernel and all the healthy stuff—the green, the leaves, the trees, have dried up. Only this grey dry nugget of life remains.

Do you think I did it then, just as they say?

I asked him this quite directly. My tone was

not polite.

Mrs Thompson—(he begins every sentence with 'Mrs Thompson' and I swear it is to professionalise things, to restate his position as my—what is it he is supposed to be, in any case? My confessor I suppose)—Mrs Thompson, perhaps it will help you if you try to remember that I am not here to judge you. I visit all prisoners in your—predicament. I am—as you have pointed out on a previous occasion—reasonably new to the profession but let me assure you that my youth does not imply a lack of experience of the world, nor of the human heart. If you do not require my services I will go away. So far, however, you haven't given me a clear indication that you would like me to. Should you do that, I will gladly leave and trouble you no further.

Now I think he was calling my bluff. The more his words sunk in—the concept that I only have to say so and he will go—the more I realised I didn't want him to. Only for the sport I suppose of annoying him so. I can't help wondering whether you have such a minister or chaplain or whatever he is to make visitations to you in your cell, Freddy, and talk to you. It frightens me, if the truth be told. I'm not such a fool that I didn't notice that Piper turned up when—when rumours began of—well, I can't bring myself to write it but I'm sure you know what I mean. I've managed not to think of it until now. And Piper's presence

228

forces the consciousness upon me, and that is too much. Although all has not gone well for us, we are surely due a fair trial at the Old Bailey and—oh, darlint, I really can't explore the future at the moment so I will perhaps end this letter before my mind travels on to it.

I want to reassure you that I do at least have Piper to talk to and unlike the wardresses, he seems to be at liberty to spend an indefinite time with me. So I am not as lonely as I was.

Don't be distraught, Freddy, about me fainting in court. I say this, but I know you will be. I have only to remember the night of my row with Percy, when he left and went to the Angel—the night I came to you in your room and how we'd been talking in the kitchen so freely—I have only to remember how tenderly you held me and how you said without a trace of sarcasm but only simplicity, poor Edie, and how loved I felt by your caring for me, by you actually thinking it mattered that I had suffered unhappiness. So few men seem to understand the power of this! To know that they could probably get a girl to do anything for them, yes, anything in the world, including all the things that I did willingly for you, and which have brought us to this point; if only they showed her the tiniest jot of genuine care for her life, her inner life, the things that go on in her head, things which men like Percy had no concern nor interest in.

Oh, I realise that I haven't told you the end

of the conversation with Piper—and there is quite a lot more but I can't remember the detail. I asked him, of course, if I could send a message to you but here he said his 'hands were tied'—such expressions leap out at me these days, have you found the same thing? So many common utterances seem to refer to prison or imprisonment. Even a phrase like the one I used earlier—*at liberty*—strikes me with the same force. I thought yesterday of the saying: As one door closes, another one opens—it chilled me, and stopped me in my tracks (I was walking round the yard at the time, thinking: if it is true, what could be the door that might open now, for me?).

I'm sorry this letter is not cheery, Freddy. Piper will come again tomorrow and I may try and practise my rusty charms on him and see if he would not be willing to smuggle at least one letter out. One letter. One tiny, tiny letter. Dear Lord, what harm could it do?

Only two more weeks until I see you in court. That at least, is something to be cheerful about. Until then I remain your loving,
    Peidi.
    xxx

*28th November, 1922*

Darlint,
Piper came again this morning. This time he
230

brought a chair! It was something of a palaver, bringing it into my cell with the wardress (Eve) propping the door open to allow him to do so, whilst keeping a firm eye and an even firmer arm out for the possibility of my making a run for it while the door was open!

The chair noisily scraped into the room, he sits down on it and offers me a customary Players.

I'm allowed more than two a day now, am I?

I'm at liberty to offer you a cigarette, Mrs Thompson, but only one.

That phrase again. Who decides, I wonder, who is at liberty to do what, from the trivial to the meaningful? Are we speaking of the Governor here or some more general omnipotence whom is in a position to decide such matters?

There was the same awkward pause. This time Freddy, I'm studying his strange patchy skin and thinking that, although now I'd put Piper's age at say, thirty, he unfortunately has not shrugged off the red pimples that usually beset a boy of fourteen.

Now, Mrs Thompson, I'm here to listen and offer guidance where I can, as I said yesterday.

I turned my head, ever so slightly to make sure that the dangling shadow of yesterday was not in the corner of my eye or the corner of the room. It wasn't. I tried to do this in a way that Piper wouldn't notice, but although he didn't comment, I had the sense that my gesture had not escaped him.

What shall I talk about? I asked brightly.

What would you like to talk about? he shot right back.

I'd like to talk about Freddy.

Another direct challenge. I watched him to see if his piggy eyes might light up. My feeling is, Freddy, that he wants to catch me out in some way. That he is sent here by someone—I don't know who—to try to get me to confess to the crimes I'm accused of or at least to drop some devastating piece of evidence into the conversation. I don't for a moment trust his minister's guise. Who on earth would take up such a profession! Surely it is only older gentlemen types, with no real possibility of a vivid passionate current life of their own who would want to tend to the spirit and soul of fallen women or prisoners?

Is—Bywaters—Freddy all that you think about, Mrs Thompson?

I thought this was a little harsh! I said nothing. I fixed my eyes on the plain black wool of his trousers, low at the ankle, and didn't raise them for what felt like several minutes. As I was staring there my mind wandered, suspended itself and a memory floated in front of me. It was of myself and Avis as children, I must have been around ten. I would be ten and she would be four. It was night-time and we were kneeling beside the bed and saying our prayers. I heard Avis's childish voice, a little too loud you know, just as she is now, blundering through the words with no real feeling and I heard them vividly, perfectly, just as if she were right beside me now, shouting them in my ear.

*As here I lay me down to sleep I pray the Lord my soul to keep and if I should die before I wake please keep me safe for Jesus' sake.*

Well I started to tremble, Freddy, because the voice was so loud and clear, just as if Avis, the grown Avis, had stepped into the room and was bludgeoning me with it and it had none of the candle-lit sleepiness of a childhood memory and all of the starkness and ugliness of a cold-hearted sermon from my sister (whom I haven't seen now for five days, since the verdict at Stratford, in fact, and yes, I confess this has worried me a great deal).

What a terrible thing to teach to children! I said to Piper. No understanding dawned on his face. In fact, he looked startled again, but I'm growing used to that: it's his most common expression.

What's that, Mrs Thompson?

A prayer we used to say. We were taught to say. We recited it every night and if ever I have children—

Naturally I stopped here. Piper was looking more bewildered than ever. I gathered myself back from the direction my comments were taking me.

It's so frightening! How could a child not be

frightened? So the idea would lodge and it would be impossible to reject it, but the intellect is scarcely formed in a child—it's unfair to terrorise children at such a young age and call it religion! Even if it is taken out and held under the light and examined later—well most of us can't give up our childish fears no matter how irrational we realise they are . . .

This was the most I'd ever said to Piper in one go and truthfully, Freddy, apart from you, it is the most forthright I've ever been with a man, where my true opinions are concerned.

Encouraged by his silence and even a faint nod that he gave, I believe I said more, something like: Of course, adult logic finds ways to clothe the feelings differently and make it acceptable but it's childish and primitive just the same. Terror of doing wrong, of losing the love of our 'father'. Terror of transgressing and being found out.

It was the moment that I mentioned the word transgressing that the conversation went all wrong. Of course, he seized on that. I can't remember his exact words but his voice was suddenly all portentous and serious and irritating in the extreme.

Transgressing? What kind of transgressions were you thinking of, Mrs Thompson?

Well this one, for instance. Would it be such a terrible transgression of propriety for you to not call me 'Mrs Thompson' in every single sentence?

You remember how Percy said that I had the most evil tongue on me and that I had learned it from you, Freddy? Well seeing Piper's surprise at my remark I was reminded of that, and have to concede that it is probably true. That I didn't often speak my mind before I met you. That I did discover in arguments with Percy—especially the later ones, the ones after you had left Kensington Gardens and we were thrown back against each other—an ability to say the vilest things.

To Piper's credit, he recovered well from his surprise and merely muttered: I'm sorry Mrs—I'm sorry. I was not aware that I had the habit.

More silence. Footsteps outside and the smell of burnt meat and floury dumplings that signify dinner. My stomach rumbled so loudly that I couldn't help a queer kind of smile from crossing my face.

How do you find the meals here? Piper asked. I paused, wondering at his inane question, but noting with gratitude that at least he'd dropped the 'Mrs Thompson'. Did he really care what I thought of the food in prison, did he actually expect an answer?

And then—I don't know how, but—a slow feeling crept into me, a feeling of sadness or resignation or even a faint desire, I suppose it was. A normal enough human desire, I think, grown from loneliness. Simply to make contact. To stop protesting and allow myself to—at least for a moment—feel connected to another human being again. So I smiled at him with my whole self and a part of me that had been dead for six weeks flared up for a moment. The first spontaneous genuine smile in a long while.

Poisonous, I said and Piper, thank God, smiled right back.


## POISON DETECTED

'In two of the organs, the liver and the kidney', said Mr Webster, 'I detected the presence of an alkaloid which gave the reaction for morphine.'

Mr Lewis (for the prosecution): 'Did you find any other poisonous substance?'

'No, I found no other trace of poisonous substance.'

'I am going to put to you one general question with regard to certain preparations and chemicals that have been mentioned in this case, and I want you to tell me whether they are poisonous. Hyoscine, cocaine, potassium cyanide, bichloride of mercury, digitalin, and aromatic tincture of opium. Are these at all poisonous?'

'Yes.'

'What about the aromatic tincture of opium?'

'That contains morphine.'

'Now ground glass, do you call that a destructive thing?'

'Yes.'

'A destructive and injurious thing?'

'Yes.'

'In either powdered or fragmentary form?'

'Yes.'

'And taken as such has been known to cause death?'

'Yes.'

A bottle labelled 'Aromatic Tincture of Opium' found in Mrs Thompson's bedroom was produced in court and Mr Howard, the chairman, asked Mr Webster: 'Does that contain enough to be a poisonous dose?'

Mr Webster replied that between one-quarter and half an ounce would be fatal. The bottle was an ounce bottle.

Cross-examined by Mr F.A. Stern, who appeared for Mrs Thompson, Mr Webster said that anyone could buy aromatic tincture of opium. If a person suffered with his heart and was not under professional skill, chlorodyne or tincture of opium would produce relief.

Mr Stern: 'And probably it was some compound such as that which produced the trace of morphine you found in the body?'

'It is quite possible.'

'The other poisons you mention are what you would call deadly?'

'Yes.'

'And in the ordinary course could not have been obtained at the chemist's?'

'That is so.'

'If taken in any quantity ground glass would have a serious effect on the lining of the stomach and the intestines?'

'It might have.'

'You could find no evidence that any quantity had been taken?'

'No.'

*Daily Mail,* 24th November, 1922

*30th November, 1922*

Darlint,

How I long for a proper cup of coffee. In a pure white cup, a cup so fine you can see the shadow of your fingers through the china. And when you set it in the saucer it makes that particular chink, a chink I haven't heard in the two months I've been here. Then pouring a little cream from a white china jug and the cream swirling into the dark brown of the coffee, helped by a spoon, until the two merge together. You would be watching me, and you might grab my wrist as I swirled this spoon a little too compulsively. We would be in Fuller's, in the late afternoon, when the chandeliers didn't need to be lit and only two waitresses stood chatting at the furthest corner of the long room. There would be the smell of good cigars and Johnson's polishing wax and a faint trace of Chanel No 5, mixing with the scent of warm buttered crumpets, to make a peculiar, fragrant, bun-like feeling. You and I would be having that conversation, the one we had again later that evening, outside the Criterion, sitting on the steps of the statue, the last time I saw you before—before the evening at the theatre. The 3rd October.

Before Percy's death.

Edie, what do you want me to do, I don't understand—

Only this time you would be listening, listening properly to me.

I want you to help me . . .

And so I would put the spoon down, leaving a pale brown stain on the white linen and you would clutch my wrists again, not harshly, but simply in that way you had, a habit almost, not seeming to notice sometimes if it hurt me, your fingers—once or twice—left a bracelet of bruises, dark as peonies. Your eyes, your expression, I try to bring them to mind, but all I can remember is my heart beating calmly, like steady oars in a river, obedient to controlling hands.

You have to ask Percy, ask him again about

a divorce, ask him this evening . . . I know you are afraid of him, it makes my blood boil to think of it. The man is despicable, Edie, he's—

And I would be promising to ask him, to try harder, as I did promise. I would take a sip of coffee then, and it would be at the perfect temperature, so much so that I hardly noticed it slipping down my throat and most certainly took it for granted, didn't believe for one second that it might be the last cup of good strong coffee in a pure white china cup in Fuller's Cafe on Aldersgate that I would ever, ever drink . . .

I don't think I will send this letter to you. This is a private letter.

It has come to the point where writing comforts me, writing is the only thing I do all day and I look forward to it with my tongue a little dry and my heart beating slightly faster than normal, understanding that writing—and Piper's visits—are the only two things which happen in my long, long day.

I don't count the other visits. Those are empty and I don't feel fully alive during them, the way I do when I write, or when I speak to Piper. When Mother visits or Avis or the rare occasions when Father visits, I worry so much about them, that I'm false, I can't be myself. I'm prevented from expressing my own fears, and I don't wish to appear downhearted. I certainly can't talk to them about you. Avis physically shudders if your name is mentioned and to watch her do that makes my stomach leap.

I know she is angry at me. I know she'd like to explode into that furious indignant splutter she sometimes has, which only makes one feel more sorry for her, since it makes her clumsy and undignified. I can picture her grey eyes deepening and her shaking her hands in that odd mannerism, like someone wanting to strangle a chicken, and instead of increasing my sympathy the picture tickles me, makes me want to giggle! (How dreadful of me.)

I know she hasn't visited you either since our letters were read in court. You might wonder how I am so certain of this but you forget I have known my sister her full twenty-three years and she is nothing if not stubborn. She may well sob about you every night—I'm fairly sure she does—but that won't alter her resolve. It's particularly the physical nature of our union that would so disturb Avis. She is a little like a fish in that respect. One imagines her always swimming along glassily, smooth and flat and untroubled by sudden hot spots in the water, or cool spots come to that. She will wonder endlessly at how—how her own sister could even undress in front of a man who wasn't her husband, let alone . . .

No, your name can't be mentioned and that's that.

I will write you another letter when I feel calmer, less agitated by thoughts of Avis. (That shadow has come back into my eye-corner and it is infuriating me today. As I write I keep wanting to brush at a hair at the side of my face and then find that none is there. But something shadowy definitely dangles there. It only does so when I'm not looking, I've decided. I have to catch it out.)

Yes, a gentler letter to reassure you. There are only six days now until the Old Bailey. I dread it but I look forward to it also, as our chance at last, a chance to clear our names.

Edith.

*1st December, 1922*

Darlint,
Stern visited this morning to talk with me a little about the trial. I like the man now, for all his fierceness. I feel sure he thinks reasonably well of me, and there is something fatherly in his presence. I mean he actually reminds me of Father.

He says at the Old Bailey I will be represented by Sir Henry Curtis-Bennet, whom I haven't yet met. I'm rather sorry that it won't be Stern, but he spent this morning advising me about the case. He says the newspapers are *like vultures,* there has been an enormous amount of interest, and he is anxious to save me the scandal and suffering of going on the stand. But I want to, Freddy! It's the only way I'll have a chance to persuade

242

anyone that our love is not sordid or silly, the way they speak of it, and that you acted on a whim and out of—from high passion . . .

It was queer, this morning's conversation with Stern. It's evident he's agitated about my letters to you being read in court, feels they weight the scales strongly against us. He went so far as to say there would be no case at all if they hadn't been found. He made the suggestion to me that I should try to distance myself from you—were there occasions, he asked, when Bywaters behaved hot-headedly? Was he a fighter or a drinker, did he have other women?

When I became upset at this line of questioning, Stern too became angry. There's no need for you both to swing for it! he said, pacing the room and then muttering to himself: The Lord give me strength! He wheeled around and seemed to take in the fact that I'm quite crestfallen, defeated. Not at all my usual defiant self. Sitting on the bed obediently like the daughter he makes of me, awaiting his instruction.

Mrs Thompson—Edith—please understand. I have listened to you talking of Bywaters, and I know you've written to him and tried to get word to him and kept faith with him. I've even heard that he has managed to write to you. But you need to face the truth. You are on trial for your life here! Nothing you've told me has led me to believe that the poisoning was anything more than fantasy to keep your young man interested in you, to keep up a game. But it isn't a game any longer. Bywaters will go to the gallows for sure for a most brutal stabbing— they have the knife now! The young fool showed them where the knife was and, my God, it's an ugly threatening, enormous specimen! Not designed to curry any sympathy, although curiously enough Bywaters is already getting plenty, by dint of being young, being handsome, being dapper . . .

By now tears were threatening to spill down my cheeks. I'm telling you this, Freddy, not to hurt you, but to show you what we're up against. Stern, even Stern—whom up until now I have trusted utterly—is suddenly advising me to betray you. He claims that the entire blame could be heaped onto you and I would be perceived as the infatuated and duped older woman but completely innocent of the crime. He says there are only two ways for women to escape from the gallows in cases such as ours. The woman must be either pure and unblemished—and now that my letters have been read out I don't have that option—or the pitiful victim of a clever, dazzling man. Those are the options he holds out to me, Freddy— innocence or stupidity and I can't accept either of them. What's more it's apparent from what Stern himself says that it's too late. I'm already considered clever and knowing—isn't that the exact opposite of stupid or innocent—so what is the point of pretending otherwise?

Mr Stern, the truth is that things got out of hand and Freddy, he . . . Freddy became impatient . . .

He murdered your husband in cold blood! He stabbed him a half dozen times in the neck and chest! He left him in the street to die and you to pick up the pieces! That's the truth and the sooner you're prepared to say so, the better it will be! That's the only way you are going to save yourself—

I didn't want to hear any more. I asked Stern to leave. I was crying in earnest by then (and annoyed with myself for doing so, because it looked like weakness and that was the last thing I wanted to show).

Raised voices brought—guess who—nosy Eve to the spy-hole. Stern left in some embarrassment, promising to return later in the week or if there was anything fresh to bring to my attention before the trial. We said goodbye stiffly. I asked Eve if she had a handkerchief. I blew my nose surreptitiously, turning my back to her. She was standing awkwardly behind me, I could hear her breathing and feel that she was just standing uncertainly. I wished it could have been Clara who'd appeared just then—Eve's sly presence only heightened my shame.

Of course, I didn't know whether to hand the handkerchief back to her, the state it was now in. In any other circumstances I'd have offered to wash it, and I said so, for want of anything more useful to say.

Keep it, Eve said. Then, after a hesitation: I'll bring you a laundered one tomorrow.

I raised my eyes to hers then, surprised by something I detected in her voice. Freddy, after all I've told you about Eve, I really did not anticipate this gesture and didn't know what to make of it.

She lowered her own eyes quickly, pushed her slipping cap onto her hair, and darted out of the room, closing the door behind her with a clang.

Now I must finish here, aware as I am that what I've written above will upset you fearfully. Just to reassure you, darlint, that there is no way at all that I would betray you like that in court, nor try to heap the blame on you. I cannot understand quite what has happened to us—the events of that night—but whatever is decided I know that it is something we have arrived at together and will face together.

Peidi.

## CHAPTER EIGHT

We are walking in Belgrave Road, our arms linked. I am wearing my brown fur collar and deep mink hat; he is wearing his black wool suit. It is midnight. We are walking in the direction away from the station, and we can still hear the Great Eastern train pulling away in the distance, a light rumble. The sound of other clicking heels on the pavement, as another couple ahead of us make their way home. A baby is crying in an upstairs bedroom, but even this sound is gentle, hardly disrupting the calm spacious streets; the double-fronted houses with their neatly trimmed privet hedges, their green-painted fences, their wooden slatted blinds and their beautiful fine lace curtains.

I imagine I am thinking about this, in a quiet, satisfied sort of way. I often think with pleasure about the order and the space in these wide clean streets and their silent, enigmatic houses, closed as blank expressions, inscrutable.

We are talking about a picture show due to repeat at the Super Cinema, starring Alice Brady. He's heard it is an agreeable film, I'm saying that Agnes claimed it was a disappointment. Then we discuss a dance we want to go to and Percy is yawning, a huge, cavernous yawn that he doesn't bother to cover with his hand, and which does not flatter his face, stretching his neck so that he looks like a wild turkey.

I lean into him a little as we walk, in the habit of those who have walked often together and developed a way of accommodating each other's gait and the speed of the other's step.

It is true that I did ask him that night again about divorce. The conversation was brief and wearying. Percy started and looked dolefully at me. Surely you don't mean it, Edie? I thought we were getting along just fine . . .

Guilt plucked at me as I realised his surprise was genuine.

He carried on, I thought things were happy between us again?

And with the words 'happy' and 'again' a great hefty door slammed on the conversation. Percy's idea of happy and mine glanced off each other. Never the twain shall meet. We fell to silence after that. Of course, I thought there would be other times. Other conversations.

So here we are now crossing De Vere Road and briefly stepping into the lemony glow from a street lamp, so that Percy's dark brown shoes and the silver buttons of his black jacket are picked out and glimmer momentarily. There is a whiff of honeysuckle climbing a garden fence beside us, some trails of the dying rusty flower scattering the pavement. Also the sound of quick snapping footsteps, a little like someone impatiently snapping their fingers.

And then we walk out of the light from the lamp, and the darkness and snapping fingers have transformed into a sudden, terrifying figure; a man, who pushes me, a sharp dig in the ribs that knocks the breath out of me for a moment and now Percy is being shoved towards a wall and it's Freddy, I know it's

Freddy, so I pick myself up and say, Oh don't, don't. But they're shouting at each other; words that I can hear but not understand; my heart has leapt right out of my body and is swooping and diving all around us like a demented bat; we are dark, small, shadowy figures on the pavement, screaming and shouting in the quiet street, but just like the worst possible dream, no one seems to hear us or to come to our aid, to rescue or interrupt the scene as it unfolds; tiny black silhouettes in their silent miniature peepshow; ludicrous, foolish, stuck. Freddy angrier than I've ever seen him, his coat flapping behind him, opening up in a great wide wing-span, so that now I'm thinking stupidly not of Freddy but of an eagle about to lunge at his prey, as in the slowest possible motion he pulls back his arm and in the dark sleeve of his coat, instead of a hand the blade of a knife glitters. I'm screaming, I'm sure I'm screaming; there is a taste so foul in my mouth—and although it is dark, everything is soaked in the most breath-taking, bloodcurdling scarlet colour, arriving from nowhere like a new kind of light.

Percy staggers horribly along the wall, leaving a shiny, long black smear along the bricks, the way a snail leaves a trail in the garden, easily visible by moonlight. The colours in front of me subside and sink into greyness again as I reach towards Percy, only dimly aware of Freddy moving, stumbling away from us.

But the foul taste in my mouth doesn't subside—I don't know what I'm doing, I'm undoing Percy's coat, I'm talking to him, I'm saying, Come on, Percy, you're fine, come on, and his eyes are open and I'm staring into them trying to hold them but they are unfocused, so I'm trying to get my arms around his chest in the white shirt so I can prop him up against the wall, but the weight of him is heavy and now with a shriek I've seen that slender black snake of blood at the corner of his mouth, and it's no good, he keeps slipping down the wall, slipping and slipping; I'm crying and pleading with him, Come on, Percy, come on! and calling for someone to, Help me, help me! because I can't hold my husband up for much longer, I'm exhausted and he so heavy and if someone doesn't come soon he will keep slipping I'm sure, I'm doing my best, I'm trying with all my strength but he is—*help me, help me!*—Percy, my husband is slipping away from me.

\*　　　\*　　　\*

Eve brings me a white cotton handkerchief, folded into a triangle. It is in the pocket of her uniform. She closes the door carefully behind her. After placing the cup and bowl and spoon on the tray in the corner and picking up the pail to take out, she hands me the handkerchief.

Thank you. My voice comes out in a squeak, surprised and childlike.

When she leaves, I turn the soft, fresh-scented cotton over in my hand. I notice some faint embroidery—ELP. E for Eve. It must be a handkerchief from home. Smuggled into the prison like a nail-file inside a cake. A soft, hand-embroidered, newly ironed handerkerchief.

So I sit down on the bed and open it out. A smell of faint lemons drifts up to me; also the most sweepingly familiar, medicated, childhood, Cuticura soap kind of smell. A smell of Eve's home, Eve's life outside of prison. Any life outside of prison. My life outside of prison.

That time I cut both knees, falling from the wall outside in the front garden at the old house. Only a small wall, but I was showing off to Avis. She was daring me. Bet you can't jump off it! Bet I can! And I did and something odd happened, I caught my foot in a slightly strange position and fell, ungainly onto both knees, scraping a pink curl of skin on each, like the whirls made on butter in fancy restaurants.

And then running in, wailing, so that Mother comes running with the Cuticura ointment and she's dabbing at both knees and Avis is standing in the doorway, trying not to gloat but gloating quietly anyway, knowing that she won the bet, because I didn't manage to jump, not properly, not without falling and crying like a baby. The smell of Cuticura on a hot flannel and the sound of Mother tutting crossly, moments afterwards making soothing babying noises, in a tone I use, too, on my dolls and teddies, a tone I associate with mothers and fondly imagine I will use one day on my own children, magically managing to convey annoyance and sympathy all in the same breath.

The hot flannel, the clean handkerchief. Laundering, embroidering. I'm thinking of myself now in my own living room, with a needle and white cotton in my hand, mending a blouse; the rhythm of the stabbing and pulling and the tucking of the material and pinning . . . tiny movements taken for granted, like patting a doll's head or jumping off a wall. Turning a key in a lock, or licking the seal on a letter.

Of course, I do sew here, in the day room sometimes. But without the purposefulness— the mending of my own favourite clothes, or Percy's—or the embroidering of baby linen, yes, I was forgetting I ever did that. A long white dress, with hem stitching and embroidery around the neck. The frailest cotton, like a shroud, the tiniest stitches of all. Why did I do that, after the decisions I'd made? Just looking at that secret little gown used to fill me with such comfort, such a shiver of chilled pleasure. It was for the future, I suppose. For some other time. Some time when it would be right. Or else it was a secret penance, a way to make myself suffer, to ensure I wouldn't forget.

I can't hear Eve outside or anyone. I've opened the handkerchief she gave me, offered me. I feel something powerful and extraordinary towards Eve. It must be gratitude but it feels like so much more. Something tremulous, thundering, surprising. It brings a drumming in my temples, the rush of tears. I bury my face in the worn, many times laundered handkerchief and think of tasks, infinitesimal day-to-day tasks. Making a cup of tea. Sewing a child's christening dress. Boiling an egg, lighting a lamp, folding down a bed. Sewing a handkerchief, laundering a handkerchief, ironing a hankerchief. Smuggling a handkerchief into prison for a prisoner, knowing it is against the rules. Knowing such a transgression would surely mean instant dismissal. Thank you, I mutter again, into the handkerchief.

I scrunch Eve's gift bitterly into a damp ball, the way a child would. A tight fist, an ugly ball; a damp sodden mess that can never be unfolded and mended and laundered.

Will never open out, be fresh, again.

*Sunday 3rd December, 1922*

Darlint,

253

Piper called again. He was overdressed in a too-tight jacket and seemed both shy and restrained and at the same time to be withholding something, perhaps a piece of information, something he is saving up for me. I can't help but hope that it's a message from you, Freddy!

Once more he tried to steer the conversation to 'spiritual matters'. Prompted no doubt by my outburst about children and prayers last week, he asked, Don't you ever feel the need to pray for guidance, or comfort, or simply to feel that you're not alone?

No, thinking about what he actually said, he didn't ask. Piper never asks. He states: I find, Mrs Thompson (he was back to that, unable to drop the habit it seems), that it can be a comfort to pray, to ask the Lord for guidance, it can help to feel that one is not alone . . .

And then he waited to see if I'd agree heartily. Presumably he could then leap in with words of cheer from the Bible and fulfil his proper function.

When I mentioned that some of us feel even more alone when we pray, feeling then the absence of an answer (or of a presence) more cogently, he became animated again. His eyes widened—he was, I'm sure, excited to be given the occasion to lecture me on not praying for something, but only to connect with God, and then went on to say that we're not punished for our sins, but by them, which I have to say is

254

an idea which lodged heavily with me, as I find there is some truth in it.

You, of course, will find this cynicism shocking, Freddy, and I know you will be much comforted by your own faith, and Lily, too, no doubt she has been praying to cleanse your soul hard enough to scour a pan.

What irritates me most is how excited Piper is by words like sins and punishment. Why else would he work in a prison, if not because he likes to rub shoulders with the foul and disgusting souls of evil women? There is one in here right now who has thrown over a dozen babies into the Thames! Imagine that. She charged ten pounds a baby to poor women who wanted to have them 'adopted', having fallen in the usual unfortunate circumstances to their employer or the husband of their employer and then she and her son (her accomplice) wrapped the miserable creatures in newspaper—whilst still crying, still alive!—and threw them into the cloudy river!

It makes me shudder to think that I'm now included in a place with such women and viewed by Piper as being in the same heartless league.

I have never yet taken a bath at the same time as Old Alice (the Baby Farmer described above) but I can't think of a way that she could be washed clean. I mean, no amount of praying or asking for forgiveness could erase that crime, could it, Freddy?

I said to Piper, Will she go to Heaven, the Baby Farmer?

Heaven—now there's a question, Mrs Thompson . . .

What I'm saying is, if I *am* innocent, but I refuse to 'confess' or ask God's forgiveness for my crimes, or to believe in him, even, won't I go to Hell, whereas someone like Old Alice, might commit all the sins she wishes to in her lifetime and then at the very last lap, say she is truly sorry and repent with much weeping and wailing and lo and behold—excuse the expression, Mr Piper—or bob's your uncle, if you like—she's in the Pearly Gates. Now, can that be fair?

Well, I think you are oversimplifying things a little. And after all, it is the Catholic faith which urges death-bed confession and I—as you know—am Methodist and, as I have told you before, I'm not here to squeeze a confession from you.

I bit my tongue and didn't snap: What are you here for then? Because I do want him to visit, as I mentioned to you before, and I'm afraid to drive him away with too much insolence.

Well, it was a lively discussion at least and whiled away the time. I've begun to feel that Piper enjoys them, too. I never did find out why I'd had the feeling that he had a piece of news for me. I asked directly in the end—Have you heard something, something about

256

Freddy? But he looked puzzled.

No, I've nothing to report, Mrs Thompson, he replies, with his eyes lowered, his hands in his lap. I don't know why I have the sensation that he is withholding something from me, perhaps it's simply a general mistrust of him.

He says he will visit again tomorrow.

I'll write soon.

Edie.

PS (later)

Funny I should write about Old Alice just then and then later today for the first time I did come across her in the bathing room. She is horribly wrinkly, with those legs which are woven with black and blue veins and a little pot belly—the figure of a robin or a fat bird on stick legs. I couldn't take my eyes from her and I know the other women feel the same way. She must be around eighty years old! A figure who, if dressed, would look like a kindly bundled-up grandmother. No doubt this is how she appeared to the luckless girls who approached her.

Our bathing rooms are like a stables— around twelve baths and a wooden door between each but a short door, easy enough for the wardress to see over. Because I'm tall, it's impossible not to glimpse the other women occasionally, although I try to avert my eyes.

I could hear Alice singing to herself while she was rubbing with the stiff carbolic soap. (Her bath was next to mine.) The foam and heat—they make sure your water is scalding hot!—made a great cloud of steam but as I went to climb into my bath, I glanced over at Alice's side—the quickest of glances—scarcely time to focus—what a curious sight! With that mist of steam all around her, and that singing and her damp grey hair curling at the edges, her shiny red skin, she looked almost cherubic, a fat angel rising on a cloud of pearly steam.

A shudder ran through me—a real shock. It was as if—she looked like—a great ugly baby herself. And a picture of a baby, dragging its slimy belly on the bank, the body bloated and swollen and truly foul, floated along a river in front of me. White bodies naked on the low damp ground.

*Well now that's done: and I'm glad it's over.*

We all hate bath times here. I don't need to tell you that it's nothing like the pleasure of a long soak at home! I wish I could keep some of the more unpleasant or powerful mental pictures out of my mind, Freddy. I used to be able to. Time was, when I could have read about all Alice's misdeeds and not felt much more than a shudder. I wish I could go back to that time, but I fear I never can.

I haven't spoken to Alice yet. I don't suppose anyone has. She acts indifferent and the wardresses are gruff with her, but she must be lonely, like the rest of us, don't you think? Do evil people suffer the same way we do, I wonder, for the same trivial day-to-day reasons? Or is her head filled with something more, memories perhaps, something so pressing it fills up all spaces, leaves no room for anything else? We all know she'll go to the gallows, Freddy, but again, no one speaks of it. Even Clara—open, outspoken, big-mouthed Clara—is silent where Alice is concerned.

*   *   *

I'm making porridge. I'm standing in my kitchen, wearing an apron—a yellow checked apron with a small egg-yolk stain on the pocket. The pocket contains a crumpled handkerchief and two pegs. I'm brushing my hair away from my face with the back of my hand. A blue gas flame hisses from the stove, boiling water and salt bubbles in a pan and I'm throwing in two handfuls of oats. I don't measure anything—I've been making Percy's porridge for years.

Beside the stove I have two bowls—pale blue and white bowls, a flower pattern in the style of a Washington, but they are not Washingtons; one has a chip on the top edge. That's my bowl. I always take the chipped mug, the smaller portion, the sausage which fell on the floor. A wife's duty—making the porridge, drinking from the chipped mug.

Stirring the oats into the water, knowing that Percy is still asleep. It's Sunday. Let him sleep. Porridge is better if it stands for three minutes and you sprinkle sugar on top while it's cooling. No sound of anyone stirring. Mrs Hester isn't up next door. There's a horse clopping past in the street outside, some children's voices in a neighbouring garden. My heart beating, the wooden spoon batting against the iron pan. No sound of Percy.

Next to the pegs in my apron pocket, a small bottle. I close my fingers around it. Turn it over and over, hear the contents softly shift from one end to the other. Take the bottle out of the pocket, turn it over in my hand, take the lid off, dab my finger at the contents. A powder, white, like sugar. The porridge is bubbling and I need two hands to lift it from the stove, so I screw the lid back on the bottle, slip it back into my pocket. Go to the door. Listen at the bottom of the stairs. No sound of movement from Percy.

Back in the kitchen. Warm and steamy—I open the back door. Spoon the porridge into the bowls. The consistency is exactly right. Porridge that slips from the server at the right speed. Stirred with powder, icing sugar white.

Mine is the bowl with the chip in it. Set a spoon beside each. A napkin.

Hear Percy coming down the stairs, slowly. The bottom stair creaks.

Percy! Your breakfast is ready, I call up to him from the kitchen, still at the stove, still stirring.

He is wearing his pyjamas with a gown over

them. No need to keep up appearances, now Freddy isn't here. No need to make small talk either. Percy's is the bowl without the chip in it. He sits down in his usual place and at the end of the table which allows him to have his back to the window and I place his bowl in front of him.

I ask him, Do you want some milk? It's still quite hot . . .

I push the bowl towards him. He grunts his reply. Pours some milk from the jug onto his bowl, so that it runs to the edges, leaving the porridge floating in islands in the centre. I'm thinking of scum, of bath scum and the rim of debris that human bodies leave on a bath. My heart beating. Percy picks up his spoon. I sit down quickly and pick up mine, too. Our spoons lift. Our spoons are good silver, a wedding present. He scoops a crescent of porridge from the top, crusted with sugar, aims it towards his mouth.

He closes his mouth. He chews; he swallows. He doesn't look up.

I try eating mine but it feels like stuffing from a pillow, like straw, it's too dry, it forms a hard lump in my mouth. I keep chewing. I keep my eyes away from Percy.

There's too much sugar on this, he says.

I say nothing; I'm listening to the spoon clinking in the bowl repeatedly, the chewing, the saliva, the porridge swilling around his mouth. The spoon hitting his teeth. The spoon hitting the bowl again.

He won't notice if I don't eat much.

Too sweet, that, he says, pushing the bowl away. His bowl clean. A fine tide mark of porridge around the edges. He looks around for the newspaper and I get up and bring it to him. My heart beating. He pats his stomach and scrapes his chair back.

I eat two more mouthfuls and rush to the bathroom.


*Monday 4th December, 1922*

Darlint,

Two more days until the trial. I'm in an odd, good mood today. Optimistic. I suppose, queer though it is, I'm looking forward to a chance to get outside, to be in the world outside again, no matter how trying the circumstances.

Piper came today. He brought me a Bible. A battered blue affair with illustrations. He urged me to 'seek comfort from it' and I tried not to stare insolently at him or ask him about the racing results. I have discovered that he lives right here at the prison. There is a Chaplain's House and a Governor's House that goes with the job here. So no wonder he is here every day and we can't escape him (nor him us).

I didn't want to appear ungrateful, so I flicked through the Bible on my knee, whilst he made small talk about some of his other 'parishioners' and reminded me that there is an extra service in here on Sundays, apart from the obligatory one, and asked politely why he had never seen me there?

You like to keep yourself separate from the others here, is that it, Mrs Thompson?

This had a faint whiff of reproach about it. I glanced down at the Bible at my knee which had fallen open on a page with an illustration of Ruth and Boaz (I had heard of Ruth of course but have no idea who Boaz is!). Anyway it was a nice illustration with Ruth in a robe and Boaz standing behind her and lots of sheaves of corn or something, so I just stared at that for a while, hoping that Piper wasn't going to start a lecture. The sin of pride, I suppose.

You can keep it, Piper said, nodding towards the Bible. He seemed pleased with his own magnanimity, mistaking, I think, my downcast eyes, for gratitude or something.

I will be out soon. I have a Bible at home.

I don't know why I said this, Freddy. I don't know why I'm always so sullen with him. I do actually like the man, in some strange way, notwithstanding his awful skin and dreadful colouring and the shabby clothes he wears without a sniff of a woman's care or attention. I picture him in his Chaplain's House with a little pet dog. I think he smells of damp dog sometimes. It wouldn't be a big creature.

263

Something small and rather pathetic. Perhaps with an unfortunately mangled tail or one ear bitten off. It would have to be a sorry soul, that's for sure.

You have high hopes for the trial then? Piper asked, crossing his legs and settling into a more comfortable position, as if he recognised that I was more willing to talk than I was five minutes ago. He offered a cigarette and I took it. I stepped towards him to save him coming towards me and allowed him to light it in that way that women have always permitted men and which, even when the man in question is a minister and the woman an accused murderess, still has a servility about it which in my opinion, is all in favour of the woman.

I took my first, eager pull on the cigarette and blurted: Most reasonable people—most people—the jury will see! Freddy acted— impulsively. I had no idea he was waiting in the shadows like that. We hadn't discussed it. There is no shred of evidence that we planned anything together, that we would ever have planned or discussed something so hideous—

I was getting quite animated. It's the most I've ever spoken about things, darlint, to him or anyone, even Stern. I hadn't defended myself to Stern particularly because I'd assumed I didn't have to.

The only bits I've found awkward and improper to talk about are—how shall I put it—the events of September last year when I was writing to you and 20th January. What would Stern or Piper understand of such things? Most men remain in a kind of willed ignorance and most women seem to think such events—if not ordinary—then at least a miserable fact of life. Something one gets on with. Look at what I told you about Eve! Remember what happened to Agnes at the shop? So few men realise how ordinary it is to us women, something we must get on with, but keep from our husbands and sweethearts at all costs. Since being here I've learned plenty, through overhearing. Increasingly (perhaps it is the presence in here of Old Alice and my thoughts on that matter) I have dwelled on such things. If you were here I would talk to you about it. Eve is back in work and I've never heard her 'troubles' mentioned again. That seems to be an unspoken rule, in here as well as outside. When one needs advice or information from other women, one broaches the subject. Once that moment is passed, all behave as if nothing was said. But since being here I've heard so many different things mentioned, things I'd never heard of before. I mean, of course, the women were whispering amongst themselves, not to me, Freddy. A syringe full of carbolic soap, one woman said. Slippery elm, according to another. And a third—I suppose that is why she is in here— claimed a knitting needle and a large bottle of

265

Lysol in case of blood poisoning, would do the trick every time. I've no idea whose advice Eve took but she has fallen silent on the subject, so I suppose it is safe to assume it worked. She looks pale a milk and thin as a sliver of butter.

I'm glad you're feeling optimistic, Mrs Thomspon, Piper said, breaking into my thoughts with his cheeriness. We blew smoke at one another. I glimpsed the dark thread I keep mentioning to you but I managed to resist the temptation to turn my head towards it. (It feels, as I said, like a fine shadowy hair hanging in front of one eye but I know that isn't it.) I looked straight at Piper to see if I could fathom his expression; what he might really be thinking. I glanced down at the Bible again, read the caption to the illustration I'd landed on: 'Then said Boaz unto his servant that was set over the reapers, "Whose damsel is this?"'

It was the oddest thing. When my eyes lifted from the page, that phrase leapt in front of me. *Whose damsel is this?* I almost imagined, don't laugh, Freddy, because queer things happen when you are locked up on your own for a long period of time, and I know you told me of some yourself, from your times at sea—I almost felt as if Piper had spoken.

*Whose damsel is this?* In a great big booming voice, like that voice which called you to your ship that time when we were milling around on the deck with Avis. I jumped slightly and

Piper, who keeps his eyes on me jumped, too, ever so slightly and then coughed nervously, so that I began to wonder: did he hear it as well? Did we both hear a booming voice from nowhere ask us a question and then fearing that we were going mad, refrain from responding? Or from even indicating to the other that we had heard anything?

When I looked at Piper's hands, Freddy (he held the cigarette confidently enough, but I wasn't fooled by that), when I glanced down at him—his hands were shaking! He tried to keep his eyes steady with mine and he had a faint smile, which I'm sure he believed was reassuring, showing all his small neat white teeth; but all about him—the grey wool sweater, the glimpse of blue knitted sock at his ankle, the ginger hair—all about him seemed to tremble, to wobble, like the bottom lip of a tearful child.

I couldn't muster a thing to say—I suppose I was even rather shocked—and so we parted dolefully and he assured me he would come tomorrow at the same time.

I almost wish I *could* find comfort in the Bible and then I would have something pleasing to report to him, could offer him some solace, some succour, some proof that his chosen field had a purpose after all.

Two presents in as many days. The Bible from Piper and the handkerchief from Eve. I placed them on the metal tray (a kind of shelf)

267

in the corner where my plate is usually put, which stands in for a bedside table. It's almost home from home, don't you think?

It's funny but it's as if there are two Pipers and he brings both with him, each time. The one who plays the Chaplain's part, who asks the right questions, who disapproves and responds as he ought; who offers comfort and words of wisdom and is dutiful and the same with all the women he visits. Then there is another man and I think of this one as younger, more vulnerable, more like you, Freddy! This one, which underscores the other, flutters beneath it like a white shadow, a ghost, is much less certain. This one likes me occasionally. This Piper gets drawn into my world. This one feels afraid and most of all, this one is not certain.

I like the second Piper. I wish he would come on his own sometimes.

I'll write more tomorrow—I need a new pencil.

Love,
Peidi.


*Tuesday 5th December, 1922*

Dear Freddy,
This morning I woke with an odd ticking feeling in my heart; ticking, tapping—I can't describe it. It wasn't pleasant. I am hoping that

this doesn't mean that my optimism has deserted me. Also, I was sick! I'm sure it's anxiety about the trial and I will just have to expect it over the next few days. If I could touch you just now I would sweep my arms around you (I picture you sitting on your squeaky bed as I so often sit on mine) and you would nestle your dark head on my breast, because if it is frightening to me, it must be a thousand more times so to you!

Well, today began like any other—a wardress, Jones, I think it was, calling through the spy-hole, All right in there? and for once I had something to say other than Yes! I said that I'd been sick and she unlocked the door and sent in a prisoner who was with her to take the bucket out and that was it. No word of concern from Wardress Jones. Then hearing this charade repeated up and down the corridor *All right in there all right in there?* several times over until, rather than words, I hear *Orwyinyer?* and quavering replies *yes yes yes* in all different tones, up and down the scale.

Then we cleaned our cells, as ever—a task I've come to enjoy, Freddy, as it keeps one from being completely idle and, in addition, I feel that without any exercise I've become sluggish and slow and a little on the plump side! You would like it, you were never one to complain about my plumpness here and there . . .

Then Jones came back to take me to the library—I'm simply devouring books at the moment, I suppose the reason is that they keep my mind from noting the minutes as they slide past at the rate of a snail with sleeping sickness. Jones is quite a reader herself—much more than Eve or Clara—she stood behind me in the library with her arms folded across her chest but tapping her foot audibly . . . I thought she was trying to hurry me along and turned around to apologise, only to have her blurt out: Oh not that, Thompson, that's dreadful! Have you read Robert Hitchens? Have you read *Felix*? I told her I had and we spent five or six minutes discussing the books, and I'm sure I was flushed, Freddy, and excited, and it was—for an instant—as if I was talking to Agnes at the shop and I almost—but not quite—forgot where I was. I wish I'd discovered Jones six weeks ago because Eve or Clara just stand in dull silence, or else Clara prattles in annoyance about something to do with the Government or another man who has brought some woman to no good and Eve just twitches her cap and sniffs like a ferret . . . Anyway, I chose *The Common Law* and will surely have read it in two days and then—oh, I hardly dare write it, but surely I will be out of here at the end of the trial, won't I, darlint. I can't see how it can be otherwise.

The busy day continued with a visit in my room at two o'clock from the Governor to say

270

that I had *three* visitors and could see them in the visitors' room rather than here (we're only allowed one at a time in here), so again I was out and about, trotting down the corridor in some excitement, into the room with the giant clock at one end and the high ceiling and the smell of overheating wood (they keep heaters on for the visitors so it is far warmer than *our* rooms) and there were Mother and Father and Avis, all sitting in a row, their hands in their laps, their expressions—their faces, like three lifeless puppets, resting on a bench. When I walked in it was as if the puppeteer tugged the string and all three of them jerked into life, smiling and sitting upright and . . .

I may not be able to write more today, Freddy. I confess that many times when I'm writing I break off to cry for a while and I feel better when I do, but I don't want to trouble you with too much of this, as I know how much you worry about me. I'm rubbing at my wrist where it's aching from the writing and my cell is dark at only four o'clock in the afternoon. I have heard the key turn in the door once and once only. One of those strange oppressive moments, which would be oppressive even if I was in Ilford now: I'm suffocating under the weight of a great blanket of storm which threatens to break at any minute now, and under the weight of silence in this place. Where are the other women? What are they doing? Why is everyone so quiet?

271

I won't go on with this line of thought, as I know you will have similar sorrows to bear. I'm thinking particularly of Lily. I know how proud she is. I saw her at court in Stratford and the look she gave me spoke all. Remember that time at Shanklin when Avis teased you about the parcel Lily sent? My heart twists, thinking of that now. Lily at home in Upper Norwood, folding brown paper around a tin of black boot polish, wrapping a pair of brand new socks, flat as kippers; two snowy white handkerchiefs, and a special treat—a bar of Cadbury's, snapped in two (half she would give to Florrie, I know she insisted always on treating you two the same); a new pack of cards with pictures of girls in red dresses on the back, the sort of pack Lily imagined sailors to like.

That first time I came to your house in Norwood and Lily was in the kitchen, her sturdy back firmly turned towards me, until you said: Mother, this is my friend, Edie, and she turned around as slowly as it is possible for any human being to turn and said something like, Charmed, I'm sure, and I wanted to not mind, Freddy; my eyes took in the tininess of the kitchen and the darns on the apron she was wearing and the pots with the broken handles, and I was trying to hate her, saying to myself. *You're just jealous, that's what it is,* trying to comfort myself by picturing my own lovely kitchen, my own lovely things, but instead I was noticing her eyes with that blue,

272

Atlantic-blue gaze and that stubborn chin and seeing how she looked so much like you, darlint, with that same gas-jet, fizzling energy; and finally recognising in the way she spun on her heels and clattered the spoons in the cutlery drawer, making a great show of being busy, how much she loved you, Freddy, how much I was not what she pictured for her one and only son. A woman seven years older. With ideas above her station. And married to someone else, to boot!

Well, as ever, I've wandered off the point. The point was to remind you that we will see each other in court in a day or two and all will be fine at last when we have our chance to speak, to explain that nothing was planned, that it was rash, foolish, all of that, but that it was not pre-planned cold-blooded murder as they speak of it.

I will finish here because I fear I'm not cheering you up as I intended with talk of Lily and of Mother and Father. I'll write again tomorrow and see you at the Old Bailey the day after!

Take heart, my love, I'm thinking of you.

Edie.

\*     \*     \*

This is what Freddy told me. He is coming home from school, fourteen years of age. He is lanky and more monkey-like than ever in his gait, but otherwise recognisable—chirpy, loud, swinging over the back gate without opening it, for no good reason other than that he can. Smoking, of course, but flinging it away before he gets to the kitchen. Pushing the kitchen door open, calling out. Something like: It's me! or: Hello, Mum!

Fourteen. 1916. I'm already married, it's the year I get married, I might even be in the first week of my marriage because Freddy could never remember the month that the news came.

His mother isn't in the kitchen and the gas isn't lit. The house is cold and it's four o'clock in the afternoon, the violet hour, darker than it should be, cold and with a faint smell of lilacs, as if Lily had been picking them, arranging them when she fell. In the living room, she is lying awkardly across the floor, on her front, her head turned to one side, so that Freddy runs to her, rolls her over, slaps her gently on the face, the way he saw his father once do; then realises that she's awake, she hasn't fainted at all, she's staring at him. She's simply lying on the floor, clutching the letter.

And Freddy, Freddy the darling boy, the beloved son, tries to lift his mother, finds her unyielding and cold, so that a terror begins to creep in him because he wants her to be back on her own two feet, he wants her strong and capable, to be Mum again; not this floppy girl, this bereaved wife. And he tries his best, puts his back into it, bends his knees, the way his father taught him once, carrying boxes in the cellar; and he manages to get his arms beneath Lily's body, stumble to the sofa, where he sets her down as gently as he can. He sits down beside her and places his awkward boy's arm around her neck and her hair has come undone at the back and tickles him; he finds that he has grown taller than her overnight, that his arms are solid and strong, compared to her limp, white arms and when she stops staring glassily ahead and blinks huge tears onto her cheeks he finds that he can feel brave; feel a cold, polished fury at the world, at the war, at everyone; he can look over Lily's head, feel her hot tears splash onto his arms but scarcely notice them; direct his gaze outwards, sharpen his anger into a keen, perfect blade.

But in the back of his mind is the muddled thought: how proud Dad will be when she tells him. Look after your mother for me, Dad said, one of the last things he'd said, like a thousand others. And Freddy imagined saying to him: I did! Look how well I looked after her, I made a good job, took care of things, of Mum and Florrie. And all for you! Because I want to be like you: a good man, a decent man, the sort of man you and Mum would be proud of.

Freddy couldn't shift the thoughts, the motivation. I know it was behind many things, it propelled him, it was his touchstone. What would my dad think of this? What would Dad have done, in my shoes? Lily said it often enough. If only your dad was 'ere, he'd have something to say about it! About Freddy seeing me, apparently. But Freddy told me once, and I believed him. Dad had an eye for good-lookers you know. He wasn't all sweetness and light.

He would of loved you, Edie.


*September 21st, 1922*

My Darling Peidi,
I've come out on deck to have a cigarette & write you. The spray & nowhere to lean my paper will mean you have to expect some blotches. It's nearly six a.m. & I'm on duty in an hour—right now we're off the Western coast of Canada & it's whaling season.

I love to sit here & stare at the sea. I've found a nook where I can't be found. It's cramped & I know every rivet, every twist of rope, every link of chain by heart from staring at it, but it means Jim won't be up here yelling at me again.

All the fellows miss their girls but they don't have the burdens that I do, knowing you are with HIM. Knowing that he's taking you dancing—you always say he has two left feet! Why are you going dancing with him? Don't go to our place Edie, *please.* I know you'll call

276

me childish. I hate it when you do that.

When I first looked out the sea was blank. A sheet of black paper, pretty still & then the sun came up & the sky dipped itself in the sheet & soaked up every shade of red & pink, but then, Edie—guess what! I saw five black fins, circling something. I thought it must be sharks, but they were huge. As we came closer, some of the fins leapt from the water & I saw they were orca, the whale they call here 'Killer Whale'; I've never seen one before. They're black, with a funny shaped nose & a white saddle-patch. They leap, Edie, like dolphins.

I could of called to Arnie or Jack but I just couldn't help myself from staring at them, it was like they were pulling me towards them, into their circle. Of course, we didn't get that close, & I made out in a while what it was that was in the centre of them—a baby seal! The thing was still alive, but not for long. It was crying & bleating, like a kind of dog. The whales circled smaller and smaller & then one of them—the biggest—dived under the seal and tossed it on its nose, threw it right up into the air & for the grandest moment it almost looked like the poor creature would sail off into the blue . . . then the next whale, then the next, did the exact same thing.

They were like cats worrying a mouse, Edie, it was awe-inspiring & terrible all at once. I couldn't rightly help myself from watching & admiring the great creatures & they didn't stop until they'd skinned the seal alive, it popped right out of its skin, like a sausage in a pan, if you get the picture, great squirts of blood flying up like sauce. Only then did they eat it. They swam off in a line, slowly, like they had eaten a grand Christmas dinner.

I wanted to sing and shout, Edie, I don't mind telling you. It churned me right up inside, watching it like that, so magnificent and so bloody. I was thinking of you & how cruel life is, how cruel creatures are to one another. You said I was entitled to 'all by nature that he is entitled to by Law'; but I want everything, Edie, I don't want to share you. I can't stand to think of his brutal hands on you. If I see him touch you again like that—I can't stand it, Edie, I've told you that. I don't know what I might do.

I will be back later this month & it's only that which keeps me going. Jack & Bill know I've got a girl but don't worry I haven't told them a thing. They make jokes all the time—can you imagine the sort—& it's true enough that I practise what they call 'solitary confinement' out here—what fellow wouldn't when he has you to think of, your hair fanned out around your head, your arms behind your head as you lie there, smiling up at me . . .

I miss you, Edie. Think of me often, be sure you say no to him, won't you. I'm lonely, I miss you.

Your darlint boy, Freddy.

278

*Wed. 6th December, 1922*

Freddy,
A note which maybe I will manage to slip to you in court tomorrow! Arriving outside the Old Bailey this morning I was longing for a glimpse of you. I was blinking, blinking, like a rabbit emerging from his warren! All those strange grey pitted stones of the building, the texture like shortbread biscuits. All those carvings of fruit and acorns. I mean, what have they got to do with anything? So many times we passed the Old Bailey on our walks at lunchtime, didn't we, and how little interest we took in it then. Those colossal, clanging gates those iron-barred windows, the gold statue of Justice on the top. At least I *presume* it's a statue of Justice, although now I start questioning everything in a fashion that I didn't then I'm rather confused.

We were waiting around a lot, hiding out really in the back of a car near the Magpie and Stump (Sir Henry said the prison van would be too obvious and I'd be mobbed) and I had time to study everything. Then Sir Henry says: Right, now, they're going in . . . And there was a break in the crowds. He hustled me and the wardress who'd been appointed to come with me and another security officer, towards the entrance.

Bundled through the archway I noticed for the first time that there were three women, naked women above the arch, and one holds a mirror and one a sword and I can't imagine who they are or what they represent. Sword of justice I suppose, but mirror? Vanity? I can't fathom what they think is so good about that, I thought vanity was our downfall? And what was the third one, what was she holding? Then I was thinking why women, anyway, why is it *we* who stand for Justice or Liberty or whatever it is in these statues but the rest, the judge, the jury, the newspaper men, the prosecutor, the solicitors, the people in court, the crowds in the public gallery, all of them; nearly every last one of them, *men . . .*

Anyway, I was thinking of you, darlint, as Sir Henry marched me through the door, giving me no proper chance to absorb anything; but the inscription I passed under sprung into my consciousness in any case and, Freddy, I thought it said: 'Defend the children of the Poor and Punch the wrong doer!'

Later I decided that the word was 'punish'.

Last night I dreamt that I had a little daughter. Her name was Violet and she had hair the colour of mine, but hers was in tight red curls, like furled flowers, like the tight tubular flowers of a hyacinth. I was looking down a long, dark tunnel and I was sleeping or tossing and turning and there was pain in my belly and blood everywhere and when I

280

opened my eyes there she was: Violet. Her eyes so sharp, so blue, so fragrant. Arriving in a sea of red: eyes of blue and light. Eyes like yours.

So I spoke to her, softly. I said: Hello. I asked her, Do men prefer redheads? I read that, in a newspaper once. I sent it to you, the cutting, you remember? They are bound to mention it. Your little girl. Your daughter, a redhead in a blue dress, shorter than anything I ever wore, a girl born in a charabanc, eating marrons glacés and french almonds and wearing blue because it makes her red, carrot-red hair redder; makes it sing. And laughing, because no one has told her not to, and shouting because no one is here to tell her to be quiet. And she looks a little like Avis, thoughtful like Avis, and giggly. And a lot like me. *And these are pearls that were her eyes.*

Goodbye, Violet, I said to her. Your mother has done something terrible. She has planted hyacinths all wrong, all wrong, and now they have grown and can't be undone and nothing can ever be right. But that's not your fault. Don't be unhappy. You will have a perfumed life of rose-pink and ivory. Your tiny little toes. Your tiny little eyes. *Goodbye, Violet, where ever you are, if you are out there, if you ever were. Freddy's love made you. Freddy's daughter: Violet, my darling. A tiny constellation in a sky of blood. Goodbye.*

I think the drugs that Dr Lynch has me on

are producing these wild, powerful dreams. That and questions, questions all the time about the meaning of my letters, especially the references to the herbs, you know. Stern and now Sir Henry have both begged me not to go on the witness stand and Sir Henry insists that men won't understand such matters and will judge me all the more harshly if I try to explain. The world of women's bodies is a mystery to them and one that they would rather remained a mystery. I think he is speaking of himself. You were never decorous like that and I've learned from the women in Holloway that there must be other men like you, men who know a good deal more than Percy ever did and who prefer not to remain in ignorance.

Darlint, have patience and faith. This really is a trial for us, of all our strength and ability to withstand scrutiny. We must simply tell our stories. Tell how you loved me and tried to make me happy. I will tell how I loved you and how happy you made me. All, I assure you, darlint boy, will be fine.

# WHO PLANNED THE CRIME?

PROSECUTION SUGGESTS MRS
THOMPSON'S AS 'THE CONTROLLING
HAND'

The following letter, long and ardent, was put before the Court today in the Ilford trial; which has attracted huge crowds, some of them gathering since 4 a.m. this morning. The letter included a newspaper cutting entitled: Poisoned Chocolates for University Chief: Ground Glass in Box.

'Don't keep the piece. About the marconigram—do you mean one saying yes or no, because I shan't send it, darlint. I am not going to try any more until you come back. I had made up my mind about this last Tuesday. He was telling his mother & co the circumstances of my Sunday morning escapade and he put great stress on the fact of the tea tasting bitter, as if something had been put into it, he says. Now I think, whatever else I try in it again, it will still taste bitter. He will recognise it and be more suspicious still and if the quantity is still not successful, it will injure another chance I may have of trying, when you come home. Do you understand?'

## WAS THERE INCITEMENT

Mr Inskip then referred to a significant passage in another letter, in which it appeared that Mrs Thompson was the dominating influence in the crime.

He suggested that throughout the correspondence it became clear it was she who was urging him on to commit the crime in some way or other in order to secure her happiness. He may have been reluctant or not, but could the jury have any doubt, after hearing these letters, that she was not reluctant?

After describing the incident relating to the crime and the statements alleged to have been made by the couple, Mr Inskip went on:

'The jury would have to consider whether the hand that struck the blow was moved, was incited, to the crime by Mrs Thompson. It might be that the passion of the young man might have led him in that direction. There was the undoubted evidence in the letters upon which they could find that there was a preconcerted meeting between Mrs Thompson and Bywaters at the place.

'If you are satisfied,' he concluded, 'that Mrs Thompson incited the murder, and that, incited and directed by her controlling hand, Bywaters committed the murder, then it will be my duty to ask you to find her, who incited and proposed the murder, as guilty as Bywaters, who committed it.'

*Daily Sketch,* Thursday December 7th, 1922

*Thursday 7th December*

Dear Freddy,
It was frustrating today, deeply frustrating, not being allowed to take the witness stand. Sitting so close to you, seeing your dark head held upright, the white of your shirt collar, the pale pink spots of your cheeks. Not daring to glance at you too often, but feeling such awareness of you at all times. I don't think I realised until this morning how very dark your eyes really are. Or rather, your eyes are as sea-blue as ever, but your brows now overshadow them more than before, as if your face has grown slightly gaunt. I do think you look a little thin, darlint. I know you try to remain chipper but to me you are strained indeed.

I concentrate so hard on not looking at you, but feel every inch of my body drawn towards you, so that sometimes I find I can't follow at all what is being said. Of course I catch the gist easily enough and I understand that it is me who is being accused (what did he say? 'the mind who conceived the crime') of planning everything. I know this is not what you have said, nor ever implied, and when we have our turn to speak, surely this will become clear.

If it was difficult for me to see Lily trembling like that in the witness stand, how much harder it must have been for you.

I'm tired and not much in the writing mood this evening. It's five to nine, so only five minutes until lights-out and for once I believe I will fall asleep almost instantly.

Strange the thoughts of you which surface when I see you again in the flesh. I was thinking of the time in Valentine's Park. I remembered the feeling of the ground hard beneath me and the shrub bushes scratching my face. The grass stain on my peach silk which I had the devil of a job to remove! And the feel of your coat buttons scratching my neck and your stubble burning the skin around my mouth as we kissed and—don't misunderstand, I'm not complaining, Freddy!—how everything chafed and burned, so much so that I began to imagine my whole body was on fire and the heat became so concentrated in the one spot—you can imagine which spot I mean!—that I truly believed I might burst into flame at any moment. Sometimes on those hurried, stolen occasions, you seemed to wonder if you hurt me. How many times you asked me anxiously: Did that hurt? I could never describe accurately—perhaps I didn't know—whether the feeling was a kind of pain or not. It's because it wasn't quite a physical pain. It was a painful sensation, but an emotional one; a fear of being alive, every nerve exposed, every vein open to invasion. That day I remember how deeply, how inevitably, you inhabited me, flooded through me.

Suddenly, writing this, I'm thinking of Dr Lynch calling me vain and silly, of the Solicitor-General saying today, How sedulous she was! meaning, of course, the poison, the efforts they claim I went to. I trust that you, reading this, will not find my sentiments beyond your comprehension; that you might say to yourself, even, yes, I've felt such things, although maybe I would keep them to myself or express them differently but, yes, they are powerful, they motivate and determine us, they can dominate us at times, but the feelings themselves are not intrinsically foolish or foreign or misguided! Only perhaps what they bring us to.

I can't shift the sense I have (I had it again today, listening to the metallic tones of the Solicitor-General reading out my letters, the emphasis he put on certain words, his raised eyebrow and tone at certain phrases) that my *letters,* the wording of my letters, the very way I express myself, is on trial. The books I read, the kind of picture shows and theatres that I went to, all are on trial. But this is the only language I have! These are the conversations

I've had, the education I've had, the words I've drunk in since babyhood, the expressions I was raised on—how can it be otherwise? Something about me is *wrong,* I know that, I sense that. I get the most powerful feeling of how those men in court consider me; *silly, vain,* those two words come back again and again. Vain to consider that our love might be a real love, on a par with other great loves. That just because you are from Norwood and work as a ship's laundry man and I grew up in Stamford Hill and read a certain kind of novel, we are not capable of true emotions, of having feelings and experiences which *matter.* Yes, we committed adultery and yes we knew it was wrong, wrong, but not sordid like they say!

I'm tired, I'm so tired that I've no idea any longer what I want to say to you, only the hope that, despite the garbled nature of this letter, you at least might understand. I looked up vain, in the dictionary at the prison library, do you remember when I first got here? But I don't think I ever told you what I found: *Vain:* a. (F., from the Latin vanus). Empty; worthless; having no substance, value or importance. Syn: unreal; dreamy; shadowy; insubstantial; unavailing; useless; fruitless; worthless; unsatisfying; empty; light; inconsistent; conceited; inflated; proud; ostentatious.

But I *do* have substance, value, or importance, surely: I am not light. I am *not all sweetness and light* a description you once used about your father, and I know you meant it lovingly, it was a compliment. Now I am driven mad with exhaustion, I've been writing this last part in the dark and I've no idea whether it is legible or not, I suspect the writing is all over the page, doubling back on itself. But darkness is not always the evil opposite of light either, is it? I find it comforting; blessed, a relief. I'm sorry, I know I'm rambling, darlint, aren't I, it's the strain of the day in court, and now, at last, to sleep.

Until tomorrow,
Your Peidi.

## BYWATERS, IN DEFENCE, SUGGESTS SUICIDE-PACT

UNFLURRIED, BUSINESSLIKE
EXPLANATION OF PASSIONATE
PHRASES IN A MASS OF LETTERS
FROM MRS THOMPSON
'I will call Bywaters.'

Mr Cecil Whitely was opening the defence in the Ilford murder drama at the Old Bailey yesterday afternoon.

The twenty-year-old boy in the blue suit, who had been sitting at one end of the long dock, separated by warder and wardress from Mrs Thompson, the frail, girl-like widow of the dead man, rose slowly and deliberately.

He crossed the wide space behind his fellow prisoner, passed through the glass door of the dock, and preceded by the usher, walked steadily through the doubled rows of craning necks to the big canopied box beside the judge. There he placed his hands behind his back and waited.

Under the strong light of the lamp above his head his long-featured, slightly heavy face, with forehead and chin inclined to recede, looked handsomer. The thick hair, brushed high and carefully upward, gave an appearance of added inches, but the man is short and inclined to be broad, older looking than his years. The well-cut lounge coat, double collar and neat tie bespoke carefulness rather than dandyism.

MASTER OF HIMSELF

He was complete master of himself and answered the opening questions of his counsel in short, straightforward sentences, but in tones so low that even the court had to ask him to speak louder.

There was handed up to him the thick portfolio of typed and numbered copies of the letters which have passed between himself and Mrs Thompson; letters almost all written by her, since his have been lost or destroyed: letters, moreover, on which the fate of one or both of them may now turn.

For an hour and a half he had listened to the reading of these letters at length, and had he chosen to turn his head across from his side of the dock to the other while counsel were taking turns in the reading, he might have seen Mrs Thompson weeping steadily and silently as her passion for him was thus again laid bare.

## EXPLAINING LETTERS
Bywaters handled the massed sheets with the facility of an accomplished clerk, who might have been dealing with documents in which he had a keen but only a business concern. He asked for page references, and then ran his fingers lightly through the leaves till he came to the one he wanted.

It was his task to explain certain passages in the letters to which the Crown point as 'indication of an intention on the part of one prisoner, or both, to commit violence to the dead man, or for the woman to poison him'.

## 'To CALM HER.'
He denied the implications easily, almost ridiculed them.

What, he was asked, was the 'compact' referred to in Mrs Thompson's letters as made between herself and him. He answered in a word, 'suicide'. But he qualified this a moment later, explaining that Mrs Thompson was highly strung and that it was she who suggested suicide as the easiest way out of their difficulties.

'I agreed to it to calm her,' he said.

Emotion in almost all its phases swept over the courtroom during the reading of the letters themselves.

Mr Travers Humphreys had scarcely begun the reading when Mrs Thompson, hitherto pale but composed, fell forward on both hands and began to weep, not in audible sobs, but silently. So she sat, bowed, motionless, for three quarters of an hour, until, when the moment came for the luncheon adjournment, she was lost to sense of movement. Judge and Jury had left the court. Bywaters, passionless and apparently heedless of his fellow-prisoner, was leaning, talking rapidly to his own solicitor. The two wardresses who sat one on the side and one just behind Mrs Thompson during the morning, endeavoured to rouse her.

At last, one grasping her firmly around the waist, the other steadying her by the arm, they carried, rather than accompanied her to the dock steps.

Bywaters was still chatting eagerly on the other side.

Mrs Thompson had regained her composure after the interval.

## TEMPTATION TO LAUGH

Up in the gallery, where men, young men, had triumphed for the most part in fighting their way to admission at the head of the queue, which started at 1.30 a.m., there was every now and then, a frank disposition to laugh at some especially ardent passage. It might almost have been a breach of promise case, or so it seemed at times. There were scarcely more than a half-dozen women who had succeeded in squeezing into the gallery, but they were many deep in the long queues of the unsuccessful, and in those who swarmed round the front of the court-house, drawn to see even the outside of the building where the great human drama is being enacted.

## COURT RESUMES

After the break there was again a stir in court as Bywaters, well groomed, calm and erect, walked across to the witness-box. Asked about the quarrel that took place while he stayed with the Thompsons, Bywaters said that Mr Thompson started to knock his wife about, and threw her across the room and overturned a chair, and on seeing this he intervened.

'Had you fallen in love with her?'

'No, I was fond of her, and we were just on friendly terms.'

'When did you fall in love with her?'

'In September, just before I went away.'

'Before you left in August did you have any conversation with Mrs Thompson as to a separation or divorce?'

'Yes.'

He added that on the day of the trouble Thompson said to his wife: 'You get a separation.' She said she wanted a separation. But from time to time he retracted. 'I told him,' added Bywaters, 'that you are making Edie's life a hell.' He replied: 'Well I have got her, and I will keep her. He promised he would not knock her about. I extracted the promise from him.'

*Daily Sketch,* Friday 8th December, 1922


*Friday December 8th*

Darlint,

I thought I might get to see you at lunchtime today? I wonder where you took your break?

Sir Henry and I were in a tiny room off a long corridor; there was a scratched wooden table, a high window which wouldn't open and the most filthy smell of old men's socks and moth balls. One of the wardresses had to sit right beside me, with her chair jammed in tightly and she wasn't someone I knew; it was a huge woman, with arms like hams, so I didn't feel able to put my head down on the table or speak freely to Sir Henry as I might have done, if I'd been in front of Eve or Clara. Furthermore there was a policeman standing beside the door, fidgeting and picking his nose and trying to hide the fact that he clearly couldn't stop staring at me. I sat up straight and drank the tea which the policeman had brought me and toyed with the paste sandwiches, which were curling at the edges and enough to choke me.

I kept thinking of you: where are you in this building, what are you eating, what are you thinking, how did you think it went?

How calm you seemed! How self-possessed. It hurt me a little to have you say that I was prone to melodrama, or what was it—'highly strung'? But I understand entirely why you feel you must put this slant on things. Also, of course, when you said we were just on friendly terms, a chill went through me. But, Fred— please don't be too alarmed by my weeping. There is nothing I can do to stifle it. I always right myself afterwards, in private. It is the exposure, so many cold eyes on me, that I find so painful.

When I pushed the plate away, Sir Henry offered me a cigarette. I searched his face—I had had the strongest impression that he disapproved of women smoking—but he gave me one of his fatherly smiles, nothing to worry about, all is going fine, that kind of thing. He looks so different without the wig on! He wears his shirt sleeves rolled up outside the courtroom and sweat often breaks on his upper lip. When I'm up close I find myself mesmerised by odd things—the way the grey hairs in his eyebrows snarl in with the darker ones, the way his nostrils flare in indignation sometimes, if he becomes heated. I know he feels the whole situation is unjust, Freddy. I know that he thinks I should not be on trial for my life but I still get the sense, over and over, that he disapproves of me, that he would like to shake me sometimes.

Then I couldn't help myself, I asked Sir Henry, why did they only put half the letters in evidence? Why did they leave some of my letters out—the ones which talk about the events in January, the doctor—which explain the herbs, for instance?

The wardress stared straight in front, the policeman's eyes slid around the room. Sir Henry sighed wearily and scraped his chair away from the table. I don't know if he was annoyed, frustrated . . . impatient with me.

296

Mrs Thompson, such matters are not in my hands. You know I agree with Stern that the letters should not have been put in evidence in the first place. The ones you refer to are deemed too indelicate for a public airing. And just as well, too. The *Daily Sketch* would no doubt get hold of them—

He glanced at the wardress who sat stonily with her practised 'I'm not really here' gaze.

*Indelicate!* You know what he means, don't you, Freddy? That a judge and jury can listen to our private correspondence on all matters of the heart, as long as a very ordinary truth about women's bodies is not mentioned. If I was to show this very letter I am now writing to Sir Henry Curtis-Bennet, to that fat wardress sitting in that airless room, to any one of them in fact, they'd act as if I'd broken wind in public. And yet we all know women are trying, through whatever methods available to them, to limit the number of children they have! Do you know that Mrs Marie Stopes has opened a clinic now, in London, near the prison, I've heard Eve and wardress Jones whispering about it and if it had been opened years ago, maybe Old Alice and others like her would not be presented with so many ripe babies for the picking. Perhaps it is your years at sea that have allowed you your sensibility, darlint, because you were never shocked nor ignorant of such matters, were you? I always suspected that you saw plenty of the kind of women I'm

297

talking about on your travels, and although I was always jealous, wasn't I, jealous of Molly, I mean, or others like her, I knew too that it was the reason you understand the—the warp and weave of us, the reason you are not afraid nor disgusted.

Well I've wandered from the point again, that was my lunch break finished and I never did get a satisfactory answer from Sir Henry. Of course the letters they've chosen to put in evidence and the newspaper cuttings I sent you all cast me in a particular light—no need to spell out which one—but it's only a day now until I have my chance to stand in the dock, to have, as they say, my day in court.

I hope you don't mind the plain speaking in this letter. Present circumstances have toughened me up and present living conditions have opened my eyes to a few things. I'm probably not the person who came in here two months ago! I know that what Percy used to call my 'evil tongue' has become more evil through close association with so many hard truths. I cling to the opinion that you would like this Edie as much as the old one and that perhaps you would understand that it is you who created her, or freed her, when you ran out from the shadows that night and altered our lives forever.

# CHAPTER NINE

Freddy has written the doctor's name on a slip of paper; the name he got from Arnie. My hand is curled over the note in my pocket. Without taking it out I can see clearly in my mind Freddy's writing, the house number, the doctor's name: Carpenter. In brackets Freddy has written 'Near Lower Thames street'. That extra direction tells me he is anxious about me, worrying that I won't be able to find it.

I'm wearing the fur, which is a mistake. Too grand, too noticeable. It falls open at the knee and the heavy collar brushes my neck, the cuffs are so big I can draw my hands up inside them, like a child. My stomach full of ice. I am waiting in a hallway, on a chair, close to the foot of some stairs, in a terraced house that smells of dogs, and damp newspapers and also, powerfully of phosphorous, it smells like the match factory. It's a funny place to wait. It's the place to wait in a poky house which really isn't big enough to have people waiting in it. A picture on the wall opposite shows three horses grazing in a field; I'm staring at these when a woman appears—a different one to the dark-haired girl who opened the door to me— at the top of the stairs. The horses still dance in front of my eyes, like spots; beautiful dapple-greys, prancing, legs raised in their green field as I raise my eyes to the woman now motioning me with one curt hand to come upstairs. Creakily, I approach her. I keep my eyes low until I reach the top stair. She is standing with her arms folded and no expression flits across her face when she sees me.

Over here—she points to a bedroom, hovering behind me while I struggle with the brass doorknob. I don't know what I'm expecting—a man in a white coat, a room full of instruments—but instead there is a shabby bedroom, the curtains half-drawn, a bowl and jug at the window, a bed with a sheet on it. Instinctively I avert my eyes from the sheet but I know without checking again that, although it's washed, there are faded stains on it.

You didn't write anything down? The address? she says, and her voice is surprising— a sweet voice, young; the wrong voice for this stiff, peg-like person, holding out her arms for the coat.

My fingers unfold from Freddy's note, so that I can hand the coat to her.

No, I didn't write anything down.

Well, I'll have the money to start off with, she says, her eyes on my handbag. My fingers fumble with the snake-catch, I'm trying to open it but I'm also fighting a rising feeling of nausea, tasting the bile at the back of my throat. I put my hand over my mouth and before I can say a word there is a bowl,

300

magically held beneath me, now splattered with orange and pink flecks. I notice, I can't fail to notice, that one of the specks lands on her thumb. She waits patiently until I've finished heaving and then as swiftly as it appeared, the bowl is whisked away. She wipes her hands on her apron; young hands, like the voice. Only her face is old—a hooked nose, and deep lines between her brows, as if someone wrote the number eleven there in furrows.

The sour smell of vomit creeps around the room. I run my hand over my dry lips and feel their cracks, but I daren't ask her for a glass of water.

All right—you can give me the money after. How many weeks are you?

Six weeks.

I'm shivering like a shorn lamb without the coat and now I've started, I can't seem to stop, a shivering that racks my jaws and seems to rattle the teeth in my head. I'm watching her hands again as she smooths out an old grey towel on the bed. I'm noting that the thumb is wiped clean and that she wears no ring and that her knuckles are prominent, the tendons ridged and raised up. She nods to me: meaning, off with your drawers then and jump up on the bed. She doesn't waste words on me. Her look says: And no need to act so high and mighty like you don't know what you're here for.

Slowly, with the same fumbling fingers that wouldn't open my purse, I start undoing the buttons at each side of the knickers, I drop them down clumsily and step out of them. I look around, wondering when the doctor is going to arrive. The girl seems in a great hurry so I climb up on the bed anyway. She goes to the window and pours some water into a large bowl.

I want to cover my face with my hands, cover my face, smell my own clean hands instead of this room, make the light flood rose-pink in front of my eyes, make this room, make this girl disappear.

Sitting up I try to ask how long the wait for the doctor will be. I thought—my friend said—Dr Carpenter . . .

Dr Carpenter! She sniffs and her dark grey eyes meet mine for the first time.

She leans forward and presses on my knees, and I feel the first cold touch of metal.

I'm Dr Carpenter if you like. If you insist, she mutters.

Her breath brushes my thighs and I think of Freddy, tears hammering at my head, I try with all my energy to push this thought away. I can hear thunder cracking somewhere, in this room or out in the street or deep in my own skull, I've no idea, but there is thunder, a great booming crackling sound and something is breaking, something is snapping in two like old twigs. I'm thinking of nothing, of nothing at all, my eyes are closed and I can see nothing but I can smell sweat and oil and the rust and glint of fresh blood and somewhere on Lower Thames Street there is snapping and cracking and a young woman with knuckles like the coldest of stones, crunching under my feet.

*     *     *

What will I say, today in court, how will I answer when they ask me about those times; first trying the herbs, the pills, then a second time, the worst time, the house? It seems like a million years ago, to think of myself leaving that shabby, dark little house, to discover a great sour fog has replaced the rain and swallowed the city. I'm tapping along Lower Thames Street, flitting from one yellow streetlamp to the next, like a moth. Is it by accident that I end up so close to the river? Suddenly, there I am and there are treacherous wet steps and iron railings, and the grey water, shining like metal, in gap-toothed pockets in the mist. I'm stopping and drawing the fur coat around me, swaying in pain and looking down at the soupy river. What am I thinking about, if I'm thinking at all?

I can remember clearly the water's ridged surface and the feeling of sickness again as I watch the tide travelling swiftly; note the debris that twirls out of the mist and disappears back into it again; and *when,* when did I notice the bag, the brown tied bag, mysteriously dry, bobbing on the skin of the water, pausing long enough in my little patch for me to observe it; lumpy, swollen, a bag of tricks, a bag of kittens, a bag to remind me of the soily bag of hyacinth bulbs that mother flung at my feet, that day, that day I was supposed to be planting a beautiful hyacinth garden.

I'm feeling for my handkerchief, but my fingers fold instead around Freddy's note. Now the bag has floated away, but it's followed swiftly by another, this one swirling gaily; the same bulky shape, the same string dangling from one end dark and stained, pulpy; these bags can't be real, I didn't really see them. These bags must be shame or guilt or terror or something else I'm parcelling up: these bags I didn't know about in those days, I hadn't met Alice, I hadn't overheard Eve, I thought I was the only one who could picture even for one second her own flesh and blood, or her own self floating there, plain and irrelevant as a butcher's bag.

\*       \*       \*

*All eyes are upon me.* That was just a phrase, I'd no idea until these last few months, and again this morning, right now, what it might mean. That eyes have weight, they can land on

304

your clothes and your hair like a swarm of moths or bees, form a great cloud around you. A cloud which feels heavy, strenuous to walk through.

As I'm walking to the witness-box I hear those in the gallery leaning forward, hear the creak of wood as they crane to see me, the whole room lean towards me, like a ship tilting it a vast wave. I hear—or feel—a great stirring from the balcony above as I take my place in the canopied box between the judge and the jury. I keep my eyes fixed on my gloves, carefully removing them. I note the trembling in my hands with the same glance that I note the glass and jug of water in front of me. Just as I note my heartbeat, pounding ferociously.

A male voice in the gallery warns those up there to be quiet, to remain in their seats. I do not glance up at them.

For the first few seconds I hardly hear what is being asked of me, I fumble my replies and the oath and the details of my name and my address but a little voice in my head is urging me: *Only concentrate! Pay attention!* So I try to block out all other things: block out the wardress standing behind me, the green leather chairs of the court-room, the oak panelled box with the jury in it (which seems to be only inches from my nose), block out Mother and Father somewhere amongst the seated people, he with his arm tightly around her, she with her hands in her lap, her white gloved hands, lifeless as two great handfuls of paper. I lift my head up an inch higher and feel my neck creak, I'm so out of practice. I swallow, straighten my shoulders, try to raise my eyes to look at this person, this man in his black robe and his grey wig, who is staring so intently at me.

And was the marriage a happy one?

No, not particularly so. I think I was never really happy with my husband, but for perhaps two years it was better than it had been.

After a lapse of two years were there constant differences and troubles between you?

There were. My husband and I very often discussed the question of separation, long before the June of 1921. I had known the family of Bywaters for some years before 1921. I cannot say that my husband knew them well, but he knew them. In June 1921 I went with my husband to the Isle of Wight for a holiday. The prisoner Bywaters accompanied us, along with my sister. We remained there a week, and then we returned to our house in Ilford, along with Bywaters, who remained there, living with my husband and myself, until 5th August.

During that holiday in the Isle of Wight, and while Bywaters was at your house, had you conceived an affection for him?

No . . .

\*      \*      \*

306

Have you at any time from your marriage until the death of your husband done anything to injure him physically?

Never.

Have you ever been in possession of poison?

Not to my knowledge.

Have you ever administered poison to your husband?

No.

Have you ever given him ground glass in his food or in any form?

Never.

Now come to the letter dated 20th August, 1921 (exhibit 12): Come and see me Monday lunch time, please, darlint. He suspects. What did you mean by, 'he suspects'?

I meant that my husband suspected I had seen Bywaters; I think it was on the Friday previous to that date.

Now, Mrs Thompson, look at the letter (exhibit 27) where you say: I had the wrong porridge today, but I don't suppose it will matter, I don't seem to care much either way. You'll probably say I'm careless and I admit I am, but I don't care—do you? What were you referring to?

I can't really explain.

The suggestion here is that you had from time to time put things into your husband's porridge, glass for instance?

I had not done so.

Can you give us an explanation of what you had in you mind when you said you had the wrong porridge?

Except we had suggested or talked about that sort of thing and I had previously said, 'Oh yes, I will give him something one of these days.'

By Mr Justice Shearman: Did you mean that you had talked about poison?

I did not mean anything in particular.

Turn now to your letter of 10th February (exhibit 15): Darlint, You must do something this time—I'm really impatient—but opportunities come and go by—they have to—because I'm helpless and I think and think and think—perhaps it will never come again. What did you mean by 'You must do something this time?'

I meant he must find me a situation or take me away altogether without one. I had discussed the question of Bywaters finding me a situation and also the place where he was to look for one for me—Bombay, Marseilles, Australia—in fact, anywhere where he had heard of anything.

Come now to exhibit 16 where you write: . . . This thing I am going to do for both of us, will it ever—at all—make any difference between us, darlint, do you understand what I mean? Will you ever think any the less of me—not now, I know, darlint, but later on—perhaps some years hence—do you think you will feel any different, because of this thing I shall do? Darlint, if I thought you would I'd not do it, no not even so that we could be happy for one day, even one hour, I'm not hesitating darlint, through any fear of consequences of the action, don't think that, but I'd sooner go on in the old way for years and years and retain your love and respect. I would like you to write me, darlint, and talk to me about this . . . What was the thing you were going to do for both you and Bywaters?

I was—I was going to go away and live with him without being married to him.

*　　*　　*

My legs are beginning to feel wobbly from holding me so stiffly, my eyes to ache and sizzle from staring, from concentrating so hard. But my voice is louder, a little firmer. I am no longer afraid to speak. This is my one chance, this is what I've been waiting for: to find the words, the exact words to persuade them, all of them, that they have got it wrong.

*　　*　　*

Have you any clear recollection now of what happened when your husband was killed?

Except what I have said; I was dazed.

Is exhibit 4, the short statement, everything

309

you remember, and is it true?

It is true.

Was the statement you made to the police, which I will read to you, your recollection at the time, or was it deliberately untrue: We were coming along Belgrave Road and just past the corner of Endsleigh Gardens when I heard him call out 'O-er' and he fell up against me. I put out my arm to save him and found blood which I thought was coming from his mouth. I tried to hold him up. He staggered for several yards towards Kensington Gardens and then fell against the wall and slid down. He did not speak to me. I cannot say if I spoke to him. I felt him and found his clothing wet with blood. He never moved after he fell. We had no quarrel on the way, we were quite happy together. I did not see anybody about at the time. My husband and I were talking about going to a dance . . . Now did you intend to tell an untruth about the incident?

Yes.

Was that to shield Bywaters?

It was.

In your statement you say: We were coming along Belgrave Road and just past the corner of Endsleigh Gardens when I heard him call out 'O-er' and he fell up against me . . .Does that suggest that he was taken ill, and that nobody was present?

Yes.

Did you intend when you said that, to tell an

untruth?

It was an untruth.

And you intended it to be an untruth?

I did.

Was that to shield Bywaters?

It was.

Were you going to shield him from a charge of having murdered your husband?

I did not know my husband was murdered.

Did you not know your husband had been assaulted and murdered?

The Inspector told me but I did not realise, even at the time, that he was dead.

Inspector Hall had told you your husband was dead?

He had.

Later, when you saw Bywaters in Stratford police station and realised he had been identified by a neighbour and arrested, you became distressed and said I must tell the truth.

I said something like, Why did he do it? I did not want him to do it. I must tell the truth.

Meaning, I must tell the truth about the murder?

Meaning, I must tell the truth that Fred—that Bywaters was present.

Had you any doubt when you were asked by the police about it that it was Bywaters who was there and was the man?

No, I had not.

May I take it that when you made the long

statement, the first statement (exhibit 3) you left out Bywaters' name in order to shield him?

I did.

\*      \*      \*

But the point where my voice cracks, where I have to take a sip of water, where the noise of my own swallowing nearly deafens me and the glass panes in the ceiling threaten to splinter and land on me, is not during cross-examination by the Solicitor-General. I'm exhausted after that, but mostly steady now, I have to remain at the witness stand until Sir Henry completes his questioning. I know I have been flustered and confused and what I have done and said has come out sounding more deceitful, more deliberate than I intended.

Then comes one small question from Sir Henry, gently asked. And did you love him very much? And it's so, so hushed again in here and I feel, not eyes this time landing on me, but breath; as if all those in the public gallery have opened their mouths as one and would now like to swallow me right up.

I did, I say, brokenly, with the words, *I do*, echoing in my head. I understand somehow that Sir Henry has phrased the question in the past tense so that my answer will not come out like a wedding vow. At this moment, he wants no reference to marriage or adultery to exist in the minds of those listening. Only the word *love*. He is a clever man, a brilliant, powerful, wonderful man. He asks me if I did everything in my power to help Percy, after he was attacked. I assure him that I did. Everything I possibly could. The court adjourns.

*       *       *

Sir Henry knocks on the door and says, Be brave, Mrs Thompson, bear up. It's time now. The jury have reached their verdict.

The wardress takes a loud breath and stands up, the policeman shuffles towards the door. I stand up, too. I feel like my eyes are closed; all I'm aware of is her arm, the woman at my left; the grip of her fingers and the snap of her heels on the scuffed wooden floor.

*       *       *

I have my eye on the one lady in the jury but she won't return my gaze. I skim briefly the four or five other women in the room but my eyes return to her. She is a thin lady, young, with a navy blue velour dress and a Napolean-shaped hat in almond green, and the hat is not one of ours. I'm trying to tell from the trembling under her chin, from the trembling in the room in general, what it is that the judge is saying, but although I'm listening and

313

listening, I can't hear a thing. It's like that time when I sat in the police cell at Stratford, whispering to myself Percy is dead Percy is dead but I couldn't make it feel true. The judge is wearing a queer black square over his wig and he says: there taken to a place where you shall be . . . and may the Lord have mercy . . . and his mouth is moving and words are floating out from his lips and they are wafting over all our heads, like the finest plume of smoke and there is silence, absolute silence, where blood stops and breathing ceases and yet his mouth is definitely moving, something important is most surely being said.

THE ILFORD MURDER TRIAL

A murder trial which, for no very clear reasons, has absorbed the public attention came to an end at the Central Criminal Court yesterday. A Mrs Thompson and her paramour, Frederick Bywaters, were both found *Guilty* of the murder of Mr Thompson and sentenced to death. There were no circumstances in the case to evoke the slightest sympathy. The crime was pre-meditated and long contemplated. There was a multitude of love letters, which as Mr Justice Shearman said in his summing up to the jury, showed that the woman was seeking the assistance of Bywaters 'in the removal of her husband by the administration of poison'. Apparently no poison was given, but Mr Thompson was stabbed to death by Bywaters in a lonely road. The whole case was simple and sordid. As the judge said it was an ordinary charge of a wife and an adulterer murdering the husband. For that reason it is hard to understand why the entrance to the Court has been besieged day by day by men and women. It is extraordinary that persons should squat outside a Criminal Court at midnight in the hope of gaining admission next morning to hear a trial which presented really no features of romance, and which provided none of the horrors that appeal to the morbid mind. There were, no doubt, some of the elements of the *crime passionnel*, but that extenuating term has never received a welcome in this country.

*The Times,* Tuesday December 12th, 1922

\*         \*         \*

It's after lights-out and I'm trying to fall asleep; I'm heavy and full with medicines from Dr Lynch. It's as if the stupor of a heavy meal is weighing me down; but every time I close my eyes I can hear the hiss of a match striking against a shoe and the room is filled with a sudden yellow flare and I can see his mouth again, the shiny snake of blood seeping down his chin, and then I'm sitting up with my heart leaping and leaping and the room is black and someone is screaming, the most distressing kind of scream in all the world, and then footsteps are outside the door and there's shouting and jangling of keys; then there are arms around me and a pillow near my face, and the rough texture of their grey flannel uniforms, the bulk of Clara, her arm cradling my head saying, Ssshhh now, come on now, Mrs Thomspon, Edith, that's enough now, and the smell all around me again, that same smell that was in my nostrils that night in October; it's a human smell, I think that human beings produce it, maybe it is even me who is producing it. I think it is what fear smells like. Then the prick in my arm from another of their needles and the screaming evaporates. For an hour or two at least, I know I'll be able to enter the warm dark sleeves of a longed-for sleep.

*December 17th, 1922*

Darlint,
I'm sorry not to have written sooner. I know you must be terribly worried about me. I'm going to try really hard to get Clara or Eve, I think probably Eve, whom I sometimes feel I

316

may have won over, to smuggle a letter out to you.

Actually I've been in the prison infirmary since the trial and have just been allowed out. I can't remember much about it, so there is no need for you to worry. You would smile right now if you saw your Peidi, for despite everything—I'm gaining weight! Dr Lynch thinks it's extraordinary, but he has no explanation to offer. He does not wish to examinine me properly for the reasons I once gave to you—the man is ludicrously fastidious and can't bear to touch women if he can avoid it. He's more concerned to fill me full of various medicines which, I must agree, do seem to dull any kind of mental pain and make me positively light-headed. Of course he doesn't administer them for my benefit; it's to stop me screaming and moaning, as I disturb the other prisoners.

I didn't mean to mention the screaming there and I want you to forget that I said that.

It is quite different now that we are not on remand, is it not? I am in a different room now (I will call it a room and think of this place as the Holloway Hotel. I found a little poem on the inside of one of the books in the library: *Oh where shall I spend my holiday? Is often the Londoner's wail; Well, if you fail your rates to pay, You may spend* it *in Holloway Gaol!*).

This room is near the exercise yard—I mean near the sweeping hotel lawns—so that in the mornings if it is not my turn, I can hear the steps of the other women, going round and round. The biggest difference of all is that now I am expected to work! I'm not permitted to sit in my cell room all day by myself, but have to sit beading cloth or making bead curtains in a viciously cold room, right next to the kitchens, so that the boiled cabbage and carbolic smell seeps right into my skin and all day long the rattle of beads rings in my ears, only punctuated by a sudden splash and hiss when a whole box of them is knocked to the floor.

Worst of all, Freddy, is that now I can't escape the gaze and chatter of the other women, although so far I have not said one word in reply. The wardresses treat me differently too—coldly, not on account of the verdict, but because we are never alone together and there is no chance for privacy.

I am sure all can tell that the drugs are stupefying me and put my rudeness down to that. But in truth it's rather frightening. Guess who has the sharpest eyes and the quickest fingers in the whole of Holloway and has therefore been put to work in the beading room? Yes, Old Alice. She sits right across from me, with her nasty little tongue darting out of the corner of her mouth as she threads and her legs crossed so that the prison dress which is stretched too tightly across he makes her look like a bundle of beads herself, about to burst right open and explode all over the floor . . .

The other women don't talk to her but they talk amongst themselves. It is easy enough to conjecture what they are in here for: the young ones who titter occasionally at their own obscene jokes and call each other Dollymop or Judy in all freedom are the prostitutes. Their stay is usually fleeting it seems and they treat the rest of us with scorn. The shoplifters are the poorest and although I never noticed this before, I mean in the world outside, it's easy to tell somehow from their skin, a certain quality of their skin, where it seems not to fit their bones, as if they never had flesh enough beneath it to fill the space, that they have probably been poor from the moment they were born.

Then there are the drunks, abortionists and the fraudsters. Murderesses are something special as far as I can gather. It seems that just at the moment, or as far as it is possible for me to know, there's only Alice and me and one other woman in here right now. The other woman seems almost a child—she looks little more than sixteen. She killed her baby, locking it in a suitcase and leaving it in a railway carriage, when she was afraid her family would find out that she had given birth. I remember hearing of it six months ago, do you, Freddy?

So even here where you might think there is no social hierarchy I can take pleasure in the fact that whenever I walk into the beading room, with Eve or Wardress Jones or one of the other wardresses behind me, a little ripple runs through them all, like the ripple that runs through a bead jacket when you shake it. I suppose they have heard of my sentence. Of course, I have a sense that everyone is treating me with kid gloves. You may be surprised at my mentioning 'the sentence', darlint, but the stance I took in the very beginning, of not thinking at all, well, I've decided that that didn't get me very far. In any case with so much strychnine flooding my veins I really feel numb and don't mind if my thoughts occasionally land on the subject and pause there—like a fly exploring a cowpat—for a hovering moment before moving on.

Sir Henry has visited me once but that is another difference about no longer being on remand. I can't have visitors every day and have to wait until Thursdays. (Don't be alarmed by this letter by the way, I'm endlessly pricking myself in that dreadful beading room and blood has just smeared over the page. I hope you can read this writing.) You mustn't be anxious if I don't write as often as I used to—one because I'm not always lucid these days and two because I have less privacy and time to myself and my fingers are always occupied with beading.

I can have visits from Piper however and he will be coming tomorrow morning. Sir Henry said that there will be an appeal on 22nd

December—only five days away, and as ever I remain optimistic about that, as you must too, darlint. According to Sir Henry many people are against the sentence and an appeal for clemency has been circulated which thousands are signing. Last time Avis came—before the trial—she said that she had spoken to Florrie about you and Florrie said that you were playing draughts with your warders an seemed hollowed-out and pale but not otherwise distraught. I know you best and I know what such behaviour hides.

For once, for the first time, I don't know what to say to you. Only that I love you and am thinking of you, but, Freddy, this is going to sound cruel, and also an understatement.

I wish you hadn't done it.

Edie.

\*　　　\*　　　\*

Piper, young Piper, here he is again. He flicks through the Bible, he folds down the pages with comforting passages. But he's premature. I'm not quite ready yet. His neck is red as a rash, he trembles still, I notice the trembling in his hands as he sits with the Bible he gave to me on his knee and the wet dog smell seeps into the room with him. It seems to cling to his suit and his hair and I'm tempted to ask him, does he actually keep a dog, has he a secret dog hidden in the Chaplain's House, that he feeds milk to and permits to sleep on his knee . . . I know it would be forbidden.

He watches me smoke, holding the matches as he no doubt has instructions to, lest I set fire to the whole prison. These days, too, he calls me 'Edith'.

I draw on the cigarette, rocking myself a little, making my bed squeak. The noise makes him uncomfortable, his colour rises a little.

I'm sure I saw you in court, Chaplain. Were you there or was I—mistaken?

I've noticed that my words come out slowly these days, they join together or break up in the wrong places, the way a drunk's words do. It must be the after-effect of so much strychnine pumping through my system. It is a pleasure to watch Piper flush. Watch the deep scarlet flood up his face from the neck upwards. It reminds me of my years at school, how we would tease certain boys who reddened more easily than others.

I was there once. Yes. Not from prurience you understand. From concern for you, Edith.

I've noticed that you don't ask me to pray for a—reprieve . . . do you think I'd be wasting my time?

I'm rocking harder, the noise a satisfying kind of purrpurr squeak purrpurr squeak and the steps of a curious wardress can be heard outside. Piper glances at the spy-hole and then back to me and seems to bite back something he wants to say.

It is never a waste of time to pray, never a sparrow falls but God hears it, Edith . . .

Yes, but what I mean is—will he grant my prayer if I ask him, or will I be wasting my breath?

I can't begin to speak for Our Lord and how he operates. His will is a mystery to us.

The squeaking is loud now and I'm aware that I'm doing it but I'm not sure I'm able to stop. It's the medicine again. Everything feels as if I'm under water. Outside noises, events, people filter through but inner ones have equal strength and it's hard to judge how loud something is, how silly or extreme. For instance, maybe the squeak is a tiny sound, maybe only I can hear it.

Let me put it this way. If I'm innocent, God won't let me—let my—let the sentence be carried out, would he?

Again, that is not for me to say! His voice is rising and his hands clasp at the closed Bible and he is squeezing it, squeezing the pages in a very strange fashion. Innocent people do suffer, Edith. Look at our own dear Lord who suffered on the cross—

I hope you're praying for me, Chaplain, because surely you have more sway.

I am praying, Edith, I am!

This comes out as almost a shout. The Bible slips from his knee to the floor with a great thudding crash and he bends, flustered, to pick it up, placing it instead on the tray where my food is normally placed. Amidst all the noise, the squeaking bed and the tray rattling I try to speak carefully and softly to be sure that he will hear me beneath the cacophony.

If I was—a good Christian—a believer, do you think I'd have more chance to be saved? I thought you said—I'm sure you said in chapel last week—that like the lost lamb, God cared more for the one sinner—the one—lost sheep than he did for the other ninety-nine who were safely at his side . . .

I think I'm saying this in a deathly small voice, pale and flat. Again it's hard to tell but Piper looks alarmed, I'd say he looks as if he's panicking.

Only the Lord can truly judge us, Edith. Mere mortals make mistakes.

Ah ha!

Now I leap up and Piper makes a sudden movement, a swift intake of breath in a loud gulp, like someone slurping their tea.

You think the judge was wrong, don't you? You think my sentence should be commuted!

Oh, Edith, it's not for me to say. It's not for me to raise your hopes. My job is to offer solace, to pray for you and with you if you want me to, and to prepare you—prepare you—

A sob breaks and Piper sinks his head in his hands. The room seems to shake and blur as if someone had hold of it and was shaking both of us together inside it, throwing us from one end to the other like passengers in a ship, buffeted by enormous waves. Now I can't tell if I'm crying or Piper is, but the sound of sobbing is racking the air around us.

All those people praying! A million signatures you said, on a petition! You know I'm innocent! Freddy will be praying and Mother and Avis, and you and you and—

Piper raises his head from his hands, his eyes are dark and sunken and they are full of something so terrible, that I can't stare into them, am afraid to dive in, lest I never resurface. Piper is mumbling, over and over, Our Father who art in Heaven, Our Father who art in Heaven . . .

But he can't touch me. He can no more rise from his chair and put his woolly arms around me than I can get up off this bed, spread my wings and fly right out of here, free as a bird.


*21st December, 1922*
*9 p.m.*


Darlint,
I have a terrible terrible headache as I write this—I feel as if a great lump of coal was alight in my head—but realising the date, I've roused myself from my bed to write to you and to try to raise your spirits, knowing you will be, as I am, thinking about tomorrow, the appeal hearing. (The headache seems to be due to the

325

fact that I'm now constantly squinting to see that troubling shadowy thread in the corner of my eye which shifts from vision whenever I try to look at it head on.)

I'm so sorry that I don't feel well enough to attend the appeal hearing tomorrow—I don't want you to worry if I tell you this, but over the last few mornings, my waking sensation is of a powerful and somewhat frightening nausea, and in the afternoons I can hardly stay awake—but I want you to know that I am there with you in spirit. Every minute of every hour tomorrow I will be hoping and trusting and knowing that so many prayers are being sent our way that I am sure good sense will prevail. Sir Henry has been for a brief visit and told me in his great booming voice to 'have faith' and to 'pray for common sense' to triumph.

I always did have the ability, didn't I, Freddy, to believe that all would come out right in the end? You told me many times it was a quality you loved in me.

You remember I told you once that if you didn't like the endings in novels, you should do as I do and make up your own. I believe I've always been good at that. I've struggled since the sentence was read out in court to believe that this would not be my end. I continue to believe that, darlint, and you must, too. I believe we create our own destinies through the power of our imagination, through the

326

things we will for ourselves. Despite all Piper says to me, I can't believe in his version of God's design, God's plan for us. We can be happy, I'm sure of it, but perhaps happiness has to be clawed at, scratched and dug up, the way a dog digs dementedly for a bone, with the scent of promise in his nose to spur him on. The thought that it is there, it is there, somewhere!

I always had that sense. I knew it was possible and it will be, it *will* be, Freddy.

I will not sleep at all tonight. I will keep this letter to you under my pillow, safe in the knowledge that one day soon I will be able to give it to you in person.

Your own darlint Peidi.


*22nd December, 1922*
*(early hours of the morning—I've no idea but the light trickling in through the window is pink)*

Darlint,
Since I wrote my last letter to you I've thought a lot, and somewhat coolly about the events of 3rd October. Seeing the knife in court—that huge, rusty knife! Hearing the details all over again—a new thought struck me for the first time. I have to write this, painful though it is, because I have to tell you, Freddy, just in case I don't have another chance to—that I saw you clearly for the very first time today. As if a pea-

souper had cleared all around me. I know I was dazed, I know it is true that it all happened so quickly and so suddenly but last night I saw you, not with your sea-blue eyes, but with your deep cleft of a chin, the cleft that I told you in another letter reminds me of a child's bottom! I saw you absurd and silly and cruel and mistaken and bloody and angry and I saw what you are capable of. *Three stab wounds on the body. One wound penetrated to the spine.* The knife raising up and back, up and back, and sinking through skin and flesh and bone and glistening with blood. *A second wound was situated at the right side of the neck and a short distance below and behind the angle of the jaw.* And I'm crying and crying—*Oh, don't!*—and poor Percy is struggling and making that horrible gurgling sound, but you keep right on. *It passed upwards and inwards and penetrated into the floor of the mouth.* And I thought: that is Freddy. That is the man I know. But did I know that he was capable of that, for all that we might have talked of it? No. Until today, I had no idea. I could not really see what you did, even though I was there. Today, just as I was waking, I witnessed it with my own eyes.

\*       \*       \*

Now the Governor is standing in my cell and there can only be one reason. He has a letter

328

in his hand, a letter from the Home Office, he has Piper standing beside him (although, in truth, Piper seems to be edging behind him, a naughty child hiding behind his big brother) and with the key dangling from a long chain, there also is Clara, her great broad arms folded, her expression as blank as a piece of wood.

Yes, I hear perfectly what the Governor is saying. From the moment he opens his mouth to utter, I'm sorry Mrs Thompson, . . . I know exactly what is being said and my legs are turning to liquid and a thin dark tunnel is rising up in front of me but I'm fighting to keep breathing, struggling not to enter it. The Governor waves his letter in front of him, the white letter, the red seal; a bloody handkerchief, a nose bleed, the night at Shanklin we ruined the pillowcase. The Governor waves his letter, fearfully, defensively; not like a handkerchief, but more like a flag.

Piper and Clara dart forward and hold out their arms. I suppose I must be crashing towards them from a great height. The grey room retreats to a pin-prick.

*  *  *

*Judy leaves the baby with Punch, the baby cries, so Punch throws it down and kills it, then Judy returns and quarrels with him and of course he*

329

*kills her too, and also the Policeman who comes to arrest him and the Black Man and the Crocodile. The boxers have a round of fisticuffs for no reason whatsoever. Then the ghost of Judy comes to awaken Punch's conscience and Master Marwood the Executioner comes to carry him off. Master Marwood has staring eyes and a down-turned mouth and a little wooden gallows in one hand. He has a pink tennis ball for a face and a bald patch on the middle of his brown-painted head. He has a grubby black dress and a white collar at his throat—he doubles up as a priest. He has a gallows with a swinging rope, flopping around with him, thumping heavily onto the stage sometimes, making the audience jump.*

*Everyone else boos at Master Marwood, but Freddy is laughing.*

*Master Marwood the Executioner with his ridiculous parody of an unhappy mouth, the shape of a segment of orange. He's just a jest, he's a jape, he's floppy, meaningless, a jack-in-the box joke, nothing to worry about at all. I'm me, I'm Edith, this can't happen to me!*

*A gallows, a tiny wooden gallows, to entertain a crowd.*

*And now at last I know what that thread is, distracting me, teasing me, making my head ache, hanging over me. I probably could have seen it all along, if only I'd opened my eyes just that little bit wider. Master Marwood with his orange segment mouth, ready to flip over and play the part of the priest at the drop of a hat.*

*Master Marwood waving the gallows in one hand, the loop of rope in the other.*

# CHAPTER TEN

Marriage—it's not all it's cracked up to be you know, I am saying to Avis. I don't know why you're in such a hurry to tie the knot.

I'm not! Avis's voice with its familiar squeak, rising an octave at the insinuation. We're on the top deck of the number 25 from Cranbrook Road, travelling up to the West End, to Simpson's, to be exact. Avis wants to do some Christmas shopping. I haven't seen her in a while and this seems like the perfect occasion for a proper talk, to find out where she and Freddy really stand. But the conversation keep taking off at a tangent. (Perhaps knowing that Avis is the wrong choice, utterly, the wrong choice to confide in about Percy, but persisting any way, a roundabout route to finding out if she has seen Freddy, or heard from him.)

There's so much that's just routine and work and everything loses its—glow—when you have to do it night after night, whether you want to or not . . .

Avis starts to blush, a deep pink chasing up her throat to her cheeks.

But—well, Edie, I think you're only speaking for yourself—about yourself and Percy and—not everyone feels the way you do—

Not everyone's married to Percy Thompson!

The tartness in my voice makes her turn to stare at me. The colour is still in her cheeks but in her usual stubborn way she is persisting, acting unembarrassed.

Percy does love you very much.

This sentence stings me and I stare away from her, out of the window.

Sometimes . . . (I say this quietly, less forcefully, daring myself.) Sometimes, I'm really quite afraid of him.

Great clumps of grey snow float to the street below, dissolve into slush, coat the tops of cars, the tails of horses, the shop awnings, umbrellas, the signs outside the theatres on Shaftesbury Avenue. I don't know why her remark that Percy loves me irks so. Isn't it what I'd expect? Avis sticking up for Percy. Refusing to see just how bad things might be. Even that time I showed her the trace of a bruise fading on my cheek. What was it she said? It's the drink. He's a good man, really, except for the drink.

All marriages go through bad patches, she blunders on.

Bad patches! This has been one big bad patch for the last seven years!

Her obstinate cheeriness goads me, makes

me want to tell her other things, worse things. I reach in my handbag for a cigarette, offer her one, knowing she'll shake her head. An elderly gentleman in the seat behind us makes a tutting sound with his tongue, as I light it, so I try my best to blow a smoke ring over my shoulder, in his direction.

I really think I shall ask Percy for a divorce.

Edie! You wouldn't!

The shock in her voice is satisfying. At last *something* has hit its mark. Now I feel that the entire bus is listening, although in truth that would be very difficult, over the sound of the engine and the general hubbub and chatter of children at the back. It's our stop next; we both stand up and move towards the stairs, Avis suddenly running back to the seat for her gloves, rejoining me, a little breathless as the bus jerks to a halt at Piccadilly Circus.

I'm thinking: Another missed chance! How can I ask her if she has seen him—if she has feelings still for Freddy?

But I think now that if I'd really wanted to know the answer, I'd have found the occasion during that year, that long year of letters and meetings and dreaming of Freddy. I'd have found the moment somehow.

*25th December, 1922*

Fred,

I'm sorry I haven't written to you sooner.

Today is my birthday, as you know.

Avis came to visit and Mother and Father.

We had carols in the prison chapel. I can still hear them now, the women with their dreadful wispy voices.

*God rest ye merry gentlemen, Let nothing ye dismay . . .*

As I fainted I have been brought back to my room.

There is a cup of cocoa turning cold on my tray. They make it with water you know. I'm hardly eating a thing, but I'm gaining weight at a remarkable rate! It's quite strange and combined with the nausea in the mornings, and the natural miss that I've had since I've been inside, I find myself wondering—but what is the point of wondering? Sometimes they weigh me up to three times a day! In court, I remember the question, is there any reason why the sentence might not be carried out—a question they asked only of me, not of you, darlint, and the official next to me whispered: Is there? And I said, in a daze, not knowing what she meant: No. Now I understand her. My life is worth nothing. But if I'd been carrying another . . . But I can't think straight. I think it must be too late.

*Remember Christ Our Saviour was born on Christmas Day*

*To save poor souls from Satan's power . . .*
I never can remember the third line.

I don't know what to write any more, darlint.

I love you. I thank you for what you gave me. *Glad tidings of comfort and joy, comfort and joy, and glad tidings of comfort and joy . . .*

What a strange carol to sing in a prison.

Love, Edie.

*7th January, 1923*

My Dear Avis,

I'm writing this just before bedtime, which is the one moment I get in a very busy day to be quiet and to be left alone and to think a little. I need some extra pills to help me sleep but I need to be lucid to write this so am avoiding taking them.

I feel dreadfully sad that whenever we see each other here, real conversation is impossible. The presence of the wardress like a great dark crow in the corner of the room, the strain of remaining optimistic, of relating trivial news to one another, of trying not to waste the hour in weeping and wailing . . . all of these things prevent an honest discourse between us.

I know that Mother and Father aren't strong; the job will fall to you to take care of them. I can see already how you are doing this,

335

how much you have grown up in the last few months and I congratulate you—truly!—for surprising us all in this way.

Now you are not to waste time in regrets about anything, anything at all, for I know that you have laboured for me in all respects, I know that you have written to the King, I know that you have sacrificed all your dignity and shyness in speaking out and seeking an audience when you would naturally want to hide in the house, but you knew it had to be done. And I appreciate all of it, Avis. If it all comes to nought it will not be for want of trying, of that I'm sure.

Please don't be shocked that I can write in such a pessimistic way. I am no longer hopeful of any kind of reprieve and the effort of trying to remain so has been exhausting. I have to get these matters off my chest. Writing frees me from some of the sensitivities that still constrain me in person. That, I suppose, is why I love to write so much. I know that you said you could not have believed I'd written those letters, unless you had seen them with your own eyes. I know that you intend this disbelief as a compliment to me. But in truth, I am puzzled by your remarks.

I am not sure which parts of my letters you are so convinced I could not have written. Do you mean my ardent lines to Freddy? I can't believe that you really did not know that your sister was not modest or delicate or afraid to express herself openly. I'm sure you had some inkling or another in all our years together of my robust physical nature, just as I had a sense—without us needing to speak of it—of your chaste nature, so different from mine.

I suppose what you are really saying is that you can't believe your sister would write those things about poison and pieces of light globes. But, Avis, I don't think it's true that you didn't know I was unhappy. That I had grown to dwell night and day in the most compelling way, on the possibility of a way out of my situation with Percy, however desperate or remote that possibility might be. Suicide, murder, escaping to another country, running away with Freddy—surely anyone suffering as I was and with my impassioned nature would have dreamed of such things. It is not a crime to daydream, to *imagine*, is it, Avis, after all? But perhaps it *is* a crime to write such thoughts down in black and white.

Avis, I know you are only trying to be loyal and struggling to maintain the best opinion of me that you possibly can and I can't blame you for that. But I must be honest now with you, as this may be my very last chance. It feels as though you don't really see me properly, as though you are trying to block out a side of me. Like those dolls we had, do you remember them? One way up the skirts fell in pink and lemon lace, then flip them over and underneath they wore a witch's black skirt and carried a broom! No need to remind you which of those dolls you loved best, which one you never flipped over to play with.

When I remember the summer we spent in Shanklin I picture that photograph we had taken on the beach, all four of us. Percy sucking on his pipe and Freddy squinting into the sun and me without a hat and you, you broad-brimmed and healthy, clutching at your white gloves. I try to keep from thinking this, but the thought won't stay away. That a year from now, of the four of us, only you will be able to look at that photograph again. You know what I am saying, Avis. Like those glass phials of coloured sand. Only the one strand would be left and all the others ebbed away without a trace. And that one strand alone will feel pointless, lost, broken . . . bewildered, trying to exist without the others. I do know that.

Sometimes in the past, I have wondered why it was that no matter how bad things were, I never seemed to be able to enlist your sympathy. I remember how infuriating and hurtful I found it when I told you about Percy or tried to talk to you before our wedding, or . . . or the time not so long ago when I hinted, I hinted really heavily about having had a miss and you . . . you just seemed to ignore what I was saying. How maddening I found it, I don't mind telling you, that you dismissed things so readily, that you persisted in wearing your cheeriness like a kind of armour against anything ugly, any kind of truth I might try to introduce. One remark stays firmest in my mind, it was when you said, Oh, all husbands are like that and I thought: but you don't have one, how can you know? In that respect I thought you were so much like Mother. Always advising me to accept my lot, or to remember that others have life harder than me, rather than the other possibility which also exists: that there are those who have things easier!

Lately, I have felt sorry for harbouring all these petty angers towards you, Avis, and I want so much to get them off my chest, to tell you that I realise now that the remarks you made were never intended to hurt. I think you always intended to comfort me, trying to chivvy me out of a despair. Perhaps you were envious. It must have been hard for you, seeing that your sister was loved, despite all her waywardness, while you who never hurt a fly, who deserves love above all others, sometimes were denied it. Perhaps you felt frightened for me, perhaps you saw long ago the direction my dissatisfactions were taking me in.

I have decided lately that there are two kinds of people in this world and what will make one kind happy, will never work for the other. Some people desire nothing more than to be comfortable, to offend no one, to create no waves. I used to think that such people were cowards, hiding from their true nature, unlike me, who was in active and painful pursuit of it. Now I believe that they are not hiding from anything, they truly do want nothing more than to find a safe corner in the world and curl into it, like a cat finding the sunniest spot in the house.

But for others, for me, that would never do. Just because something hasn't been tried before doesn't mean that it can't exist. Such a lot has been made of my imagination—yes, I admit freely it has a lot to do with my current predicament. 'Gush'—isn't that what the judge said, about the books I read, the writing of my letters? If my crime in their eyes was to have too much imagination I think it was also to have an excess of sentimentality. But was it *sentimental* to find the way Percy treated me intolerable and to long sometimes, to escape? Is the private world of the bedroom really so irrelevant, when it is also the theatre where the most significant dramas of a woman's life are spent? Most of the women in Holloway seem to be here due to one or another act on that particular stage.

I hope some of this is making sense. I am not trying to criticise you, only to say that I understand at last that you and I are not the same and neither can change who we are. There is only one respect where I think that we are similar and that is one which many of our sex might be said to suffer from. I believe we both have an unnaturally exaggerated sense of guilt. It has been hard for me to claim innocence, when in so many general ways— and there are still things that I could never talk to you about—I do indeed feel vaguely guilty. But, as I say, it seems our lot as the fairer sex to carry this feeling more than men do. I've never heard a man even speak of it.

A lady has been to visit me in here, you might have heard of her—Mrs Margery Fry? She tells me she is 'quite exercised' by my case and will be doing all she can on my behalf. She knows some very important people she told me, Mrs Virginia Woolf and Mr T.S. Eliot, and she's quite an influential person. I don't think she likes me much but she is trying her best, Avis, so you must always hold your head up high, wherever you go, safe in the knowledge that there are others who believe as you do, in the injustice of my sentence.

But it's now so important for me to say, Avis, that you were always the warmest of sisters, so kind, such a good sport, so generous. The business with Freddy—how difficult we've found it to talk of it and yet I know that you knew, long, long ago and I know that you chose to say nothing, in your typical way, through a mixture of love and loyalty I suppose, or perhaps wanting to believe the best of your sister.

I'm sorry for mentioning Freddy. Thank you

for all that you have done for me . . . if there is anything of mine that you want, anything you can bear to keep . . . the blue velour dress, my best fur. Please give Florrie the mole-coloured cloche and the lilac suit that Freddy bought me, if she will accept them. My gold and purple knitted jacket, the mauve voile dress with the embroidered bodice and hem; that silver beaded bag you always loved . . . do, please, keep it.

I only ask one thing of you. I don't ask it of anyone else, not even God, for I have no need of it, but I do ask you, Avis. Please forgive me for everything, if you can find it in your heart to do so.

Your loving sister,
Edith.

*     *     *

A bell is ringing, a tiny bell, shaken in someone's hand. The sky is rosy and the birds are twittering to each other; the happiest, most melancholy sound in the world. And now the door is opening and here's Eve. She's crying, great tears streaming down her face. She puts a finger to her lips, she looks like a teacher. I know I must be silent.

Opening her palm to show me what she has brought and then closing her fingers again.

I step into my shoes without lacing them. My eyes are only half open and I cannot say whether I am awake or dreaming. I follow Eve down labyrinth corridors and out into the yard, follow the click of her pointed heels, the big bow of her prison apron.

She turns once.

I'm leaving today. I've said I can't do it. I can't go into that wooden box with you tomorrow and I've lost me job over it.

I open my mouth but no sound comes out; like dreaming, like nightmares. Mute screaming.

In the courtyard the square of earth at the centre glitters with frost. I've never been here when it is empty like this. The sky sits on top of us like a neat pink box, like the inside of a mouth. Eve takes me to the centre square of earth and kneels beside it. She takes her big key, hanging from a chain at her waist and begins digging. The tears keep flowing, bouncing off the end of her chin, splashing her hands and her arm. My own face is dry and iced over, like the frosted ground. I'm shivering from head to toe.

Four mouths to feed! Four mouths to feed! What am I going to do? She sits back on her heels. Her tiny eyes are swollen, her nose red and pointed. She is holding out her palm again, holding three hyacinth bulbs and showing me the rough pockets in the ground she's made for them.

And so I take one of the bulbs and turn it in my palm and then bring it to my face to smell the earthy blue smell. Something like new eggs still warm from under a chicken, stuck with the odd feather. I press it into the earth. I scatter earth on top of it. I feel the earth seeping under my nails: this will be the last texture, the last egg-shaped object. This digging, these birds, the last sounds. This person, this ferocious little woman I hardly know. I could say thank you to her. I try out the words quietly. My voice comes out like the sound a bird makes; a squawk; meaningless. Eve gives no sign that she's heard me.

And then I'm fainting or sleeping or waking again, I'm not sure which, but there are shiny green shoots already sticking up, just like fingers; balled-up fists at each centre I bend to sniff them and the smell rises up to me; a plump, haunting, grassy smell. I almost want to bite into them but she is at the window, she is calling me from inside the house. I dust my knees and run in, glancing back at the flower beds. Thirty green gloved hands, slender fingers clutching at the air, waving to me. The ivory white flower is L'Innocence, the midnight blue is Marie, or perhaps Madame Kruger; the rose pink is Lady Derby, the magenta is La Victoire. Spreading their fingers wide, waving their gloved hands like a great swarm of colourful school children, standing on the platform while the train pulls slowly away from the station.

The garden, shortly after we moved to Manor Park. Mother was so proud of that garden—I know that it signified everything to her. I must have been around six. I remember the sight of her white cotton gloves, the machine-embroidery in a pattern of leaves at the cuffs; pale flat shadows of her hands on the grass beside us, and the dirt under my own nails, my childish stubby fingers. I was digging deep, just for the joy of it, the black earth rolling under my fingers, making little pockets for the hyacinth bulbs to pop into.

I think she was watching me. I was aware of the cold hard grass, damp seeping through my skirt and into my knees, and wanting to lift the skirt, and let my stockinged limbs out, free them. I felt her gaze before she sat back on her heels, in one hand a bulb, fat and smooth, turning it over and over as she spoke.

That's your trouble, Edie. I can see it right enough. You expect too much. You think it's a right, happiness, or something to wait for. It isn't. You'd be better off learning that right away. Save a lot of heartbreak, in the long term, a lot of disappointment.

I sat back on my heels in deliberate mimickry and I pushed my fringe away from my eyes to stare back at her. I knew from some instinct that she didn't like it when I did that and soon she dropped her own eyes, began busying herself putting bulbs in the homes I'd made for them. Wanted to act, I thought, as if she hadn't spoken at all.

I may have been only a child but I felt it strongly, remember it vividly. My thought was this: you're speaking of yourself. That's not true, that's not true for me. *Edie, don't expect to be happy.* I was happy, happy in a way that she has never known, albeit briefly. I'm sure of it. It's funny but at the time I felt myself trembling with rage, trembling with dislike of her. *That kind of advice is not going to help me, because I'm different from you and you don't know everything about me.*

We worked together in silence after that. She was proud of the garden and of the success of her work, she was proud of having a garden at all, after the little terrace at Stamford Hill. But when the hyacinths flowered that spring I was in trouble again. I'd mixed up the bulbs. I'd handed her ones randomly, from different, carefully labelled boxes, which I'd chosen not to read. She was at the other side of me, she couldn't see the boxes. All the colours all together—L'Innocence, Lady Derby, Distinction, Gertrude, Chestnut Flower, Queen of the Pinks, Queen of the Blues, La Victoire; a riot of colour and not what she expected at all. She wanted an entirely blue patch of earth, in the style popular at the time, then in the next bed a pink square bed, and so on. And instead of this she had an unruly blaze that was due to my mischief.

I think it was that moment when the chalk fell on a particular square, when I hopscotched and leapt right onto that square, marked with an arrow and the words, *This way, Ediel!*

I can't blame Freddy, no, not really. If I trace it back that far, I have to admit. At that time, Freddy Bywaters wasn't even born.

*     *     *

Send them away, I don't want to see them, I scream, I can't see them—send them all away! and I'm putting my hands up in front of me, as if someone is coming to attack me. Someone is: it's Dr Lynch again with the strychnine, rolling up my sleeve and catching me gracelessly as I slump to the bed.

So Eve marches over in her official capacity and pretends to be lifting me to an upright position on the tin-sounding bed, but under her breath she's whispering: Selfish, you are . . . bloody selfish . . . think of *them*! So that dimly, yes, I'm aware that she has lost her job, that tomorrow, when I'm no longer here—and it's not that the phrase has any meaning but it can *form* in any event, in my mind, as phrases are wont to do—tomorrow her struggles will continue. Her four little mouths to feed.

So she and Dr Lynch and then Piper, too, half walk, half carry me, into the visitors' room with the one wooden desk, the metal waste paper bin, where the Governor is standing with Mother, Father and Avis. Never did a set of people ever look so much the same, so patently cut from one piece of cloth as these three people do, just now, staring at me, with faces like three stark white clocks, stuck on one hour, one moment.

I'm scarce even here, if truth be told, but with what consciousness I have left, I'm trying to move forward, to offer myself to each. My eyes are closed but I smell Avis with her scent of roses, of geranium and wood. I hear her pearls crashing together, only I'm sure she's not wearing any; I hear her sobs and Edie, Edie! somewhere in a child's voice; then I feel Mother in her good wool coat, throwing her arms around me. Weeping shakes her body and her little pointed face is wet, as if she threw a small damp circle of cloth onto my dress. I feel it soak, soak through and I can barely stand, but Eve is there, Eve is somewhere beside me, somewhere shadowy, her words ringing in my ears; making me know that I have a choice in this, even this, especially this.

Choices are tiny now, minuscule: I could lie down or I could make this one last effort to stand. Lastly, here is Father, his great arms enveloping me until I'm almost a miniature doll and I know it can't be true but I hear Freddy say, *Bear up, Edie* and I hear singing, my Father's lovely lilting voice, up and down the notes, up and down; someone is walking up a long staircase, then trundling back down again. I'm cradled in his arms and being rocked to and fro, so that I can only imagine that it must be my very first moments, my first breath on this earth, my first great open-mouthed bawl.

\*      \*      \*

It's 8.15 a.m. and Freddy is polishing his shoes. He works hard buffing with the blackened rag until he can see a smooth round moon in each toe. He straightens up. His curly hair is neat, a prison crop. *Those are pearls that were his eyes.* His stomach gargles with the last cup of tea, hastily drunk.

And that last conversation we had, 3rd October, 1922, the night before the theatre, I keep going over and over it . . . We were in Fuller's, in the late afternoon, when the chandeliers didn't need to be lit and only two waitresses stood chatting at the furthest corner of the long room. There would have been the smell of good cigars and Johnson's polishing wax and a faint trace of Chanel No 5, mixing with the scent of warm buttered crumpets, to make a peculiar, fragrant, bun-like feeling. Fred and I were having that conversation, the one we had again later that evening, outside the Criterion, sitting on the steps of the statue

349

of Eros, the last time I saw him before—before the evening at the theatre. The 3rd October.

And Freddy was distressed, saying Sshsh now, the way you would to a child; and I know he put his arm around me and his sleeve smelled of smoke and wax, and I know we could hear the water from the fountain; from fishes' mouths gawping above us, spraying their white endless spume and I probably leaned my head against his shoulder, tipped my head back a little, saw the arrow and the cupid and didn't care who saw us, but what was it I said?

I think I said something like, something like (but I can't remember), . . . I think it was: I'm desperate, I really am. Did I say that? Did I use that word, the word *desperate* and if I did, if I did say it, is that the reason, is that what pushed him, pushed him *to blazes,* that would be his phrase; so much power one word might have, so much could some words matter and yet I can't remember, I can't remember properly, exactly, I couldn't have persuaded them in court, even if they'd asked me, if my life depended on it, which it did of course, which it does . . .

The warder is unlocking the door, the Chaplain, the prison Governor and the strangers, the two new young men, all enter the room and Freddy stands up. He stands stiff and formal, no hint of a tremor, as if for duty on ship. They all nod to one another. The

Governor, maybe he even greets Freddy, shakes his hand. *How brave he's been, that young man,* they'll say. *That's the kind of lad this country needs.* They'll even disapprove, some of them. *We've lost enough young men already.*

Freddy has been weighed and measured like me. Calculating the drop. Everything is prepared.

The Chaplain saying: The Lord giveth, and the Lord taketh away . . .

They walk in a convoy along the corridors, with the Chaplain at the back, intoning. The rooms are silent, there seems no one else in the entire place, only the six of them, walking, with no particular hurry, Freddy's polished shoes tapping a beat along the corridor, Freddy's heart tapping another beat, and Freddy thinking of me, his heart twisting at the thought of me, of what he has heard from Florrie, that I am not bearing up well, not like him.

*I'm desperate, I'm scared, Freddy, I wish you could help me . . .*

And into the courtyard where a cold blast of air will snip at his cheeks and sting his eyes before the Governor nods at the shed and the door is opened and there is one step up, one last step for Freddy to hesitate, to falter and he does, one slip! One error, for a boy, the kindest boy in all the world, but the hottest temper.

The Chaplain saying: He cometh up and is cut down, like a flower . . .

The hottest sense of justice, a boy allowed only one mistake in a lifetime, one slip . . . so here he is slipping, ever so slightly, held at the arm by one of the young strangers, the other holding out the white cap which they pull over Freddy's face so that now all he can see and taste is white but this cover is not for his benefit, although they tell themselves it is one last dignity for the prisoner, it is surely for their benefit; so that they will not remember, they will not have to see his face. My sweet boy, with the limpid blue eyes. My ship's writer, afraid of the water. *Fear death by water.* The men around him are white canvas shadows, the Chaplain saying: I am the Resurrection and the life (saith the Lord:) he that believeth in me, yea, though he were dead, yet shall he live: and whosoever liveth and believeth in me shall not die for ever.

With the white cap briefly suffused with pink while the rope—no—not the rope, I can't get that far, I can't get to the point where the stranger, the young man—where Master Marwood—jumps back and kicks the lever and Freddy, darling Freddy . . .

But after all, I sacrificed myself, offered myself up, abandoned myself to Freddy. He held me in his hands and I dangled, swung and jerked, high above the little houses with their boiled eggs and tea-cosies and husbands home from the war and their old cats sleeping on rugs by the fire. I swung high, high above them all from the day I allowed Freddy to lift up the rose-pink silk of my underslip and keep lifting and peeling until only my face was covered and all else, all about me, was unwrapped.

'AND IF ANY MISCHIEF FOLLOW, THEN THOU SHALT GIVE LIFE FOR LIFE'
Exodus, XXI
Percy Thompson, his last photograph, taken by his wife.

*Daily Sketch,* January 10th, 1923

\*       \*       \*

*Here I am dancing. I'm dancing at Ilford Town Hall with Freddy, my feet are swirling, Freddy is twirling me, he is lifting me towards him and away from him and music, music floods into every cell, every pocket of this room and people, other people all you other people in this world are nothing to me, nothing at all, your faces like petals blurring in a wet storm and nobody ever danced like this, nobody ever danced like this, our feet so light so quick we could drum a hole right into this burnished floor, we could spin you others here into sticks of sugar; our bodies glittering all colours of the rainbow, all colours of a tree caught in honeyed light, the way children dance; the way leaves dance in the wind; being*

353

*alive, being me in this scarlet velvet and these ochre feathers, I'm pure as flames, I'm the only thing, the only one in this world that matters; you'll never understand that if you don't like dancing, you'll never understand, you dreary people, dreary people with your lidless eyes, your blurred petals for faces—how the leaves feel when the wind snatches them, picks them up and twirls them in his great strong arms, the way that Freddy, my darling Freddy, catches me.*

# AFTERWORD

Edith Thompson and Frederick Bywaters were both hanged on the morning of 9th January, 1923. Almost immediately rumours began that Edie had been pregnant at the time of her death. If this were true, and had she said so at her trial, her sentence would automatically have been reprieved. The dress and underwear she was hanged in were burned and part of the Home Office file on her was sealed until 2022. I have not been able to find anything to substantiate—or deny—the rumour of her pregnancy.

The executioner later committed suicide and the prison Governor retired from his post, reportedly a convert to the movement against capital punishment. The Chaplain attending Edie (whose name was not Piper and who bore no resemblance to the chaplain in the novel) retired from his post, too, later devoting the rest of his life to speaking against the death penalty.

I first came across Edie's letters to Freddy in an anthology called *Erotica,* edited by Margaret Reynolds. Later, I included some of the letters—found as an appendix in Filson Young's account of her trial in the *Notable Trial Series* (1923)—in *The Virago Book of Love Letters,* which I edited. The letters themselves spin a haunting tale—incomplete, since few of Freddy's letters to Edie survived—skittish, tantalising, inconsistent. Troubling. Extracts from some of Edie's actual letters are included in this novel (pages 206, 207, 214 and 215), but most are made up. *Fred and Edie* is a work of fiction and no offence is intended towards living relatives of any character whose name I may have borrowed in the service of telling Edie's story.

All newspaper accounts are actual ones. T.S. Eliot was familiar with the case but unsympathetic and in a letter to the *Daily Mail* he praised the paper's unsentimental attitude in demanding that the pair should be executed. Margery Fry did indeed visit Edie and Virginia Woolf makes a mention of 'poor Mrs Thompson' in her diary. Almost immediately after her death, books were written proclaiming Edith's innocence. Edie's belongings were auctioned and newspapers reported that a frenzied mob crowded onto the pavement outside her Ilford home, even resorting to stealing leaves from her privet hedge as souvenirs.

Interested readers can find details of the trial in Lewis Broad's *The Innocence of Edith Thompson* or *Criminal Justice* by Rene Weis. Filson Young's book, including Edith's own letters (mentioned above), remains the most affecting of all accounts.

I'd like to thank Carole Welch for inspired

editing, as ever; Daphne Feldt for sharing her recollections of Ilford with me; and Meredith Bowles for love and support during a strange, demanding year.

JD

We hope you have enjoyed this Large Print book. Other Chivers Press or Thorndike Press Large Print books are available at your library or directly from the publishers.

For more information about current and forthcoming titles, please call or write, without obligation, to:

Chivers Press Limited
Windsor Bridge Road
Bath BA2 3AX
England
Tel. (01225) 335336

OR

Thorndike Press
295 Kennedy Memorial Drive
Waterville
Maine 04901
USA

All our Large Print titles are designed for easy reading, and all our books are made to last.